DOUBLE W

The music faded. In the second pew, the groom's mother wiped a tear from her eye. Her son, bolt upright, glanced down at his bride. For an instant he looked puzzled.

Looked away.

Then back again. Something was bothering him.

'Dearly beloved,' intoned the Reverend Timms, 'we are gathered here in the sight of God and in the face of this congregation, to join together this man and this woman—'

But hang on. What was happening? The bride was dumping her bouquet (lilies and freesias) unceremoniously on the flagstones. Was sweeping back the veil from her face.

What on earth … ?

The groom had turned his head. Was staring with a look of utter disbelief.

'You bastard!' she screamed.

Also by Lizbie Brown

Broken Star
Turkey Tracks
Shoo-Fly

Double Wedding Ring

Lizbie Brown

NEW ENGLISH LIBRARY
Hodder & Stoughton

First published in Great Britain in 1998
by Hodder and Stoughton
First published in paperback in 1999
by Hodder and Stoughton
A division of Hodder Headline

A NEL Paperback

10 9 8 7 6 5 4 3 2 1

A CIP catalogue record for this title is available
from the British Library

ISBN 0340 71751 3

Printed and bound in Great Britain by
Mackays of Chatham, plc, Chatham, Kent.

Hodder and Stoughton
A division of Hodder Headline 338 Euston Road
London NW1 3BH

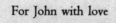
For John with love

It is a wounded heart
Wherein yet sticks the dart.
Every piece sore hurt throughout it,
Faith and troth writ round about it;
It was a tame heart and a dear,
And never used to roam:
But having got this haunt, I fear
'Twill hardly stay at home.
For God's sake, walking by the way
If you my heart do see,
Either impound it for a stray,
Or send it back to me!

From 'Good folk, for gold or hire'
by Michael Drayton

Chapter One

Five minutes to noon. The church was all but full. Groom's family to the left of the nave, bride's on the right.

Celia Hannaford kept her eye on the congregation through what she called her driving mirror above the organ seat. Her fingers could do the business (Marche Nuptiale' – Gounod) all by themselves. Should do. She'd played at enough weddings.

Never your own, said a voice in her head.

How could I play at my own? Stupid.

Awful outfits, she thought, reaching for bottom C with one deft foot. Flash. It was the only word. The groom's mother, in particular. Yellow hair, pink hat, blue frock, like a box of liquorice allsorts. And those flounces only emphasised her pronounced bosoms. (Celia always called them that.) What we have here is the lower class in full splendour – Cecil B. De Mille with knobs on. But that's how it is these days. Everything over the top. Vulgar. Elegance disappeared with oil lamps and elm trees and fountain pens that filled with ink.

The bride's lot, in the right-hand pews, were, on the whole, a touch more tasteful. A couple of ancient aunts, a tall, silver-haired man – rather distinguished – in a linen suit and a coffee-coloured girl in a cream cartwheel hat.

I know her, Celia thought suddenly. I taught her at St

Theresa's. Outlandish name. Gloria? No, Glory. She was always correcting me.

They all look . . . far away, inside themselves. Weddings are a magnet for all sorts of emotions. People get mentally unhinged by them. It's common knowledge. The angel above her head smiled his brittle smile. In the mirror, Celia saw the groom glance round expectantly.

Nothing yet. No hint of white. He looks nervous.

Don't they all?

There had once been a young man who threw up all over the vicar's surplice. Dreadful mess! But memorable. This one merely fidgeted with the buttons on his new suit. Sharp suit. Sharp haircut. Dark, springing curls; thick, muscular neck above the grey cravat.

Irish family, didn't somebody say?

Handsome face, but . . . a certain looseness. Yes, definitely somewhat weak around the chin.

The best man looked more precise, sitting as stiff as if they'd left the coat hanger in his shoulders. Three minutes to twelve. Time was going on. Well, it usually does, Celia told herself. Anything else would be unusual, to say the least.

She flipped the page, pulled out a couple of stops. Dim chatterings and rustlings, now, at the back. The Reverend Timms arriving with tardy dignity. And bridesmaids. At last. A big girl in pink satin and the obligatory little one. The photographer had them trapped in the doorway. The big bridesmaid was . . . not unattractive. Outsize, but she had marzipan arms and a full, confident stomach. Outside, the street stood wet from the overnight rain. The churchyard (or should that be graveyard? What's the difference?) shimmering with a pearly light.

'Look up, darling?' said the photographer's voice above the roar of the organ. 'That's it. Perfect! Aha! Here she is. Here she comes—'

He chased out to catch the bridal car. Stray gawpers by the

lych gate goggling at the occupants. A sigh of 'Aa . . . aah! Beautiful', was carried into the nave by a passing breeze. The bride seemed in no apparent hurry to tie the knot. Nice girl. Pretty girl. Imogen Shand. Another past pupil of St Theresa's. Celia remembered teaching her to play the violin. Good family. Old money. What's she doing marrying into this lot? She wondered. The groom's mother was now fretting. Swinging her considerable bulk sideways in a fruitless attempt to see what was holding things up.

A movement at the back of the nave. Old Thursley, waving a handkerchief. The signal . . .

Action stations.

A crescendo of chords, a lively arpeggio, then the wedding march came thundering out.

Here comes the bride . . .

Well, what you could see of her beneath all that lace flummery. The woman in white, Celia thought. A vision from another era. How girls transmogrified themselves for this once-in-a-lifetime occasion.

Once? These days?

You must be joking!

The bride came gliding down the aisle . . . Now this was odd. All on her own. No father, no brother. No male arm of any kind to lean on. Come to think of it, there was no mother either. And she had one. Celia remembered her. Louise Shand. Met her at Speech-day once. Didn't much care for her. Flinty type in an expensive wool suit.

The organ vibrated under the vaulted roof. The bride was now halfway down the left aisle. Swishing over the blue flagstones (yards of silk and lace), steaming along like a house on fire, the little bridesmaid jiggling and joggling along at the rear. The photographer was doubling back to catch them from the front. Aiming his camera at the ivory lace veil that hid her face. I hope she's wearing less make-up than her future mother-in-law, Celia thought. Inches thick. Trowel job, I shouldn't wonder . . .

3

Celia waited for the bride to take her place next to the groom; toned the music down while the vicar bent his glistening bald head and read the usual prologue. She had heard it so often, she knew it off by heart. 'They shall grow together like a twining, climbing plant . . .'

The Reverend Timms ran the local poetry society. Worse luck, said Celia's inner voice. Lengthened the service no end.

'. . . with God's help, these two young people will flourish like the vine.'

The music faded. In the second pew, the groom's mother wiped a tear from her eye. Her son, bolt upright, glanced down at his bride. For an instant, he looked puzzled.

Looked away.

Then back again. Something was bothering him.

'Dearly beloved,' intoned the Reverend Timms, 'we are gathered here in the sight of God, and in the face of this congregation to join together this man and this woman—'

Celia shuffled her music, reached for the first hymn. But hang on . . . What was happening? The bride was dumping her bouquet (lilies and freesias) unceremoniously on the flagstones. Was sweeping back the veil from her face.

What on earth. . . ?

The groom had turned his head. Was staring with a look of utter disbelief.

'You bastard!' she screamed.

Gasps.

For the bride wasn't the bride, after all. Celia's fingers hovered over the keys. Not Imogen Shand, not that sweet little thing everyone had fallen for at St Theresa's. No, this was some other young woman, her face as white as her silk train. Thereafter, several things happened in quick succession. With a spurt of energy, a sudden movement, the imposter lifted her arm and caught the groom a great whack across the side of his face.

It left a red mark.

'Two-timing bastard! It's about time they all knew what you've been up to.'

The little bridesmaid stood there with her mouth wide open. No one had primed her on what to do if war broke out.

'I'm pregnant. And it's your baby and you didn't want to know. You make me puke! You make her puke, too. Imogen. She sent me to tell you to get lost.'

The young woman wrenched the pearl tiara from her head. The groom sat down hard, as if his legs had gone. There were beads of sweat on his forehead. He looked like a man trying to keep balls in the air while rearranging himself under them.

What now? Celia found that her legs were trembling. Her heart attempted to free itself, alien-like, from her chest. She wanted to turn from the mirror and stare, like all the other faces in the congregation. No, you can't, she thought. Keep the music coming.

What's that noise?

The groom's mother. Was it? Shrieking in the second pew. Hysterical. That's all we need. Bach . . . quickly, Celia thought. Drown her out. But the little bridesmaid was now adding to the wailing.

Lord help us.

The rest of the guests sat frozen in their pews.

'I hope you rot in hell,' yelled the bride, before turning to make a fast exit down the aisle; creating her own silken breeze that took the service sheets and scattered them behind her. As she reached the porch, the sun came out. The sudden blaze of light startled Celia, so that her fingers slipped. The organ let out an odd, discordant chord. Then a mighty silence, as if someone had cut the sound track . . .

Chapter Two

———⟩⟨○○○⟩⟨———

Silence.

'Bloody hell!' whispered Glory Magdalena Fraser, who had an unobstructed view of the proceedings. In front of her, the vicar, motionless, like a cardboard cut-out, while all hell broke loose around him. On her left, in the aisle, the little bridesmaid howling her eyes out. To her right, the groom's mother, her face the colour of a boiled beetroot, now vigorously shoving her way towards her son.

'You didn't tell me it would be this much fun,' said Glory's companion, who, like most men, was not a huge fan of weddings.

Glory scarcely heard him. God almighty! she was thinking. Who needs theatre? The organist struck up a tune, then added a shaky descant. 'She always had a tough streak. But that took some nerve . . .'

'You know her? The bride from hell?'

'She went to the same school as me and Immy.'

'Imogen Shand? The real bride? The one who didn't turn up?'

'You got it.'

'Cosy.' Did they share boyfriends even then? he wanted to ask, but Glory's attention had been drawn away from him. She was staring across the aisle to a spot by the font.

Her voice was disbelieving. 'That guy's still taking photos.'

'Hedging his bets.' She didn't catch on, so he was forced to

7

explain. 'If the bride and groom don't want his snaps — and I wouldn't bet on it — the tabloids might.'

'You're joking!'

'Not really. Think about it. Hey, the best man's lighting a fag. Think he'll pass them round?'

'Shut up, Ed. It's no joke.' And don't argue, her look suggested. Glory needed to think and she couldn't do that while he was being facetious.

Glory has gifts in plenty. A fine intellect, a certain sassiness, a forthright tenacity. But Glory also has a temper. She's volatile. Likely to erupt, just as much as her friend, Kat.

They are a pretty pair.

'So where's Imogen,' the young man asked, 'if she's not here?'

'Sobbing her heart out at home?'

It didn't bear thinking about. Glory stood there thinking.

With a certain sense of guilt. That had to be acknowledged.

Little whisperings, like the sound of last year's dead leaves, began to drift round the grey Norman arches. Uncomfortable rustlings and shufflings, as the congregation tried to decide where they went from here. Glory turned her head to gaze behind her. One old dear — straw hat, snow-white hair — was hyperventilating. Looked as though she might pass out.

Almost involuntarily, she tensed herself for action.

Glory was a third-year medical student at the University of Bristol.

But the danger was subsiding. Someone had come to the rescue, was fanning the patient with a hymn sheet. Glory's catlike eyes turned once more to the front pew. The best man was dragging hard on his ciggie. Not a happy chappie. The groom's mother had ditched her hat and was leaning over her son, talking hard, like a boxing trainer bringing back her man after a knockout punch.

'Remind me never to present myself at the altar,' said Ed. 'The poor guy's pole-axed.'

'Serves him right,' said Glory grimly. She had no pity for Johnny Mulligan. He'd had it coming to him.

Oh, yes.

Ed said, 'That's not very nice.'

'*He's* not very nice.' Johnny had been walking on thin ice for a very long time. Glory knew that for a fact. It was the women in his life (or on the edge of it) that you had to feel for. Kat. Imogen. And God knows how many others.

She drew herself up to her full height, a tall, slim, elegant girl in her cream silk suit and the aforementioned cartwheel hat. But appearances can be deceptive. There was a solidity about Glory – a ballsy pragmatism – that was probably inherited from her Scottish father.

Glory wouldn't necessarily have agreed with you on that point. Ask which of her now-divorced parents had most fostered her strong ambitions and she would have plumped for her Jamaican mother, who had spent the last ten years holding down a high-powered sales job with a cosmetics company. A job that entailed a lot of travelling, so that Glory had largely been brought up by her maternal grandmother.

But don't make me out to be a victim, she'd more than once told her friends. Somebody has to bring home the bacon. Mum works all hours God sends. I appreciate that. Anyway, I'm doing all right.

Call me a liar and I'll deck you.

'So where's the nearest pub?' Ed's voice said now in her ear. 'I take it the reception's off?'

Oh, ha-bloody-ha, thought Glory, dumping her box of rose-petal confetti surreptitiously under the seat. 'I can't go to the pub.'

'Why not?'

'Somebody's got to check on Imogen. She must be in a hell of a state.'

She bent down to pick up her bag, just as the groom, wearing a rigor mortis smile, shook off his mother – quite roughly – and strode back down the aisle. Generating a furious energy, he plunged from the gloom of the church into the sunshine of the graveyard.

The buzz in the congregation got louder.

They stopped shilly-shallying and got right down to it. The best gossip they'd had in a very long time.

'Jolly glad I came,' Ed said. 'Wouldn't have missed it for the world.'

Glory looked at him and shook her head. Sometimes, she thought, I really like you and sometimes you're a bit of a prat.

Which was it today?

No time to ponder the question. 'Where's the car?' she said.

'Just round the corner.'

'Good. Then you can give me a lift. Pronto.'

Chapter Three

―――❦❦❦――

Glory Fraser wasn't the only person needing a lift that afternoon.
At twelve fifteen, in a narrow, deserted alley just behind St
Bartholomew's Church, a man in a linen suit was flinging open
his car door.

'Get in,' he said sharply to the tall young woman in white
lace.

Kat Gregg stared at him with dazed, green eyes.

'Get in,' he said again. 'Silly bugger. What on earth possessed
you?'

She slammed the door on him and marched on up the alley.
The pale lace of the train slid behind her over pale flagstones.
Behind a wall and a hedge, ring doves cooed. The car – a quietly
expensive, blue Audi – caught up with her again; the door
opened once more.

'Look, stop messing me about and get in.' The man's dark
hair was flecked with silver. His mouth was wide and intelligent.
There were bags under the grey eyes, but attractive bags. He was
not classically good-looking, but had a natural sexiness.

For a second, she seemed to hesitate.

'Not often you're struck dumb,' the driver said.

Silence.

'What got into you? Dropping a bomb on them all like that?
Come on, Kat. Get in. I'm here to help.'

'You can't help.'

'Have it your own way. But let me take you home, at least.'

'I don't want to go home.'

'So where do you want to go?'

'God knows. Just leave me alone.'

'To wander the streets like a madwoman? You can't be serious?' He sat there waiting patiently. 'We'll drive around, if you like, and talk.'

At last, she gave in. Grabbing at the sweep of lace, she dragged it into the car with her. Then slammed the door behind her.

'Good girl. Let's get the hell out of here . . .'

The back streets at this time of the day were free of traffic. The car swung capably in his hands along the edge of town and turned north along yellow-stoned crescents, past high-walled gardens.

'Why did you do it?' he said again.

She stared ahead out through the windscreen, eyes brimming with tears.

'OK, so I know the answer to that. The whole world knows. You made sure of that. Too damned impatient, as always. I knew you were whacky. Nicely whacky, I used to think. Didn't have you down as nasty.'

'I'm not nasty.' This last came out as a childlike, desperate wail. 'It's Johnny I'm mad at, not her.' The wail turned to floods of tears. She wrenched off the veil, threw it on to the back seat of his expensive car.

'So where's Imogen?'

Silent weeping.

'Kat? Where's Imogen?'

Nothing.

The man moved one hand (gold signet ring) on the steering wheel. 'You must know where she is. You got hold of her wedding dress? It is hers?'

A nod of the blonde head.

'Right. So how did you get hold of it? You went to her house. The house she shares with her fiancé? Am I right?'

'I had to tell her about the baby.'

'On her wedding morning? Christ Almighty! You don't do things by halves—'

'Stop the car—'

'I'm not letting you out in this state.'

'Stop the car! I'm going to be sick.'

He pulled deftly into the curb. She flung the door open and was violently sick on the pavement.

'Here.' When it was all over, he proffered a large, white cotton handkerchief. 'You buggered up the reception as well. My wife's going to be livid. You realise that? Champagne waiting, filet mignon for seventy, strawberries flown in from God knows where. Who's going to eat it all now? Tell me that?'

She blew her nose and gave it a hefty wipe.

'What are you? A jelly brain?' he asked. 'Why the hell didn't you ask my advice, instead of bloody storming Troy?'

'What's Troy got to do with it?' She felt better now, leaning back in the seat, twisting and untwisting a strand of her hair. The physical and emotional storm had passed over.

'Sod all.' He sat there looking at her. 'So are you going to have this baby?'

'Too right I am.' He'd got through to her at last.

'You've thought about it? You're quite sure?'

She clasped her hands over her stomach, as if in defence.

He wanted her to get rid of it.

Well, she wasn't going to.

He couldn't make her, even though he was famous for sweeping juries away by the force of his personality. Particularly the women.

He didn't pursue the matter, but homed back to an earlier question. 'So where is she? Imogen?'

'I don't know and I don't care.'

'Oh, come on, Kat.'

'I don't owe her a thing.'

'You don't really believe that.' There was a stale smell of vomit. He wound down the window.

'I do, actually.'

'Never give in, do you? So damned fierce. But then, you always were.'

'Meaning?'

'Meaning you've got a terrible temper.'

'And she hasn't? Miss Bloody Sugar Sweet?'

'Well, if you want the truth—'

'All right . . . all right. She's all sweetness and light.'

'She certainly didn't deserve what she got this morning.'

This time she didn't argue with him, but sat there moodily chewing at a fingernail. A car passed down the street. A woman wearing a blue jacket strolled by with her dog.

'So you went to Imogen's house this morning. What time was this?'

'Eleven thirty. Twenty-five to twelve.'

'So the groom had already left for the church?'

'He wasn't there in the first place. He spent the night at his mother's house.'

'So who was there with her when you arrived?'

'A chap called Tim Kidston.'

'Who is?'

'An old friend of hers. He was giving her away.'

'Unusual arrangement. No father to give her away?'

'Her father's dead.'

'What about her mother? Why wasn't she there?'

'Her mother hates Johnny. They haven't spoken since Imogen moved in with him.'

'So it was just you, Imogen and her friend. So then what?'

'I told her about the baby. That it was Johnny's. She didn't believe it at first.'

'I can imagine.' Aidan Makepeace, one elbow resting on the window, seemed to have his mind on other things.

'She thought it was a joke. But when I said it again . . . she went mad.'

'What form did this madness take?'

'What do you think? She yelled at me. Threw things. Tried to throw me out of the house. I refused. I'd got it into my head that I wasn't going to budge. So in the end, she tore off her frock—'

'Her wedding dress?'

'Yes. And she went.'

'Went? How?'

'She just ran out of the house. And he ran after her. Tim Thingy.'

'Which left you sitting pretty.' He was beginning to see.

'I didn't plan it. I had no plans, even at that stage. I just sat there, feeling disgusted at myself. Feeling sick . . . But then, about five minutes later, the wedding car came back from delivering the bridesmaids. And it suddenly came to me. I'd taken it out on Imogen, but she wasn't the one who deserved to be punished. It was him I wanted to hurt most. So when the chauffeur rang the doorbell, I knew what I was going to do.'

A south-westerly wind. Grass smells. The verge had just been cut.

'Silly bugger,' Makepeace said again. But somehow it sounded more gruff. More affectionate. He started the engine and they drove on.

Chapter Four

———◦◦◦———

'I want you to close the place up, Bethany.'

'But we're full. It's our busy day.'

'I don't care.' Kat's face was flushed, her hair dishevelled, though she was doing her best to appear calm. 'Get rid of them. Say we've had a death in the family. Say the electricity's gone down. Anything. Just get rid of them.'

For weeks afterwards, Bethany Clark, who worked as a part-time waitress at the Beehive Tearooms, told anybody who wanted to hear (and there was no lack of takers) about the precise sequence of events on that never-to-be-forgotten Saturday. How her employer, on sweeping in through the door of the tiny cottage, had caught that gorgeous dress (fifteen metres of fine lace) on the chair by the door and in yanking it away, had ripped it right down the back. How, swearing hard and whipping the train over one arm, she had next caught the tablecloth on the oval table in the centre of the room; in one swift movement, crockery, scones, jam and cream went crashing on to the wooden floor.

Without even noticing.

That was the oddest thing.

'Shut the place up. Then get off home.'

Next Kat had hoisted herself and the tea-stained lace train through the arch and into the tiny, old-fashioned kitchen.

Sending a startled customer who was waiting by the cash desk, hard back against the wall so that he dislodged the copper warming pan. More clatter. At which point, Mr Makepeace came barging through the back door, looking ever so . . . well, masterful. And before you could blink, he'd whisked her — Miss Gregg — out through the scullery and up the stairs to the private quarters.

Pity really.

Just when it was getting interesting.

Bethy should have hung around. Ten minutes after the tearooms had closed and the girl had gone racing home to tell her mother about what had happened, Johnny Mulligan's car skidded to a halt on the far side of the tall box hedge that separated the Beehive from the busy main road.

And then the fur started to fly. Yes, indeed.

By this time, Kat had shed her borrowed plumes and had changed back into a white t-shirt and her old grey tracksuit bottoms. The OPEN sign had been brought in from the stretch of rough gravel that served as a car park. And Aidan Makepeace had walked over to the hotel his wife ran on the far side of the park, to see how she was coping with the abandoned reception.

Mulligan banged open the door (which Kat had forgotten to lock) with one angry thrust. Came striding through the now deserted tearooms and up the stairs into Kat's first-floor sitting room like some latter-day avenging angel. It was a wonder there were no scorch marks.

'I'll kill you . . . you fucking jealous little cow. Stitching me up like that. Ruining Immy's big day.'

'Blaming the wrong person, aren't we?' White-faced, Kat stood her ground. 'You should take a look at your own actions some time.'

'Sick. That's what you are. A bloody sick little bitch.'

'I like that! You've been getting away with murder for years.

Up to your capers . . . Oh, don't try and look innocent. You know what I mean. Pretending it's the Irish in you . . .'

'Bloody feminist. Can't stand being second-best, that's your trouble. Always was.'

Flinching, she turned aside, arms folded across her enlarged stomach.

'Aggressive bitch—'

'Only when I'm pushed too far.'

He stood in the doorway, as though blocking her escape route. 'So where is she?' he demanded. 'Immy?'

'How would I know?'

'You should know. You drove her out of my house, you sodding slag.'

'I don't know where she is and I don't care.'

'You will care, by the time I've finished with you. You'll be hearing from my solicitor. You won't know what hit you.'

His eyes fell on something that lay flung across the desk in the alcove. The ruined wedding dress, complete with tea stains and the three safety pins stuck into the long zip at the back. (Kat was a tall, large-boned girl, even without the baby bulge, and the dress was two sizes too small for her.) With a swooping movement, he snatched it up. 'I'll take that.'

'She won't wear it now.'

'You vicious little bitch—' He lunged forward and hit her across the face with such force that she stumbled on the rucked-up rug and fell half across the sofa. Arm raised, he went for her again, but this time she fought back, dragging a long scratch down the side of his face.

'I'll kill you—'

'For God's sake, man—' Someone was dragging him off.

A newcomer. The fair young man who, not long since, had stood next to him at the altar. 'For Christ's sake, she's pregnant—'

'That's her story.' The words fell harshly into the sun-filled room.

'Don't you dare doubt my word! I'm having a baby. Your baby.'

'Do we have proof of that?'

'How dare you! How dare you doubt my word! You, the biggest liar on the whole of the planet—'

Johnny Mulligan didn't deny the fact.

He just showed his contempt by laughing in her face.

'He really hurt me, Aidan. He's destructive.' It was four in the afternoon. Kat sat gazing out of the window at the dappled green garden. At a splodge of blue. Delphiniums at the base of the crumbling wall.

'It seems to be catching.' He tossed her a sideways glance. 'So, did he know about the baby before today? Did you tell him?'

'Of course he did. I told him weeks ago. He didn't want to know.'

'And that caught you on the raw?'

'What do you think? I told him that even if he wasn't interested, I'd make sure he paid maintenance for it. And he laughed. You heard him. Could I prove it was his? he asked. That was the final insult.'

'The man's a complete prat. You're better off without him. You're a strong personality. You'll survive.'

She folded her hands together around one knee. 'But I've made a pig's ear of it all.' A silence. Then, 'What will they all think of me?'

'They'll think you're a bloody witch.' His rueful smile took the sting out of the words. 'And so you might be. Bringing the proceedings to a theatrical halt like that. Christ, you should have gone on stage. It'll be in all the papers. You realise that?'

'I've already had the *Chronicle* on the phone. Think it'll be a world scoop?' An edgy joke. 'I told them to sod off. Took the thing off the hook.'

'Your best plan would be to get right away for a bit. Right away where they can't find you.'

'Oh, yes?' She turned her head to look at him. 'That would suit you, wouldn't it?'

'I don't follow.' He was pretending to be thick. An old barrister's trick.

'Yes, you do. My lease is up. Your wife wants me out. But I'm not going to oblige you, Aidan. I've got a good business and a living to earn. A child to bring up.'

'And we'd never throw you out. You know that. It's just that Anna has her own plans for the Beehive.'

'And she nags?'

'Now and again. Don't all wives?'

'I suppose so. Was she very mad about the reception?'

'Not best pleased. But she was also concerned about you. And Imogen.'

'I'm sorry. For all the trouble I've caused.'

'It's not me you should be apologising to.'

'I know. I'll go and see her. Immy . . .'

'If she'll let you.'

'If she'll let me.' She buried her face in her hands. 'Aidan, I'm really sad.'

'You and a lot of others.'

'I couldn't help it today. My temper flares. You know me.'

'Unfortunately, in this case . . . yes.' A faint grin as he lifted her chin. She found a smile in return. 'That's better,' he said.

And then the doorbell shrilled. Aidan went to answer it. When he came back, there was a woman with him. She stood, shaking slightly, in the doorway. Plump, bright blue eyes, white-blonde hair out of a bottle. The kind of woman you'd get to read your fortune at a fair.

Rose Mulligan. Johnny's mother.

'I've come to collect my things,' she announced grimly. 'I won't be working here any more.'

Pale, now, as death, Kat said, 'As you wish. Look – Rose—'

'I'll never forgive you for this. I want you to know that.'

'You don't think your precious son should take a share of the blame?'

'No, I don't. He says the child isn't his.'

'Well, he would, wouldn't he? If you believe that, you'll believe anything.'

'I do believe it. Why would he play around when he's got a lovely girl like Imogen?'

'Ask him, not me.' Kat's hands were clenched, but her voice was cool now and laconic.

'Funny you never mentioned it before. That you were sleeping with my son behind his girlfriend's back.'

'I could hardly tell you, could I?'

'Ashamed of it, were you?'

'Not proud of it, if you want to know. But he said he loved me. And I always loved him—'

'What rot! Love? That's not love – what you did today. It was an act of destruction. Pointless. Deliberate. You'll be getting the bill by the way, for the cost of the reception.'

'And I shall be slapping a maintenance order on him.'

Rose flushed, as human nature struggled with integrity. 'Cheap little whore! I know what I'd do with you.'

'Tar and feather? String me up?'

'And the rest. I know about women like you. Think I don't? Nasty. Envious. Trying to steal that pretty little thing's thunder. You want to be like her? Men falling at your feet? Let me tell you something. You'll never make it.'

Kat gazed at her for a couple of seconds – her eyes perfectly still. His all-adoring mother. Who knew bog-all about her precious son and his antics. 'Oh, get out of here.' Indifferent now. Weary. 'Just get out.'

'I'll be glad to.'

Aidan took the case that it was comic rather than dramatic. 'Another satisfied customer,' he said when they were alone again.

Kat sank back on to the sofa. 'She's a kind-hearted woman. I like her. God, what a mess—'

'Passions are messy things, darling. Let's have a drink.'

'Can't. I'm pregnant.'

'Nonsense. One won't hurt.' He went downstairs to the kitchen and came back with two glasses of red wine. Put one into her hand. 'Sip that. It'll warm your cockles.'

She took a sip and sat looking at him with a faint smile.

'What's so funny?'

'I was just thinking. My great-great-great grandfather was convicted of machine-breaking and rick-burning in eighteen thirty.'

'That explains it then. It's in the genes.'

Kat found her limbs relaxing in spite of it all. The wine helped. So did having Aidan there. Mr big-gun barrister. He'd been a good friend this last – what was it? – two years? Almost three. A rock. A rock with a bloody good sense of humour. He was a clever old stick, but he never paraded the fact. Just made you feel enormously comfortable in his company.

She took another sip.

Of course, you might just be kidding yourself. Barristers have the ability to make their clients feel they're the most important people in the world. Then, a week later, those same clients may be starting a life sentence. Think he remembers them then?

Blow that, she thought. You're not a client. You're a mate. Just think yourself lucky.

Jump-cut to six eighteen that evening. Kat, alone again, made herself a sandwich. Egg and mayo. Hours since she'd eaten anything. And there was the baby to think of. You can't run on empty. Got to start looking after yourself. No one else to do it. Not after today.

But she took one bite and pushed the plate away. Just the thought of eating made her stomach churn. And the house smelt of stale toasted cheese (Welsh Rarebit on the Specials board) and the wine had made her feel unstable. She wanted to retch, but couldn't. She walked slowly and unsteadily up the narrow staircase to her round bedroom with tiny Gothic windows. Lay on the bed for a while, tossing and turning.

Just for a few seconds, she dropped off, but fell straight into an uneasy dream. It was a wet Sunday morning. She was on the inside of a glass church and Imogen was screaming at her from outside; the screams silenced by the glass divide.

Just as well, she thought, jumping herself awake. Other people's crying pain . . . you couldn't think of it. Mustn't let yourself. Only your own. That's enough to get on with.

Downstairs everything was quiet. The phone was still off the hook.

'Want to use our house in town?' Aidan had asked before he left.

'It's OK. I'm fine. I'm staying here.'

'Is that wise?' He'd been worried about the press hammering on her door. Or Johnny coming back.

'Aidy – stop worrying. I'll call you if I change my mind.'

'I should stay here with you. But Anna's arranged this dinner . . . a friend's come over from Italy.'

'I'll be fine. Honestly. You go off and enjoy yourself.'

Fierce pressure behind her eyes. Kat slid herself off the bed, felt for her shoes, eased them on and grottily made her way over to the window. She reached for the clasp, flung the window open. Air flooded in. Soft, clinging air that brought with it garden smells. Damp earth and beech leaves . . . and the burnt musk of geraniums. There was a soft plopping under the wisteria. It was raining . . . but listlessly. Kat closed her eyes and listened. Suits my mood, she thought. Want to cry but can't. Takes too much energy. None to spare. Bloody awful day took every spare ounce.

Crying's no good, anyway. Gets you nowhere. It's time you

got your act together, considered the options. She arranged them, roughly, in circles around the inside of her head.

Stay here and keep bumping into Johnny. Face the ostracism. Move the business. Start all over again.

Top yourself. Sod that. You want the baby.

How are you going to keep working and look after it?

In circles the options remained. Her brain kept going round them and getting nowhere. Then, suddenly, something snapped. 'Oh – bollocks!' she thought. Lurking here with the doors locked and bolted. It's pathetic.

Bravado now. Defiance. And a stiffening resolve. I'll bounce back if it kills me. What you need is to get out of here. Get some fresh air.

It's raining.

Only drizzle. Anyway, it's stopping.

But first, this place is a tip. Bed unmade, pots in the sink, clothes strewn where you flung them down. First clear the place up . . .

An hour (and ten minutes) later, she closed the door behind her and locked it. In each hand was a black poly bag full of rubbish, along with her car keys.

The trees were a ghostly presence straddling the parkland. Silver bits in the shadowy masses. She shivered in her thin cotton t-shirt and turned to look back at the old stone cottage.

If only . . . If you could turn back time? You can't. The past is the past. But what the heck? I'll pack it away. Hide it somewhere.

The child wriggled inside her, like a little fish. No storm can touch him or her.

If only she had known . . .

Chapter Five

Two hours earlier, Marcus Finney had opened the bottle that he kept on the walnut chest next to the Staffordshire figurine. He filled a single glass, then turned Bach's Toccata and Fugue up to full volume.

He had good reason, having just completed a bit of business that was most advantageous to him; having sold a French mantel clock with two draped nymphs for twice what it was worth to a Yank with a wallet as big as Texas. Marcus loved giving them the old sales patter. With enormous satisfaction, he recalled the course it had taken.

'Exquisite, don't you think? My wife found it at a country auction. She has a real eye.'

'Sure is pretty.'

'I don't really want to part with it. You grow fond of things. Had it home with me for a couple of years, as a matter of fact, above the fireplace next to a divine piece of blue Delft. Feels like a member of the family. You know? But it's like women. If you kept every single one you fell in love with—'

'You'd be in one hell of a pickle. So . . . what if I took this particular dame off your hands? How much is she going to cost me?'

'Well, for a special customer . . . and I can see you're a man of taste . . .'

'None of your dashed blarney, now.'

'Wouldn't work, sir, on you. I know a head for business when I see one. I might let her . . . it go for . . . shall we say eight thousand?'

'Holy Moses! You think I'm made of money?'

'Can't do it for much less, I'm afraid. I'd be cutting my own throat. But I'd like it to go to a good home where it'll be appreciated. I could do six thousand. Can't go any lower.'

'Alrighty. Now – that bit of Delft you mentioned. Don't suppose that's still hanging round at the back of the store—?'

Marcus had sold him a Delft straining bowl that had never seen the inside of any of his homes (and these had been many and varied), telling himself that he was a frigging genius. Life was looking up. And it all boiled down to one thing. Returning to Bath to live. That decision had been a turning point. Yes, indeed.

The pendulum was starting to swing back.

He took his glass over to the window and stood gazing out through half-closed eyes across the sharply sloping alley that was Bartlett Street. Late afternoon sun settling on stone with a hint of honey. Bath pavements. Buildings close enough to look each other straight in the eye. And at the corner of the street above, the Assembly Rooms. Marcus lifted his glass, sipped at it and stood perfectly still, gazing at the tall chimney stacks. What could be more civilised? The place . . . this shop, full of beautiful things.

Not a crack in sight.

Beauty is an opium. It buoys you up. Helps convince you of your own status.

Marcus slid his glasses down his nose and looked over the top of them at his reflection in the window. Tall, fair-to-greying, pale blue eyes, blue shirt, yellow spotted bow tie. Looks intelligent, knowledgeable. The tie helps. Yes, definitely. He took another sip of the malt and gazed voluptuously round the elegantly crammed window. Life is a fugue. Round and round it goes and in the end, you come back to where you started. I could never tire of this city. Not true. You couldn't wait to get out. Ah, but that was years ago, when I was young. I'm young now. Oh, come on. Tell the truth. Well, youngish. Not bad for your age. And getting fitter all the time, thanks to that rather splendid health club you've joined up at Cheyneys.

That rather expensive (no, bloody expensive) health club. This thought appeared to amuse Finney and give him an inordinate amount of pleasure. What the hell? You can afford it now. The five-star hotel, the pool, the sauna and all the other first-rate facilities. Not forgetting the rather nice class of female that you meet in the café afterwards. Lean, tanned, animated young women. Modern . . . with precisely synchronised bodies and minds. Out of this world. Out of your world. Not necessarily. Not these days. Things have changed, remember?

Finney turned away from the window, put the glass down, wiped a speck of dust from the chest of drawers (early eighteenth-century) to the left of him. Have they? Have they really changed? Not in one department. Not at home. Christ, I'd give anything—

Anything?

Anything. All this. Whatever it takes. But there are some things you just can't alter, try as you will. Some things money can't buy. Nothing can. Nobody. Tough. You have to learn to accept, that's what that wet little social worker said. No, I can't. Won't accept. Why should I? Live with it then. Oh, but I do. God knows, I do. Every single fucking day of my life.

He locked up at five thirty, shoved the keys in his pocket, mooched up the hill to Alfred Buildings where the car was parked. The sale now forgotten, his mood suddenly and inviolably changed. Thoughts of the boy penetrated his nervous system.

The boy.

That's what Finney called him. Never anything else. His son, now eight years old. One of twins. The other one had died. The perfect one and they were left with – He wouldn't say it; couldn't ever say the words.

Downs Syndrome.

The phrase still sent a nervous charge right through his system.

A mongol, he'd once heard some old woman whisper after passing them in the street. Sometimes he dreamt about the incident. Hacked me apart. Put me in a black mood for weeks. I took it out on Jan. So what's new? Partly she brings it on herself. All that guff she tries to put out about Downs children having special gifts. Bringing warmth and love and this golden glow into your life.

Golden glow? You must be joking!

It's like a perpetual cloud hanging over you. A shadow that moves with you wherever you go.

For the millionth time, Finney asked himself: Why, oh why, should it have happened to me? Because you're too old. Jan was too old. Chromosomes. Faulty ones.

Yes, but for what offence? It's not fair. All I ever wanted was a son to play cricket with, to josh with, to drink with, like other blokes. Not much to ask, really, is it, bloody God? But you chose to stamp on me. OK. So you can't blame me if I occasionally hit back.

'These came for you. The post was late.' His wife met him in the hall, handed him a bundle of letters and glanced at him quickly as if to assess his mood.

He took the mail and, still heading for the stairs, shoved them into his pocket.

'Marcus – I told Lucian you'd help him with his project.'

'Project?'

'On Roman mosaics. You know an awful lot about that kind of stuff. I thought—'

'Well, you can think again. What's the point?' He gave her a look which hadn't yet exploded, but which threatened to, some time in the near future.

'It wouldn't take long. Ten, fifteen minutes. Please, Marcus. He's been so looking forward to it.'

'Know that for a fact, do we?'

'Yes, I do, actually. Why don't you ask him?'

The boy was sitting on the floor in front of the television, studying the screen with a completely indifferent look on his face.

'Lucian? Tell Daddy about your project.'

The boy didn't move.

'Lucian. Turn down the sound. I'm talking to you.'

The boy turned and looked, but his attention lagged somewhere behind. The upturned eyes inscrutable. Self-contained.

'Daddy wants to see your project book.'

'Oh. Right.'

A complete blank. No current. No aura. It was like he absorbed everything, but gave nothing back.

'Go and get it, then.'

'Now?'

'Yes, now. Please.'

'Oh, for God's sake—' Finney's patience was gone. 'I don't have time to bugger around.' He hurried out of the room, pushing past his wife, without a look and shut the door behind him, leaving the two of them on the other side.

Upstairs, he showered swiftly, changed into tracksuit and trainers and immediately felt busy again. Focused. He found the bottle that he kept in the bottom of the wardrobe, unscrewed the cap and took a long swig.

He had replaced the bottle in the pocket of an old tweed jacket and was shutting the wardrobe door when he remembered the letters and took them out of his pocket. Mostly bills. But thank God the loan sharks were no longer breathing down his neck.

Finney shoved the bills back in his pocket. Left in his hand was a slim, blue envelope. Typed, but personal. He examined it with something like recognition, then opened it.

A photograph fell out. A snapshot of a child. Fair hair, blue eyes, sweet smile.

There was also a piece of paper, three inches by four. On it was written: *Fruit of your loins. Wouldn't you like to meet him? Watch this space.*

Finney stood there staring down at the photograph. So shocked that he had to get the bottle out again and give himself another shot. Rain spattered against the window, but he didn't hear it. The muscles in his face were working, though it was impossible to tell whether this was from upset or excitement; his eyes lingered on the typed words as he wondered who the devil the letters were coming from . . .

Jan said, 'You're going out?'

'I think that's what I said.' Sarcastically, he pretended to study his memory. 'Yes. I definitely said I was going out. Do I take it that you object?'

'But — you haven't been in two minutes.'

'And now I'm going out again. OK? I'm meeting a client at the shop.'

'But there's . . .' Something slippy and slithering about her voice. Same with the look she gave him. Like she's making some kind of protest, but trying not to cause offence. A thin, dark woman in a black top and skirt. Thin, as opposed to lean. Too thin. No colour in her clothes or her face. Not much life either.

Mad Bohemian once.

Wouldn't think so now.

He made a meal of facing her out. 'There's what?'

'I cooked dinner.'

'Not hungry.'

32

A pause. Then, 'Look . . . Marcus . . . I know you find this difficult . . . but Lucian needs you—'

'For what, exactly?'

Her face was very pale. 'To talk to. To play with. He needs a father.'

'Well, I'm sorry, but I can't fulfil that role. I don't feel like his bloody father.' He looked at his watch. Six forty-five. 'I'm off. I've got a key.'

She looked at him for a second without speaking, then said in a low voice, 'That's right. Go on. Detach yourself. Not that you've ever done anything else.'

'What did you say?'

'Nothing. It wasn't anything. Forget it. Go on out.'

She wasn't going to get away with it that easily. 'It's OK. I've got five minutes. You can tell me. Pour your heart out.'

'It doesn't matter,' she said, not looking at him.

'But it does.' He couldn't refrain from the boozy baiting. 'Of course it does. So tell me. Don't hang back.'

'It doesn't matter. Don't start. Please.'

'Don't start what?'

'You know.'

'No, I don't.'

The boy appeared suddenly in the doorway. Stood with one hand fumbling at the handle. Clumsy, Finney thought. A good boy, as they go. But grotesque.

'Tell me. Get it off your chest. Come along—'

Silence.

'Tell me, before I lose my temper.'

'You'll lose it anyway.'

'Sorry? Didn't quite catch.'

'Yes, you did.' Her eyes suddenly came up, blazing for once.

That was better. Having the desired effect. Finney preferred his victim to put up some sort of defence. More fun. Definitely. 'All right. I did. But humour me.'

Her face, as it looked at his, was still defiant. But there was

33

also a hint of fear. She was looking round, surreptitiously, for a means of escape. 'I said it's Saturday night. You'll get mad at me. You always do.'

'So there must be a reason. Don't you think?'

'Yes, you've been drinking.'

The boy went on gazing at them and fumbling with the door handle. 'Do you know, Lucian,' he said, breaking his own rule, 'your mother gets these moods on her. Can't think why. Seems to want a fight. We shall have to do something about that – don't you think?'

She pretended not to know what was coming. Her very stillness angered him. 'Don't you think – my love?'

'No!' And suddenly, she moved. But he moved faster. Caught her with the flat of his hand as she lunged for the stairs.

His inner rage boiled over.

Inadequate, to hit a woman and to go on hitting her when she was down? Of course it was. Finney knew it, at rock bottom. But the condemned man had to have some kind of recompense for his prison sentence.

He looked at her crouched there, weeping. 'I'm off, then,' he said.

But before he went, the phone rang. He picked it up quite coolly. 'Marcus Finney Antiques . . .'

Chapter Six

At ten thirty a.m. the following Monday morning, Max Shepard came bounding into his partner's quilt shop, Martha Washington, in Pierrepont Mews and dropped a copy of the *Daily Mail* on the counter.

'Seen this?' he demanded.

> ### REVENGE 'BRIDE' SHOT DEAD
> 28-year-old Katharine Gregg, the girl who on Saturday scuppered her lover's wedding to another woman, was shot dead in a back street near the Assembly Rooms in Bath that same evening. Johnny Mulligan (33), the man on whom she wreaked an infamous revenge, was last night charged with her murder. Mulligan was freed on bail for a substantial sum, raised by his mother, Rose Mulligan (55).
>
> Local antiques dealer, Marcus Finney, discovered the body and immediately called for help on his mobile phone. A wristwatch belonging to Mr Mulligan was found next to the body . . .

'Uh-huh.' Elizabeth Blair's attention was still on the newly dressed window. You made a pretty good job of that, she told herself, even though I say it myself. The Spinning Stars quilt in one corner . . . blue and gold and rose, like Wyoming in October. The Boston Commons (1930s) in the other. And the Double Wedding Ring — a real dandy in every shade from pink to ripe blueberry — draped over the pine chest, dead centre.

'You think you're going on honeymoon,' Max said, 'and you wind up in a cell down the nick. They arrested him last night. Mad or what?'

'Sad,' Elizabeth said. 'For both those young women.'

'Rare old ding-dong at the church, by all accounts.'

'That's love for you. Nuclear war or nothing.'

Max looked thoughtful. 'Pretty spiteful thing to do, though . . . confronting him at the altar.'

'Hard to tell until you know the circumstances. Anyway, she paid the price.' Wry green eyes, distracted by the magnificence of the quilt, gazed candidly across at her young business partner.

'Telling me. I smell cake.'

Didn't he always?

'Coffee cake with cinnamon, raisins and sugar. Home-made.'

'Count me in.'

She already had. 'Ginger's warming it in the microwave.'

'Ginger's supposed to be upstairs looking after the office.'

'It's quiet this morning. I thought she deserved a break. Any objections?'

'Would it matter if I did?' Max watched as she bent to give the quilt one last shake. 'Great design.'

Ironic, considering. 'It's called the Double Wedding Ring. Great American classic quilt . . . always popular. Spread like wildfire in the thirties. Very old motif, probably based on the gimmel ring that came to Pennysylvania with Germanic settlers . . .'

'I only said it was pretty. Didn't ask for an illustrated lecture.' Max went mooching into the tiny back room in search of the cake. Came back a minute or two with the loaded coffee tray and plonked it down on the counter. 'Did I tell you about the job that came in yesterday? Surveillance?'

'Surveillance of what?'

'You'll like this. There's this chap called Mold. Nouveau riche . . . He wants us to watch the street where he's thinking of buying a house.'

'What on earth for?'

'Apparently he had a bad time in his last place. Hellish neighbours. They're moving down from Birmingham, where, apparently, burglary and noisy neighbours are rife. So he had this brainwave. Or rather, his girlfriend did one night in the pub.'

Ginger's auburn head popped round the door. 'That figures. It's always the women who have the brainwaves.'

Max ignored the remark. 'What Mold wants us to do is sit outside his dream house in Exmoor Avenue and report on possible problems before they sign the contract. Look for people who use the lawns as a dog toilet. Look for signs of madness in the neighbours, appraise passing kids for vandalistic tendencies and noisy ghetto-blasters. And if the local Neighbourhood Watch system works, someone should report us to the police for loitering.'

'Mad as a hatter . . .' The rest of Ginger came through the doorway. Freckled face, tiny granny glasses, skinny grey mini skirt.

'Who cares, as long as he pays well?'

Ginger poured Elizabeth a coffee, then picked up the *Mail*. 'Nightmare,' she said. 'Poor girl.'

'Which one?'

'Either. Both.'

Elizabeth said, 'And just think of all that money down the drain. Glad-rags, cancelled reception, wedding presents . . .'

'Trust a Yank—'

'Well, you've got to consider these things, Max. Weddings these days. They're state occasions. Cost a fortune.'

'Don't I know it? Cheaper to live in sin. That's what I always say.'

'To whom?' Ginger enquired.

'To my sisters when they got married.'

'How many sisters?'

'Three. Back home in Manchester.'

'Good God – no wonder you're like you are.'

'Which is?'

'Spoilt rotten.'

Max carried on philosophising. 'A wedding . . . it's like a juggernaut once it all starts. It's ritual ordeal. Not to mention a huge marketing ploy. A spend-more-than-you've-got exercise. Video cameras, photographers, Moss Bros outfits, wedding cars. Everybody eats too much, everybody gets drunk, they turn the disco up, you finish up with a hangover that lasts for a week. My doctor told me to keep well away. Marriage is bad for your mental health.'

'So how many of your sisters are married?' Ginger asked.

'All three of them.' He grinned. 'I'm the family failure. The one that got away.'

'I love weddings,' Ginger said.

'Fun to watch,' Elizabeth agreed. 'All those frocks.'

'Cinderella and her Prince.'

'Ugly Sister and her Prince in this case.' Max nodded towards the newspaper.

'Marriage is . . . comfy,' Elizabeth said to nobody in particular.

Max grimaced. 'So's an old sofa.'

'Loving someone for a long time.' She was still thinking aloud.

Ginger said, 'You don't need to be married to do that.'

'No, but—'

'But what?'

Elizabeth didn't know. Was marriage a lot of hoo-ha about nothing, after all? These two young things were making her feel ancient and outdated.

'She's got that look in her eye,' Max told Ginger. 'Any minute now, we're going to hear about her wedding.'

'Best day of my life. November fifteenth, nineteen fifty-nine. I was as nervous as hell. Like a quaking aspen. I had a beautiful new pair of shoes that pinched. And it was blowing a perfect hurricane. Rain wrestling with the wind all day long. There was a power failure. We got spliced by the light of candles. And I remember promising to love, honour and obey.'

'Obey? You?' Max was laughing.

'I did, too.'

'That one soon got broken then?'

'No. Jim wasn't much of a one for giving orders.' She looked him straight in the eye. 'So tell me . . . what in particular have you got against the married state?'

He thought long and hard. 'You have to get permits.'

'Permits?'

'To go out at night. Charlie does.'

'Charlie?'

'Fran's husband. Fran's my oldest sister. She's mustard. Charlie gets the rough edge of her tongue if he's late back. The poor bloke lives a dog's life.'

Ginger didn't believe a word of it. 'Getting married's OK. It's getting unmarried that's the bummer.'

'Hey – don't mock the most lucrative of the three D's . . .'

'The three D's?'

'Death, divorce and debt. That's what keeps the Shepard Detective Agency going.'

Upstairs, the phone shrilled. Ginger shot off to answer it and returned, five minutes later, with an odd expression on her face. 'You're not going to believe this,' she said. 'That was a Rose Mulligan.' She waved a hand towards the newspaper headline. 'The groom's mother. She says her son's innocent, but the police won't listen. She wants us to help clear his name.'

Chapter Seven

Two thirty that same day. Rose Mulligan came puffing her way to the door in laceless trainers. A big, blonde woman in a wild blouse (huge lotus-flowers) and bulging jeans. Swollen feet, swollen ankles. She had telephoned the office twice more, to make sure that someone would come.

'Come through to the patio. It's tidier there. The place is a tip.'

The flat was a council one in a Georgian block in Henry Gardens. It smelled of cats. As they passed through a long hall, Elizabeth caught a glimpse of a sitting room stacked with untidy piles of this and that and a shabby upright piano. But the garden was something else. A tumbled, English, herbaceous paradise. Willow herb and ragwort. Delphiniums and old-fashioned roses. Shaggy trees behind the harbouring wall.

'My refuge,' Rose Mulligan said, removing a trowel from a wicker chair. 'Have a seat.'

'I'm so sorry to hear about your . . .' Elizabeth pondered her choice of word. 'Your problems.'

'Kind of you to say so.' Rose Mulligan sank her considerable bulk into the chair opposite, shook a cigarette from the packet in her hand. 'I thought my life was entering a peaceful phase. Fatal, that.'

'It would help if you filled me in. Better still if your son filled me in.'

'I asked him to be here today, but it's difficult. He doesn't approve of me calling you in. Says I can't afford it and—'

'And?'

'And private detectives are a waste of time and money.'

'That may be true of some. Would you tell him we'd like to see him as soon as possible. So, your son is on bail charged with Miss Gregg's murder. Is that right?'

'That's right.'

'Pretty substantial bail, I imagine.'

'Yes.'

'Do you mind me asking how you raised the sum?'

'Anna Makepeace. I work for her – cleaning – up at the hotel. Cheyneys. You must know it. Beautiful place. Anna came straight down to the police station and fixed it all. She's been very good to me. She's a lovely lady.'

And generous to a fault.

Rose read her mind. 'I've worked up at the hotel for years. Mrs Makepeace has known Johnny since he was a little boy. She knows he didn't do it, Mrs Blair.'

'According to what I read in the *Chronicle*, they have evidence found near the body.'

'The wristwatch? It wasn't even working. He lost it a couple of months back.'

Good story, Elizabeth thought.

'Nevertheless, he had a motive for killing the girl. I'm sorry to have to press you on this, but I like to go thoroughly into the background of a case.'

'He had a motive, I'll grant you. The best in the world – but he couldn't have killed her. He was here with me until about five thirty on Saturday night and the rest of the evening he spent with Ashley.'

'Ashley.'

'Ashley Lewis. His best man. Ash spirited him off for the night to his parents' house in Gloucestershire. We had the press on the doorstep and swarming all over the wine bar. Couldn't move for them.'

'Wine bar?'

'Johnny part owns Mulligan's wine bar in Richmond Parade.'

'So what time did the police pick him up on Sunday night?'

'Around eight o'clock.'

'At this house in Gloucestershire?'

'Yes. They'd tried him at home . . . the house he shared with Imogen. Then they came here and I gave them the address.' Rose picked up the glass of orange juice that was on the table. Took a long swig. Then said, 'I'm sorry. Can I get you something?'

'I'm fine, thanks. Tell me about this girl who ruined the wedding. Kat Gregg. Did you know her?'

'Should do. I cleaned for her as well.'

'At the Beehive? And what did you make of her?'

'We got on OK until this happened.'

'Did you know there was a liaison with your son?'

'There's only her word for it.'

'Is there? Did he deny it, then?'

A look of unease. 'I asked him about it and he said he went out with her when she was still at school and she'd never stopped carrying a torch for him. She knew he loved Imogen, that they were getting married, but she had to sleep with him one more time to prove she still had some power over him. Covetousness, that's what it was. Kat by name and cat by nature. Divorced women of her age will crap on anybody's doorstep. Sorry. That was crude. But you know what I mean. According to Johnny, she invited him round to her place one night a few months back, pretending she wanted to book the wine bar for some do or other. Anyway, when he got there, she opened a bottle of wine and then another and, before he knew what was happening, he was in bed with her. Just the once.' She must have seen Elizabeth's face. 'Oh, I know it sounds weak, but he hated himself for it and he would never have done it again. Certainly not after he was married.'

Elizabeth nodded. It didn't mean she believed the statement.

'Her body was found in a back street above the Assembly Rooms. Any idea what she was doing down there?'

'No idea at all.'

Okey dokey. Try another tack. 'So tell me about your son's fiancée. Ex-fiancée. I gather she's now back home living with her mother?'

Another sip of the orange juice to fortify her. 'Yes. Johnny kept ringing, but they took the phone off the hook. So we went round there . . . he had Imogen's wedding dress, you see. He'd been up to the Beehive and made that cow give it back. But the Shand woman — Immy's mother — wouldn't let us through the door. The dress neither. Keep it, she said, and put it on a bonfire. Some people . . . well, they're miniatures. Know what I mean? Little and narrow. That's Louise Shand. I don't blame Imogen. She's a lovely girl. It's that snobbish mother of hers. Wouldn't even come to the wedding. We weren't good enough for her ladyship. She never approved of Johnny. Called him a fly-by-night and a Casanova.'

With some reason, perhaps.

'The thing that upset me most was my veil. The one I wore to my own wedding. Old lace. Something borrowed. Johnny didn't think about getting that back. Lord knows if I ever will now.' Rose Mulligan pulled at a chunk of her hair, went rambling on. 'OK, so Johnny sowed a few wild oats before he met the girl he wanted to marry. Don't they all?'

Elizabeth appeared not to have heard the question.

Rose dragged on her cigarette. 'Johnny's father . . . he used to say that women are the flowers of life. Sniff the flowers, he used to say when he'd had a few too many. And took the advice himself, more than once. He used to spout a lot of nonsense, when he'd had a drink or two. Mulligans are the fallen Kings of Ireland. Stuff like that. Buy you a soap-box for Christmas, I used to tell him. We had a few happy years together.' She brought herself back to the present. 'Johnny and Imogen . . . they didn't even get to the altar. Might yet, though. You never know.'

Rose Mulligan was an optimist, obviously.

'And the baby?' Elizabeth said quietly. 'Your grandchild that might have been? How do you feel about that?'

A shrug that tried to hide considerable agitation. 'Who's to say that it was Johnny's? From what I've heard of its mother. God rest its soul, anyway.'

The wind caught a pile of papers on the garden table and scattered them. Elizabeth helped gather them up. One or two caught her eye. 'A series of lectures on eighteenth-century music in Bath at St Bartholomew's by Peter Brendon, lecturer in music at Bristol University. That sounds interesting. Are you going along?'

'Not my scene. Must have picked it up after Evensong.'

'Do you attend regularly?'

'I'm in the choir there. I'd planned to sing a solo during the signing of the register. "O Holy Love".'

Something was puzzling Elizabeth. 'St Bartholomew's is south of the river. Quite a long journey across town for you.'

'I don't mind that. The church down at the end of the road here is a bit toffee-nosed. Full of Bath ladies. Know what I mean? Camel-through-the-eye-of-a-needle types. They make me feel uncomfortable. St Bartholomew's . . . well, it's much more . . . normal. A mixture of people. My friend, Rita, is a regular there. She picks me up of a Sunday and we go together. We're on the rota for flowers and help do the brasses and such.'

One other thing was puzzling Elizabeth. 'The reception up at – let's see now – Cheyneys Hotel. A very grand hotel. Who was paying for it? I hope you don't mind my asking.'

'Johnny was. Well, him and Immy. I couldn't afford it and her mother certainly wouldn't have anything to do with it.' She swept up the pile of papers and shuffled them into some sort of order. 'Bloody bitch. She'll be over there laughing her head off.'

Chapter Eight

Marcus Finney was cleaning a discoloured silver dressing-table box in the back room of his shop in Bartlett Street. Wiping it with a soft cloth in warm, soapy water and scrubbing its recesses with a soft toothbrush. Then he would rinse it in hot water and dry it with a clean, soft tea-towel.

Pity you couldn't rub your life up in the same way, when it had tarnished. Buff it up. Clean out all the stains that have gathered over the years. Marcus examined the muck in the recessed area of the central cartouche. My life? What, until now, has it ever amounted to? Rubbish, mainly. Educated at a minor public school. Hated the place. No alcohol, no girls. Beatings and barracking. All those years wasted. A bloody blank. Expelled (thank God) at the age of sixteen. Thrown out for cheating in a maths exam. Grabbed at the tail-end of the swinging Sixties. Smoked a bit of pot, drifted off to join the only commune in the whole of bloody India where free love hadn't caught on. Met Jan. Was obsessed by her for a while, admittedly, but that was pretty soon knocked on the head when the boy was born.

Was that when the black stuff started? The violence? No, not straightaway. A period of deep depression came first. Then the drinking and finally . . . But we won't think about that. Not today. Finney passed a hand over his receding hair. Very slowly let his mind turn to the snapshot he'd been sent through the post. Slowly; because he hardly dared let himself believe it could be true. Another son? A perfect one this time. Calm down. Deep breaths now. Calm yourself. How can I when it's like getting an unexpected Christmas present? The best you could possibly imagine. Something you've desired so ardently . . .

Might not be true, though. Thought of that? Might be some kind of elaborate hoax. Blackmail. That would be a laugh. Somebody turning the tables on you. But who would do that? What would they – she – be after? What do blackmailers usually want? Money, of course. Maintenance. Bit bloody late now, isn't it? What kind of nutcase would wait that long before making contact?

Marcus thought he might have an inkling.

He'd been thinking about it for days.

There was one woman. Long time ago, though. How long? Eighteen years, give or take a month or two. Think of it. A son of eighteen.

Marcus couldn't stop thinking about it. Dared not hope, until . . .

Until his investigations came up with something concrete. He'd done a bit of ringing around. A bit? Hours and hours.

Suddenly the door jingled. Finney brought himself back to the present, dropped the cloth, wiped his hands dry and emerged into the shop, casual this morning in dark jeans and a black polo-neck jersey that disguised his expanding waistline.

A girl stood inside the door. A girl in a green jacket, the colour of fresh pesto. Finney didn't look surprised. In fact, he'd been expecting her. Glory Magdalena Fraser. What a name!

What a girl.

Marcus stood openly admiring the line and curve of her. Sexy shoes. Strappy, high-heeled sandals on bare, brown feet. Tall, highly polished heels that made her look high and mighty. The ankle strap with its hint of bondage. The shoe providing an arc that set off her long legs. Sensual. Under-statedly erotic. Made you imagine her barefoot in the bedroom. No – the bathroom.

Marcus had a bit of a shoe fetish.

In fact, he'd asked her to wear this particular pair. They turned him on.

She's hot for it, he thought.

Glory Fraser's face was a total blank. She looked at him as if he were sick. Dirty old dork, she thought. Ogling. Fancies himself.

'Coffee?' he suggested unctuously.

'No. I'm short on time.'

Not short on attitude, though, Marcus thought. 'Better get our skates on, then,' he said with an intimate smile. And led her into the small office at the back of the shop.

Chapter Nine

You had to go just inside the gates of Cheyneys Hotel, high up on the hillside to the north of Bath, to find the Beehive Tearooms. A pretty little Regency cottage with a beehive on the front lawn. Deep gables and Gothic windows. Round (hence its name), with a porch and two over-tall chimneys, like one of those Staffordshire pastille burners. It had once been the lodge to the great house,

Elizabeth stood looking up the long avenue through the great green glade, past the stone temple and the ring of woods, to the terraces and the central pedimented portico and the stabling of this very fine example of the English country house hotel. The air smelled of pinks. They were feeding through the camomile and wild sage that had been planted on either side of the Beehive porch.

'I'll meet you there, if you like,' Aidan Makepeace had said on the telephone.

'It's not open for business?' Elizabeth had asked.

'Not just at the moment. To tell the truth, we don't quite know what to do about it, now that Kat's gone. We're waiting on my wife's lawyers to sort matters out. Anyway, you said you wanted to see the place. I've got a key. I'll meet you there if it will help.'

But he was late. Busy man, she supposed, this famous,

campaigning barrister who was passionate about issues like police corruption and forced confessions, who got fan mail, particularly from women who had heard him on the radio, who collected valuable pieces of art and furniture, gave good parties and whose wife owned (and ran) Cheyneys Hotel.

Elizabeth had had a busy morning, digging out cuttings from the *Chronicle* library and knocking on local doors, asking nosy questions.

Makepeace had shot to the top of his profession with extraordinary rapidity.

High society? You could say that again!

'Mrs Blair? Elizabeth Blair?' She heard a voice call out from the direction of the porch.

Elizabeth shook hands with him and kicked off the conversation with a compliment. 'Beautiful spot.' Somewhere up in the beeches, a ring dove called. They stood there listening. The path still showed signs of last night's rain. The greenness pierced, here and there, by a diamond of sunlight. 'And a nice little property.'

'You should have seen it when we bought it. Grunge wasn't the word.' He wore a crisp, blue shirt and beautifully cut cream trousers. One leg was crossed elegantly in front of the other as he leaned against the porch. Something Edwardian about him, Elizabeth thought. It's the distinguished air of confidence.

Nevertheless, he looked shattered by recent events.

'Kat was the one who really pulled the cottage together. The one with the drive and the flair. She was always so active. Never stopped. I really can't believe she's gone.' For a moment, his eyes filled. He had to look away. Then he got himself together. 'Come in. We can't talk out here. Let's get this over with.'

Inside was one small, round room with five tables. Blue calico cloths, shelves with jampots (like you'd fallen down Alice's rabbit hole); a new conservatory, also circular, had been tacked on at the back, with wickerwork chairs, old chamber pots filled with plants, framed fashion plates on the walls. There was a certain eccentricity, but it worked.

'It's charming,' Elizabeth said.

'Kat's doing. She knew how to make the old place look good. She had a huge amount of energy. Wanted to squeeze every drop out of life. Got too fired up at times.'

'So I gather.' Elizabeth's voice was dry. 'So how did you meet? How did she come to be running this place?'

'I first met Kat about five years ago when my wife ran a Jane Austen convention at the hotel. We converted the stables so that we could run study weekends and activity holidays and we host craft and antiques fairs in the old Orangery. Painting weekends, cookery, weaving. You name it, we do it. Anyway, I was helping my wife host a reception evening for the convention and Kat made a beeline for me. She took the initiative. She was very upfront, very open. She asked if she could lease the Beehive from us. It was so run down that I thought she was joking. But she talked us into it. Plagued us until we gave in. There was something special about her. She was always so buoyant. There was a vigour about her. Vitality. Raw energy.'

He liked her.

'She was unusual. A one-off. That young fool – Mulligan – wasn't anywhere near good enough for her. That was the tragedy of it. Why do perfectly bright women fall for arseholes like that?'

Why indeed? But it happened all the time. 'So you and Miss Gregg were friends?' Elizabeth said.

'I'd say that. Yes. We had jolly times. Lots of laughter.' A half smile, as he remembered. 'She could be very fierce in a childlike sort of way. No side-tracking. She upset people with her honesty.'

'Like when she spattered dung all over her lover's squeaky-clean wedding?'

'He deserved it,' Makepeace said irritably.

'And his fiancée? The real bride?'

'Imogen? Oh, God, it was bad for her. A nightmare.'

'You're acquainted with the lady?'

'She works as a receptionist at the hotel.'

Talk about keeping it all in the family! 'That's why they were holding the reception here?'

'Exactly. Imogen was a nice girl. Pretty girl. My wife's very fond of her.'

'And you?'

'I hardly know her. My work keeps me too busy to get enmeshed in the running of the hotel.'

'But you knew Kat? Miss Gregg?'

'I told you. She made it her business to know me. She was full of energy. I like people like that. She had a great sense of fun. She made me laugh. Her observations could be very funny. She made fun of my big car. Called it a petrol-guzzling monster. She drove this battered little Saab.'

'So who paid for this place to be renovated? You said it was in a state when she took it over.'

'She had some money saved up. I paid some of the bills and she paid me back.'

Elizabeth must have looked sceptical.

'It's the truth, I assure you. I mean, look at this place. Right on the main road, half a mile from the M4. She used to get busloads of Japanese and Yankee ladies stopping by for English tea. It was a little gold mine.'

'So you were friends and you helped her financially. Forgive me asking this, but there was nothing else between you?'

'Good God, no. I've been happily married to the same woman for almost thirty years. Kat and I were just very good friends. You always felt better for seeing her. She could be exhausting. Never stopped talking. Could she talk? Especially when she'd a glass or two of red wine inside her.'

'So she was basically a happy sort of a person?'

'Happy? Not sure if she's have used that word. You can't always expect to be happy. But she could get inebriated on life. She'd send me silly faxes that I couldn't read. Her writing was atrocious. I'd have to ring her up and say, "What?" '

'Did she ever upset you? I mean, did you ever quarrel?'

'We had niggles, but we never quarrelled.'

'Niggles? What about?'

'Oh, trivia. You know. She had this thing about spring-cleaning. She would suddenly have to clear the decks . . . do the place out, paint it through. I'd say, for God's sake leave it until the place closes down in January, but she was totally unreasonable about it. If she decided it looked scruffy – and it never did – she'd cancel everything and – whoosh! That makes her sound very screwed up and she wasn't – well, only about Mulligan. She said once that she cleaned to put her life in order.'

'Did she have rows with other people that you know of?'

'She had a temper. Can't deny that. She'd flare up. Always apologised afterwards, but, by God, when the volcano went up, you knew it. And she could be very blunt. Some people find that difficult, but you always got an honest reaction from her. She could never tell a lie. She wouldn't know how to. It all came straight out. I admired her honesty and courage.'

'Even when she did what she did last Saturday morning?'

'That was stupid. I told her so. But she changed when she got involved again with Johnny Mulligan.'

'You knew the affair was going on? She told you?'

'Yes. She couldn't stop talking about him. I think he was the only person who ever deeply upset her in her life. She really did think he was going to break with Imogen and marry her. She changed when she realised it wasn't going to happen. The effervescence went out of her. They talk about people being lovesick. It's true. Her obsession with Mulligan . . . it was like an illness.'

A fatal illness, Elizabeth thought. 'You say you talked a lot. Did she tell you about the baby?'

'Yes. That last night before she was . . . before she died.' He told her about that last night; stress, now, all over his face. He struggled to get control of it. 'Johnny wanted her to have an abortion. No way, she said. She loved kids. She was great with them. Held parties here sometimes for the kids from St Dunstan's. It's a local school for the mentally handicapped.'

Elizabeth nodded. She had heard of it. 'So . . . where were you the night Miss Gregg was murdered?'

'I was having dinner up at the hotel with my wife and a very old friend. The Contessa di Stresa. We had such a lovely evening, but – I wish to hell I'd popped over to ckeck that Kat was OK. She might not have gone down to town—'

'You've no idea what she was doing in Alfred Buildings?'

'Not a clue. Sorry. She'd have got over Mulligan, you know. She loved it here. Loved the business. She'd have bounced back. I know she would. If only she'd been allowed to . . .'

He broke off. Eyes troubled.

'You said she was pretty blunt with people. Was there anyone else – besides Mulligan – that she might have fallen out with?'

'Can't think of any. There was the battle with the Twinnies about using the roadside verge as a car park. But—'

'The Twinnies?'

'Sorry. The Benson sisters. Hope and Vanessa. Live in the cottage a hundred yards down the hill. Hate change. They had a go at us when we turned the Hall into a hotel. They threatened to take Kat to court. But she was a good little fighter. She liked all that kind of stuff.'

'You mean she was naturally belligerent?'

'Yeah. She certainly wasn't the passive type. Left that role to her ex-husband.' It was said tongue in cheek.

'She was divorced.'

'Yes. Her ex is a teacher. Well-meaning but useless. That's how Kat described him.'

'One last thing. I wonder – would anybody mind if I took a quick look around her private quarters?'

'I'd . . . better check with the police.' For the first time, he seemed faintly rattled. 'I'll give you a call. OK?'

Chapter Ten

Two strains of music vied with each other at eight fifteen that evening in the church room at St Batholomew's. 'Rejoice greatly, O daughter of Zion' from Handel's *Messiah* tinkling out from the battered piano, while more faintly from the church next door – joined to the church room by a bit of a vestry – organ and choristers rehearsed: 'Bring me my bow of burning gold. Bring me my arrows of desire . . .'

A riot to the senses, Elizabeth thought, when the bells up in the tower decided to join in with a hollow, lofty peal by way of a bonus. But she could do with that tonight. Music swelling, no matter how mingled and mangled. The emotional, not the rational. (Though the odd matter-of-fact thought occasionally emerged via the back door, so to speak – casually, subconsciously – while your senses were overflowing.)

Outside, an early autumn evening. A gusty wind, wisps of cloud, wisps of leaves, traffic whisking up the hill into town.

The piano stopped.

'Coffee break,' said the baby-faced lecturer. 'Then we'll take a look at a very public quarrel in the pages of the *Bath Chronicle* in January seventeen seventy-two about a series of concerts at the New Assembly Rooms.'

The pianist – short, dark, fly-away hair and dark eyes, slightly fey – tidied her music. The woman in the chair in front of

Elizabeth gave a start, tried to pretend she hadn't been asleep in the first place and heaved herself up to head for the coffee queue. Elizabeth didn't bother. She had more important fish to fry, like ferreting out the Reverend Richard Timms.

When she had rung the vicarage at ten that morning, he had come across as a lively, enthusiastic soul. 'Yes, come along to the lectures by all means. Plenty of places left, I understand. Seven thirty in the church room. You know where we are? Bottom of the hill, right by the roundabout. Will I be there? Well, not at the lecture itself, but I'll be next door in the church. Yes, I could spare you five minutes. You're a private detective? An American?' He hadn't known quite what to make of that, but he assured her that he positively guzzled detective stories. 'Chandler, of course. And McBain. These mean streets.' His voice positively glowed. 'Jolly good stuff—'

Tonight, he was sorting hymn books at the back of the church. A tall, dark man whose eyes exuded natural sympathy. When younger, he would have written poetry to the girl he loved. Or at least, he would have looked sonnets.

He remained shocked by what had happened in his church on Saturday. 'Quite a disturbance to our usually quiet domain. Shocked some of my elderly lady parishioners, I can tell you.'

How long had he known the two families? The Mulligans and the Shands?

'Mrs Mulligan I know very well. Splendid woman. Helps with coffee after church on a Sunday morning. And I'd prepared the bride and groom, of course. But they were not, shall we say, of a spiritual bent.'

'Not regulars?'

'I'm afraid not.' A wry smile. 'Moderation in everything, Mrs Blair. Isn't that what the Anglican church rests upon? I have to say that it's the perfect church for those who don't go to church.' There was a twinkle that expressed a great deal of tolerance. 'But young Johnny seemed a perfectly pleasant young man. Very gentle with his intended bride. Loved her deeply . . . that was clear to see.'

'Would you say he was capable – forgive me asking – of committing a murder in her defence?'

The Reverend Timms heaved a long sigh. 'I very much hope not.'

'But you think there's a possibility?'

'I've been asking myself that ever since his arrest. And I have to say that, after what happened on Saturday and given these very extreme circumstances, I can't make up my mind. Who knows what we're capable of when the passions boil over?'

'You know, of course, about—'

Elizabeth didn't get to finish the question. A sudden footstep in the aisle made them turn. An elderly man with dishevelled greying hair came swooping (it was the only word) down on them. He wore a Fair Isle jumper over a striped t-shirt, red, white and blue. More colour-blind than patriotic.

'There you are, Vicar. That chap's here about the electrics. Wants a word.'

'I'm popular tonight.' Reverend Timms left, but promised to return.

'Brian Thursley,' said the swooper, briskly introducing himself to Elizabeth. 'Should be ringing tonight, but I've put my back out.'

'I'm sorry to hear that,' she said.

'The bell is considerably heavier than the ringer, as I've found out to my cost.' He passed a hand over thinning hair, head ducked to one side.

'I imagine it is.'

'The bell I usually ring is six times heavier than I am.'

'Is that a fact?'

'It's a matter of skill over strength.' His body went into a sudden lean as he whipped a service sheet from a red hymn book.

'Or should be.'

'You've got me there. Good ringers don't need osteopaths.'

61

Elizabeth was beginning to wonder how she could slide past him. But then she had a thought. 'I don't suppose you were here for the wedding on Saturday?'

'I was here all right. Not ringing – well, nobody was ringing. They didn't get as far as the bells . . .'

The bells . . . the bells! Elizabeth shoved away all thoughts of hunchbacks and waited for him to go on.

'But I lead the band, so I came along to keep an eye on things.'

Plenty of things to keep an eye on, on that particular morning.

'Well, as I said, there we all were, five ropes, hanging about in the tower and nothing to do. Waste of a perfectly good Saturday morning.'

'I don't suppose, by any chance, you knew the groom?'

'Only second-hand, so to speak, from chatting to Rose over coffee on a Sunday after service. Salt of the earth, that woman, but she's had a hard time of it. Married a drunken pig who treated her like dirt. Oh, she'd never say so, but you can read between the lines. Still, she stood up to him over some things. Wouldn't have the kids brought up as Catholics.' He nodded hard.

Ridiculously, Elizabeth found herself nodding too hard as well, like a TV interviewer caught on camera.

'Her boys were everything to her and Johnny the favourite. Always on about him, she was. That ruddy group of his. Came along and played for some fund-raising do last year. Didn't care much for it myself, but you couldn't say so. Irish fiddles and booze behind the piano.'

Elizabeth sounded both interested and distant. 'Do you think Johnny was capable of killing the woman who broke up his wedding?'

'I think he was a squalid little toe-rag who was capable of anything. Listen to that peal. I don't suppose you know this, but there are over five thousand towers with bells hung for full circle ringing in England and less than two hundred in the rest of the world.'

Odd facts (and odd people) are one of the perks of the job, Elizabeth thought, as she drove home that night. Rainy, dark, now, as she approached the village of South Harptree. And deathly quiet, except for the soughing of sycamores behind the churchyard wall.

The lane that ran round the front of her terraced cottage was wet with fallen leaves. They had gathered in soggy clumps on the lawn and by the porch. Plenty of work there for the weekend. Worse luck.

She'd only just got inside the door when the phone rang. It was Dottie Marchant's bossy, old-maid's voice. 'You're late tonight. Can you come in? I can't get into this blasted aspirin bottle.'

Elizabeth's heart sank. Dottie had been her neighbour for a number of years; she had this habit of seizing you just when you needed to shut down for a while.

She found the old girl in her old, blue dressing gown and minus her teeth. In fact, Dottie looked haggled and impatient, disturbingly unlike her usual ebullient self. 'There you are. Been waiting ages . . .' She was mumbling a bit. Unusual. Dottie was not a mumbler. Quite the opposite, in fact. 'Get this top off and fetch me some water. Feel like two ha'pence worth of nothing . . .'

The kitchen, like Dottie, had an eccentric personality all of its own. There was a butler's sink on legs; an old boiler that Dottie still used to boil her smalls in. A couple of bentwood chairs, one with a pot plant on and the other holding a cast-iron saucepan. She had bought the cottage just after the war, when property was at rock bottom and precious little, as far as Elizabeth could see, had been done to it since.

'Headache?' Elizabeth asked as she watched the pills go down.

'Splitting.' Her small, round eyes seemed bright with fever. 'Had a blessed 'flu jab. Wish I hadn't bothered.'

'I should get to bed.'

'Intend to. Can't think where I put the . . . the . . . Oh, you know . . . the thing I get the stuff out with.' Dottie had hold of her knitted tea cosy and was twisting it round and round in her fingers, pleating the yellow and red knitted edge, while she struggled to find the missing word. 'Can't remember the name of the flopping thing.' She seemed in genuine distress. Elizabeth had never seen her in such a state.

'You'll think of it later. Look — why don't I fill a hot-water bottle while you get yourself into the sack?'

Dottie was still fussing, tucking her fingers into the hole for the spout. 'The thing mother used to use. You know. In the days when station waiting rooms had real coal fires.'

The doctor, Elizabeth thought to herself. Will he come, if I ring now? He'll have to. I'm worried about the old girl.

Max rang next morning at nine. 'You sound bleary.'

'I feel bleary.'

'Don't tell me. You were out all night on a bender.'

If only. 'I was up half the night, tending the sick.'

The doctor had thought it better if someone could stay. Nasty reaction to the 'flu jab. It happened. Should be fine by the morning. And he was right. Dottie was less feverish, though she had refused any breakfast. 'So what was so all-fired urgent?'

'Nothing, really. I just wondered what your plans were for today.'

'I thought I'd talk to Imogen Shand. And you?'

'Not sure yet. Probably a spot of Neighbourhood Watch.'

'I'd like you to call Rose Mulligan and ask why the hell her precious son hasn't got in touch with us. You'd think he'd need all the help he can get. And then I'd like you to check out where

Aidan Makepeace was on Saturday night. Find out if he was at the hotel.'

'Can do,' said Max.

'In fact, I've had a thought. Take Ginger along with you.'

'Why?' He sounded suspicious.

'Tell you later. Anything interesting in the mail today?'

'Nope. But we had an unexpected visitor.'

'Who was that?'

'Caroline.'

'My Caroline?'

'The duchess herself.'

It was an accurate description of her lady-like shop assistant. Elizabeth's voice sharpened. 'Something wrong down below?' Caroline had orders never to leave the shop unattended.

'Not that I know of. She just came up to issue an invitation. She wants to take us for a drink tonight. Me, you and Ginger.'

'You sure you got this right?' Caroline never — but never — lowered herself to socialise. Well, only for Christmas drinks.

'Positive. Nineish OK? We get to choose the venue.'

Elizabeth was stunned. 'So what did you say?'

'I told her Mulligan's wine bar. Kill two birds with one stone, I thought.'

Chapter Eleven

There was one more call before Elizabeth made it to the bathroom for a well-earned shower. Her daughter, Kate, from New York. 'Mom? That you?'

'Sure is. What's wrong?'

'Why should there be anything wrong?'

'Listen, it's four in the morning, New York time.'

'So?'

'So you don't normally call at this hour.'

'So when did I ever do anything normal?'

Good question. Kate had always marched to her own drummer. 'OK. Have it your way. Let's talk about the weather for a while.'

'God, you're crabby! I wonder why I bother.'

This conversation was going in circles. Elizabeth's patience hadn't yet snapped, but it was being stretched. 'Look – Kate. Is everything OK?'

'Everything's fine.' A pregnant pause. 'In fact, everything's damned near perfect.'

Which meant only one thing. 'So who is he?'

'Who's who?'

'This wonderful new guy in your life?'

'Mom – the world doesn't have to run on romance.'

'I never said it did. So who is he?'

A brief silence. A long sigh. Then, 'OK. So I rang to say I'm moving in with this guy. You'll need my new address.'

Such tact. Such preparation. Such care over your old mother's feelings. So how come, Elizabeth thought, I land a son who gets himself in a sweat about creeping forward an inch and a daughter who leaps blindfold into chasms?

'Mom? You still there?'

'I'm here.'

'And disapproving. I can tell. You think I'm making one huge mistake.'

'How would I know, when I never met the guy? When you've this minute let on about him?'

'You're mad at me. It's in your voice. You think people should get married before they live together. I should tell you now. Saul thinks marriage stinks.'

Saul. We have a name, if nothing else. But that's not fair. You left the kids to come live on the other side of the Atlantic.

It had been a hard night on Dottie's camp bed. Elizabeth felt suddenly exhausted. 'Listen – Kate. I wish you joy with your Saul. But I'm late for work. Give me your new address and phone number. I'll call you tonight.'

She put the receiver down. Stood looking at her mother's wedding picture on top of the china cabinet. Oval frame. Papa stiff and awkward in his one-and-only dark suit. Mama in 1920s ankle-length frock and strapped shoes. Married for sixty-two years. I'd like to say with never a cross word, but that would be a lie. Spent their first night together (and it probably *was* the first night) in a room in Papa's father's house in Lovett Street. Correction. First two years. Not a cent to get a place of their own.

Four quilts (hand-made, the only pretty things she had) Mama had in her hope chest when she moved into the Lovett Street house. Six quilts and two babies by the time she left.

Real particular about colour and stitching, Mama was. You had to take out the stitches if they weren't straight and true and even.

Kate's picture was right next to Mama's. There had been a pleasure in putting the two of them together. The one dead and gone before the other was born, but they looked a lot like each other.

Same face.

Different times.

Sex now entirely divorced from procreation. Makes life easier. Or does it? Kate, at thirty-three, already had three broken relationships behind her.

And now this Saul. Would he be the right one at last? I hope so, God knows. Weariness hit her. Elizabeth dragged herself upstairs and into a hot shower.

Max, meanwhile, was searching for his car keys in his tiny office above Elizabeth's shop. Without much success.

'Tried the piano stool?' Ginger asked.

'The piano stool?'

'I saw you drop them in there when you were looking for paper clips.' One thin, brown wrist flicked sideways to grab an envelope. She looked particularly crisp and efficient this morning in a striped shirt thing and a short, grey skirt with a sort of flirty fishtail thing at the back.

Pleat. Max struggled to find the right word for it.

A sunny morning. A light wind blowing through the open window; a constant flow of tourists in the alley below. Max lifted the seat of the Victorian piano stool. There were the keys.

He glanced at his watch. It said ten past eight. 'So what time do you make it?' he asked Ginger.

'Nine thirty.'

Damn.

'Stopped again? You should ditch that old thing. Buy yourself a new one.'

She was always telling him what to do.

The phone shrilled. Ginger picked it up. 'Shepard Agency. Can I help you?'

She said a few words, laughed and put it down again.

'Who was that?'

'My flatmate.' She offered no further information.

A pause while Max gave the watch a tap and put it right. 'So where is it that you live?'

'Hamilton Row.'

'Nice.'

'Expensive.'

'Bet you're glad she pays half the rent then. Your flatmate.'

'Actually, she's a he.'

'You share with a bloke? You didn't say.'

'Why would I?' Her grey gaze was very open.

Why indeed? He turned his attention back to the day's work.

He heard the kettle flick on and cups rattling. 'You stopped,' she called out from the tiny kitchen.

'Stopped what?'

'Fishing.'

'Who's fishing?'

'You were.'

In the window box, geranium leaves burned brittle around the edges by summer sun. Parallel strips of shade and sunlight on the wall behind. Weaker than the summer stuff, but somehow more beautiful.

'He's a medical student,' Ginger said.

'Oh – right.'

Max's youngest sister – Susy – had once gone out with a medic. Posh accent, blond-streaked hair, supercilious bastard.

'He came in drunk last night and broke my favourite teapot.'

So they hadn't been out together? She hadn't gone out with him? Then they had to be just mates. And yet the conversation had sounded . . . intimate. Her laugh. There had been some remark about him paying for it tonight.

'We went on holiday together last year. Italy. Florence and

thereabouts – backpacking. And we got on so well, that we decided to find a flat together. And before you ask, we're just mates. OK?'

Ginger went on tap-tapping round the floorboards in the kitchen and rabbiting about her holiday in Italy. Max was only half listening, the rest of his mind skimming levelly over the print-out in front of him. Eventually, he became aware of her standing behind him.

'There are all sorts of mistakes in that. Did you know?'

'In what?'

'In that thing you're reading.'

'Looks all right to me.'

'Yes . . . well. The arrangement's a bit cock-eyed. If you don't mind my saying so.'

And if he did? 'I suppose you could have done it better?'

'Probably, but it's not my job.'

Exactly. It's my firm, Max thought. So you know what you can do with your comments. She'd only been here twelve months and she'd already gone through the place like a tornado. With Elizabeth's connivance.

'You know this Aidan Makepeace? I read a newspaper article about him the other day.'

'So? Anything of importance?'

'It was one of those Sunday profiles. Quite interesting though. Media barrister. Human dynamo. Success story all round. Three homes, wife runs a top-notch hotel. Apparently he set up a charity to provide representation for people on Death Row in the States. They say he's amazing in court. Talks to the jury as if he's one of them. Wins nearly all his cases . . .' She paused thoughtfully. 'Mind you, when you think about it, that probably means only one thing.'

'What's that?'

'Well, not all his clients can be innocent.'

'So?'

'So it just goes to prove that barristers can also be bare-faced liars. Ever thought of that?'

Chapter Twelve

By ten fifteen a.m. that same morning, Elizabeth had talked her way into Louise Shand's six-bedroomed house behind Great Pulteney Street, built from locally quarried Bath stone and draped all round with rampaging Virginia creeper.

Mrs Shand could give her five minutes and five minutes only.

She hadn't the slightest intention of helping clear Johnny Mulligan's name. She didn't give a damn what happened to him. They could lock him up and lose the key for all she cared.

'I fully understand how you feel.' Elizabeth sat on the edge of the Queen Anne chair that had been newly covered in rather a splendid red-and-blue tulip design. Arched wall cupboards held a collection of china teapots and Staffordshire figures. In the centre of a group of paintings on the opposite wall was an imposing oil painting of a young woman in a blue blouse and an incandescent blue stare.

Portrait of the bride's mother as a young woman?

Very possibly.

'I have daughters of my own. It's bothersome when they bring home young men from the wrong side of the tracks. And they all do, at one time or another, believe you me.' A heart-felt smile. 'From what I hear, the young man was trouble from beginning to end?'

'Too true. But my daughter was besotted with him. Arguing

with someone who's blinded by sexual attraction is next door to useless. Imogen is a very receptive girl. Too receptive at times. That ... womaniser took her in completely. She was in a complete daze. Floating. It was as if she'd gone through some transcendental experience.'

Mrs Shand smoothed the tweedy skirt down over her knees. An attractive woman at first sight. Chestnut bob, good diamond rings on delicately boned fingers. But the eyes were too coldly blue. She had one of those bland faces, like a book that would never open.

'But you never accepted Johnny?'

'I saw through him from day one. He wasn't half so clever as he thought he was. There was no way I was going to accept him and he knew it.'

'Did that cause problems between him and your daughter?'

'Not that I'm aware of. She went off to live with him.'

Probably helped on by your disapproval.

'And you chose not to go to the wedding?'

'She was about to make the biggest mistake of her life. I wasn't going to go watch her doing so.'

Can't honestly blame you, Elizabeth thought. On the other hand, how could you stay away?

'I tried to tell her, but she wouldn't listen.'

Self-confidence as high as a tree. Don't tell me. 'So how is your daughter at the moment?'

'In a very precarious state. Exhausted, distraught . . .'

'Did she get her wedding dress back, by the way?'

'No. The coloured girl — Glory Fraser — went over to Mulligan's house to fetch it back, but Immy told her to keep it.'

'Coloured girl?'

'One of Imogen's schoolfriends. The dress is ruined anyway, all torn and stained. And the veil's disappeared entirely.'

'How come?'

'I've no idea. Apparently the Mulligan woman asked the Makepeaces to find it for her, but it wasn't at the Beehive.'

Odd. Elizabeth went on to the next question on her mental list. 'Your daughter is staying here with you, I gather? I'd like to ask her a few questions.'

'Yes. She's come back home to live, but she won't see anybody and I don't blame her. The press have been absolutely foul, hammering on the door day and night.'

'It's been pretty bad for Rose Mulligan too. All kinds of problems.'

'Don't talk to me about that woman—'

'Well, you know, I liked her. She was kind of good-hearted.'

A real down-her-nose stare. 'Those sort of people can always take you in.'

'Those sort of people?'

'Irish peasants.'

'Rose isn't Irish. She married an Irishman.'

'Well, bigger fool her—'

'So you didn't get on with any of the Mulligans?'

'I most certainly did not!'

'But you kept in touch with your daughter?'

'She dropped in now and again.'

'She needed to see you?'

'I suppose. Imogen's very young for her years. She went to live with him, but she was only half independent.'

'The other half of her still needed her mom? And did she talk to you about the relationship? Was she happy with young Mulligan?'

'She didn't talk about him. She knew better than that.'

You wouldn't let her.

'But . . .' A hesitation. 'They had a row a few weeks back.'

'About what?'

'That she wouldn't tell me, but I could see she'd been crying and she was reluctant to go home. Hung around here until I offered her a bed for the night.'

'Did she take you up on it?'

75

'No such luck. She went home at about a quarter to midnight.'

'Can I ask? What are your feelings about the girl who blew the wedding ceremony? Katharine Gregg . . . I suppose she did you a favour, in a funny sort of way.'

A shrug of the shoulders. 'I can't deny it. Of course, it hurts to see my daughter hurting, but there would have been a lot more pain in the long run.'

'If she'd married him?'

'Of course.'

A pause. 'Imogen worked up at Cheyneys Hotel, I believe?'

'As a receptionist. Yes. Glory Fraser got her in there.'

'How come?'

'Glory works there part-time. She knew the other receptionist was leaving.'

'Does your daughter like her job? Is Mrs Makepeace a good employer?'

'Very good . . . or so she tells me.' One slim ankle rested over the other one. 'I've never been up there.'

'You haven't met Mrs Makepeace? Or her husband?'

'I've seen them from a distance.'

'But they were guests at your daughter's wedding.'

'I told you. I had nothing to do with the wedding.'

'I'm sorry. I have to ask this. Where was your daughter between seven thirty and eight last Saturday night?'

'She was upstairs, flat out. I made her take a sleeping pill. Now, if you've quite finished, I have a busy day in front of me.'

Back in the car, Elizabeth called Marcus Finney, but he'd gone off on a buying trip. His wife said she'd get him to call back as soon as possible.

*　　*　　*

By twelve thirty p.m. Elizabeth was talking to Kat's ex-husband in the playground of the Philip Ward Church of England school five miles north of Bath. Hundreds of hollering seven-year-olds raising Cain all around.

Like flights of raucous starlings.

Peter Gregg was thin, with limp fair hair and a limp handshake. (There wouldn't have been a handshake at all if Elizabeth hadn't forced it on him.)

Not a mover and a shaker, that was for sure.

He said the marriage had broken up because of Mulligan. Kat had just walked out. Bored rigid, she'd told him.

'She said I was hopeless. That I took her for granted. That all I wanted was a surrogate mother and a cook-housekeeper. She called me wet and sad and immature and pathetic and a lot of other things besides.'

He kept his eye on the children all the time. There was a cramped-up look about him. A lonesome guy, if you ever saw one.

They had wanted a baby, but it had never happened. His fault, apparently. Low sperm count. They'd had treatment, but it hadn't worked. Were thinking about another lot when Mulligan came back on the scene. 'Perhaps she thought it would be easier with him,' Shaw said bitterly.

'Mr Gregg. Kieran pinched my lolly—'

Gregg went off to sort the matter out. Returned a moment later wiping his fingers on a handkerchief.

He seemed bewildered by the murder.

Still in love with his late wife? Maybe, Elizabeth thought. Maybe not. In love with what she had once been, perhaps. Or what he'd thought her to be.

'Did you ever meet Mulligan face to face?'

He shook his head. 'Flash type, so I heard. Flamboyant. She said he was exciting. She was desperate for some fun. Well, she got that, all right. Before it all caught up with her.'

The starlings were at full volume, so he went walkabout until they quietened down.

'She didn't call you last weekend – or come over?' Elizabeth asked on his return.

No, he hadn't seen or heard from her this last six months.

'I have to ask,' Elizabeth said. 'Where were you the night she was murdered?'

Anxiety before his answer came. Definitely. 'I went home to see my parents.'

'And they live where?'

'Stroud. I was there from the Friday night until Sunday afternoon.'

And the Makepeaces? What did he know of their dealings with Kat? This bit was interesting. According to Gregg, they'd taken no end of money from her business. She'd had a row with Mrs Makepeace about it. That woman wasn't half as classy as she made out.

'And Aidan Makepeace?' Elizabeth asked. 'Is it possible your ex-wife had a sexual relationship with him? Or with other men besides Mulligan?'

He wouldn't be surprised. 'Kat's brash exterior . . . it was all an act. Underneath it, she was lonely. She was a very emotional woman. She'd take her comfort where she could.'

'So who do you think killed her?'

'He did. Mulligan. He treated her badly and when she got her own back, he killed her. She had her little adventure and she paid for it with her life.'

Eleven a.m. Elizabeth was serving a customer when the young man walked into the shop. Dark, curly hair, sharp suit.

'. . . the pink-and-cream quilt? It was pieced in Nova Scotia around nineteen forty-seven. So it needed to be warm. Hard winters up there . . .'

'Are you Mrs Blair?' the young man asked with scant regard to his place in the queue.

'I am. But this lady—'

He wasn't interested in other customers. 'I believe you wanted to talk to me. I'm Johnny Mulligan.'

Chapter Thirteen

Mulligan's face wore a blank look for most of the time Elizabeth spent interviewing him. No sign today of the charmer who'd had more women than hot breakfasts.

Allegedly.

'So, Mr Mulligan, we meet at last.'

'I didn't have to come here.'

'Granted. But it might be in your interests.'

'You think?'

'I do. Unless, of course, you're looking forward to being put away for a long time.'

'That won't happen.'

'You seem very sure of that.'

'I am. I didn't kill her.'

'You're absolutely innocent?'

'That's right.'

'I might remind you that the newspapers are full of Innocents-in-Clink stories.' Elizabeth decided to go straight for the jugular. 'Did you kill Katharine Gregg?'

'No. I didn't.'

'The police believe you did. They have certain forensic evidence.'

'I had a fight with her earlier that day. But I didn't kill her.'

'Your watch was found next to her body. How do you explain that?'

'I can't. Unless—'

'Unless?'

'Unless somebody planted it there.'

'Such as?'

'I don't know. You find out. That's what my mother's paying you for.'

'Do you have any particular enemies? Besides Miss Gregg?'

'Louise Shand. She hates my guts.' He sat there staring at his hands. 'Look – I wasn't anywhere near Alfred Buildings that night. Ask Ash's parents. I was out for the count.'

'That could be faked, I imagine. You could have got out by the back way after they dumped you on the bed.'

'No way. Ash kept looking in to see if I was OK.'

'And people lie to help their friends.'

'Look – I was nowhere near Alfred Buildings and I didn't kill her.'

'You hated her enough to kill her. You have an Irish temper. And you were heard threatening her.'

'It doesn't mean that I did it.'

'OK. So we'll assume that you didn't kill her. In that case, how do you feel about losing your child as well as your mistress?'

Under the belt, Elizabeth. Yes, I know. But it's necessary. And this young man is no prude when it comes to hurting other people.

Mulligan flushed slightly. Looked acutely uncomfortable and sat picking at the edge of the counter in front of him.

'It bothers you? Yes?'

'Of course it does.' A flash of temper now in the blue eyes, but it was held under control. 'I'm not a complete monster.'

'Like the papers are saying. So tell me about Imogen. Your ex-fiancée. The girl whose wedding you ruined. What do you imagine she's feeling?'

'Leave Immy out of this.'

'You wish.' Elizabeth's firm green gaze went on studying him.

'Yes – I do wish.'

'I bet you do. I take it you don't want to think about all the times you cheated on her?'

'Look – I didn't mean to hurt her. I was faithful to her for a long time.'

'How long?'

'Months and months.'

'Big deal!'

'OK. You disapprove. But you weren't in the relationship. And it was the only time I'd ever been tied down. The first time there were rules.'

'For you to break?' She couldn't resist that one. The lazy blue eyes sullen now. He didn't appreciate the lecture.

'Say what you like. You don't know the first thing about me and Immy. It . . . wasn't all plain sailing.'

'You're saying there were problems in the relationship?'

'Not problems exactly. But—'

She sat there waiting.

'I love Immy – but it wasn't always easy.'

'In what way?'

'In bed . . . for a long while, at least.'

'You're saying she was frigid?'

'No. Not exactly. She held back for a long time . . . physically. She was scared.'

'Any particular reason?'

A shrug. 'She was young, I suppose.'

'Does that make any difference these days?'

'Not usually. But it did with Immy. She was young for her age.'

'So that was why you cheated on her?'

'That was part of it.'

'Why you cheated on her over and over again. So tell me something. Why were you marrying her, if you weren't altogether suited?'

'Because I love her.'

'Plenty wouldn't believe you.'

'I know that. Believe you me! This last week—'

'I take it you're not the most popular guy in town?'

Silence.

'But you still love her.'

'Yes.'

'Even though she won't see you? Even though she never wants to see you again?'

'Yes – damn you!' In tears, Mulligan was another man, younger, more vulnerable. 'Jesus, Mary and Joseph! No matter what you think of me, no matter what I've done to hurt her, no matter how much she hates me now, I still love her and I'll always love her. So just keep your rasping tongue away from her, you bloody old witch!'

'I upset him,' she told Max later. 'I thought he was going to wring my neck.'

'That would have made the headlines. Second Body: Elderly American. So what did you make of our Johnny?'

'Weak.' A young man whose will was as the wind. Perhaps not altogether a bad young man. (Or so his mother said.) But one who gave in to his appetites far too easily. And who thought he could extricate himself from trouble without too much difficulty.

Until now, that is.

'So is he guilty or what?'

'Not sure.' The police had hard evidence against him, but she was far from certain. 'I might make a trip up to see Lewis's parents. Got a little job for you, too.'

There must have been something in her tone. Max looked suspicious.

Elizabeth reached under the counter and handed him a leaflet. 'I picked up this at Rose Mulligan's the other day. Thought you might be interested.'

It read as follows:

Getting married next Spring? Thinking of an April wedding?
Why not visit our Bridal Exhibition in the Orangery at Cheyneys.

'Oh, no——' he said. 'Not my scene. You go.'

'Max, honey – no one's going to believe I'm the blushing bride. A trifle long in the tooth, wouldn't you say? But you two . . .' Elizabeth stood gazing at Max and Ginger, a glint of enjoyment in her green eyes. 'You'll look the part. It's the perfect excuse for you to have a quiet little sniff around the place.'

Twelve noon. Max and Ginger found themselves standing around like a pair of prunes on the waxed pine floor of the expertly converted Orangery that was expertly filled with soft drifts of silk, with gauze as thin as a vapour, with ribbons and bows and veils and broderie anglaise, with antique lace and garters and frills and ruffles. And then there were the flowers. Lorry loads of them, stinking the place out. Tiger lilies, gardenias, white roses . . . And bloody Cupids everywhere . . .

Not to mention violins. A thin rain of strings falling finely and incessantly.

It was enough to make a man turn ashen.

'Get me out of here——' Max said.

'Something wrong?' Ginger enquired.

'Gruesome——'

'Agreed,' said Ginger.

He shot her a surprised look. 'I thought women liked this stuff?'

'Not me.'

'But you said——'

'I said I liked weddings. The occasion. Drinking champagne, gawping at what people are wearing. I didn't say I wanted to get married. This stuff's gross.' Demeaning, quite definitely, she went on. Who wanted to look like a Barbie doll and anyway, they all got divorced again in a couple of years.

'Can I show you anything in particular?' a voice said behind them. The lazy, well-bred voice of a professional saleswoman.

'Yes. The way to the bar,' Max said.

'I see. Nerves.' The saleswoman – blonde with strawberry-coloured lipstick – found a quicksilver smile.

'No. I need a beer.'

'He's not usually like this,' Ginger said sweetly. 'He's a real romantic underneath.'

'I'm sure.' She gave Ginger a commiserating look.

Have a word with the receptionist if she's about, Elizabeth had said. Imogen's friend.

Glory Fraser.

Peculiar name.

'Can you spare us a minute?' Max asked, handing her his card.

Glory, a lithe, coffee-coloured girl, with a bouncy grin, eyed him up from the other side of the reception desk. 'Not right now,' she said. 'I'm on duty. But if you come back later. Say two o'clock?'

Anna Makepeace had her eye on her chef, who was enjoying himself chatting to a gaggle of American guests in the foyer. Anna leaned over the carved oak staircase built by Sir Charles Cheyney when he married into money in 1790 and decided to upgrade the ancient Elizabeth manor house belonging to his new wife's family.

Anna liked to keep an eye on things. One of those English-women as reassuring as Harris tweed. Fine-boned, but as reliable as a Raleigh bicycle.

Must speak to Chef, she thought. Wandering around the

place chatting guests up. This isn't a Huddersfield chip shop. He was gifted, but a touch cheeky for Anna's liking. She would have a word with him.

At that moment, the sun came out. Up on the top floor – once upon a time, the nursery floor. Rose Mulligan (a real grafter – no need for pep talks here) said a naughty word as a smear suddenly appeared on the middle pane of the window she had just polished to a gleaming perfection.

Or so she'd thought.

But that was life. Just when you were feeling pretty well satisfied, along came a dollop of trouble.

Time and time again.

Max hadn't intended to have a posh lunch at Cheyneys, but they got nobbled by the chef as they hung about in the lobby trying to decide how to spend the next hour and a half.

'You two strayed out of the Orangery?' he asked cheerfully. 'Are you aware that we do a special pre-nuptial lunch at a bargain price – this week only?'

A picture-book chef in a tall, white hat. Thirtyish, chubby, jowls to die for.

A chef whose accent Max was immediately familiar with.

'Rochdale,' he said. 'So – what's a nice northern lad like you doing in a place like this?'

The chef nodded towards a couple of American matrons in the corner sofa, fat feet spreading in their white ankle socks, gawping reverentially at the array of brochures. 'Teaching them to eat mushy peas with their foie gras. The Yanks love it.'

'I bet.'

'Almost as much as they love my chocolate truffles in a light mango sauce.'

87

'Wonderful,' Ginger sighed. 'I'm a chocoholic.'

'The sauce is sharp, not sickly,' said the chef, as a shaft of sunlight fell on Ginger's red hair. 'Go on. Treat her. She's worth it.'

Chapter Fourteen

'So how long have you worked here?' Max asked Glory Fraser as she led them out through a back door to a herb-lined terrace behind a façade of Georgian stucco.

'A couple of years. I'm only part-time, earning precious money to keep myself alive. I'm at uni in Bristol. Third-year medical student.'

'So you travel over from Bristol to work?'

'No. I live here in Bath with my Gran. It's cheaper to live at home. It's not easy, trying to work and study at the same time, you know? Sometimes my Gran's the only thing that keeps me going. Food, shelter. Encouragement. You can do it, girl, she says. Just keep right on going. When I get qualified, I'm gonna pay her back. Buy her a proper house. Anyway, what's this all about? I know. My library books are a month overdue. They sent you to collect them.'

She got serious when Imogen's name was mentioned. 'Yes. We were in the same class at St Theresa's. Immy's mother paid her fees, I was a scholarship girl.'

'She's not back at work yet?'

'What do you expect?'

Watch it, Max. 'But you're good friends?'

'The best. Can't think why, because we're complete opposites. Immy was quiet and good. I never stopped talking. I got sent out all the time for talking back. I was so bored! Then they found out I was a couple of years ahead of the rest of the class, that's why I was bored. Anyway, I suppose I used to sort of look after Immy. There was a group of girls who tended to bully her. She was young for her age. Náive . . . you know? Actually I used to envy her that. I had to grow up fast when my dad left. Too fast.'

'And you're still close? You and Imogen?'

'Yes. She's just a really lovely person. You know? She didn't give a damn that I lived in a council house. She knew I had a vocation. Does that sound pompous? During our third year at St Theresa's, we got sent to do some voluntary work in a home for the mentally and physically handicapped. St Dunstan's. That's when I got interested in medicine. That's the field I want to work in. I'd like to do research. Some of those people . . .' She shook her head.

Max said, 'So you and Imogen are good friends. And you were at the wedding on Saturday?'

'The wedding that wasn't.' Glory still couldn't believe it had happened. 'Neither could Imogen. I went round to her mother's straight from church.'

'You saw her? What sort of a state was she in?'

'What do you think. Poor little devil. She was hysterical. And her mother wasn't helping any. Kept on and on about how it was a good thing and she was well rid of him. I mean, you save all that stuff for later. You don't go on about it when the poor kid's sobbing her heart out.'

'You don't like Mrs Shand?'

'Slight understatement. She's a starched woman. You know? Stiff upper lip. Stiff everything. Straight-laced. She didn't like me coming home to tea with her daughter, I'm afraid. Or to birthday parties. Or anything, if it comes to that. She smiled, but she always spoke down to me. You could read her thoughts. A coloured girl at St Theresa's? Whatever next? I once heard her describe me to one of her friends as "the coloured girl". Excuse me, I felt like asking, but what colour? At least, specify. Coloured is an insult. Just as white is not an accurate description of your skin, dear pink Mrs Shand!'

Max had to laugh. He liked Glory. Some people you like instantly. You do or you don't in the first ten seconds.

Opinions ready to go, that was Glory.

He said, 'So do you know Imogen's ex-fiancé? Johnny Mulligan?'

'That prick! Sorry. Not polite language, but it's the only word for him. He wasn't half good enough for Immy. I said to her, you're an intelligent person. What are you going to achieve in life living with a dickhead like Johnny Mulligan?' A forlorn shake of the head. 'She needed her head examining, but she wouldn't listen. They never do, do they? I hoped she'd grow out of it, quite frankly. I thought if she lived with him for a few months, she'd find out what he was really like. Hard way to learn, but . . .' A quick shrug.

'So where did they meet?'

'At a club in town. I remember because it was my eighteenth birthday. He started to chat her up. He couldn't take his eyes off her. She moved in with him a few weeks later. Lived with him ever since.'

'But he had affairs behind her back?'

'Several. Girls . . . well, they got pulled towards him like he was a magnet. It was pathetic. He'd start something and then, when he'd had enough, he'd slip out of it again, like a snakeskin. And they'd let him. Mostly.'

'But he wanted to marry her. He must have loved her.'

'In his own way, I suppose . . .' Glory tugged at a sage leaf and crushed it in slim fingers. 'But what you have to understand about Johnny is that he has to have women where he wants them . . . mostly horizontal.'

'But Imogen Shand thought a lot of him. Isn't that right?'

'Listen – I'm not saying that he wasn't without a few endearing characteristics. He had a romantic streak. He was always sending her flowers. He was the life and the soul of any party. He could be kind. Like when her cat got killed . . . she cried for a week. Most men would have said don't be so bloody wet, but he stayed in with her night after night and mopped her up.'

'So did she know about the other women? You obviously knew. Did you tell her?'

'No point. She wouldn't have believed it of him.' She saw his expression. 'You think I should have. But you don't know Immy. How can I explain it? For Immy, life was like a fairy tale. At least, she wanted it to be. She was Sleeping Beauty and her prince had come. She's like . . . how can I put it? Like an intelligent baby, as far as Johnny was concerned. A beautiful but innocent child.'

A child who recently had had to grow up very fast.

'Did he ever try it on with you?'

'Once and once only. I said, piss off, plonker.'

On the subject of Kat Gregg, she was a touch more cagey. Yes, she'd been friends with Kat as well, though Kat was several years older. 'She was in the sixth form when Immy and I started at St Theresa's. I mean, Kat never knew we existed . . . not then . . . but everybody knew her, because she was the star of the school drama group. God, she was good!'

That would figure.

'She was a prima donna even then,' Glory said. 'There was one memorable rehearsal . . . must have been *Joseph and the Technicoloured Dreamcoat*, because Immy and I were in the chorus dressed as Pharoah's handmaidens. Anyway, Fanny Hanny was being particularly useless and Kat blew her top and told her exactly where to put her violin.'

'Fanny Hanny?'

'Miss Hannaford. The music teacher. Everybody used to play her up. Cruel, really. But she had no idea how to control a class and kids take advantage.'

Max was mulling things over in his mind. 'So, if you didn't

actually know Kat Gregg at St Theresa's, when did you become
friends?'

'She walked into the hotel one day when I was on reception.
She said, I know you from somewhere. St Theresa's, I told her.
The Technicoloured Dreamcoat. That's it, she said. The only hand-
maiden that didn't need fake tan. If anyone else had said it, I'd
have gone off the deep end. But Kat could get away with it. She
made me laugh. She was good fun. We had a right old chinwag
about St Theresa's and after that, she'd drop in now and again
for coffee and a chat.'

'Did you know about her affair with Mulligan?'

'No, I didn't. I knew she'd once been keen on him. Johnny
came to the hotel one day to pick Immy up from work and Kat
saw them and . . .'

'And?'

'Well, she changed completely. One minute we were laughing
over a coffee and the next, she'd got a right strop on and was
saying Immy ought to watch herself.'

'Meaning what?'

'Meaning that Johnny had a record of shagging women and
then dumping them. He'd done it to her.'

'To Kat?'

'Yeah. She was eaten up with jealousy, you could see that. But
I never guessed—' A sad shake of the head.

'You didn't see Kat after she turned up at the church?'

'If only . . .' Glory said. 'I feel bad about that. Should have
gone up there. But we weren't mates. Just acquaintances really.'

'And you can't tell me anything about her relationship with
the Makepeaces?'

'I'm sorry. I only help out here part-time.'

Fair enough, Max supposed.

'Do you blame Kat for what she did on Saturday?'

'How can I? It was a bit extreme, but that was Kat. Good for
her, I thought. Maybe I'd have done the same in her position.
No, I wouldn't. Wouldn't have had the nerve . . . or the gump.

But he treated her badly, didn't he? Left her in a hole. And she wasn't the kind of girl to be intimidated. She wanted to show him up in public and by God, she succeeded!'

Certainly did.

'Tell me,' Max said, 'do you think he killed her? Johnny Mulligan?'

The nearest thing to silence Glory had come to. 'Maybe.'

She couldn't stand the bloke, yet she didn't see him as a murderer. Interesting.

'So if it wasn't Johnny, then who?'

Some tension was beginning to show in Glory's face.

'Imogen?'

The answer came swiftly. Perhaps too swiftly. 'Oh, no. Not Imogen. She's definitely not capable of it.'

'How do you know?'

'I know Immy, that's all.'

'So how was it?'

The chef was still lurking in the foyer when they left the dining room.

'Delicious!' sighed Ginger.

'Except for the waiter,' Max felt impelled to add. 'Banging down coffee cups with existential gloom.'

'Kenneth?' the chef laughed. 'It's his old woman. She's a real old cow. Stopped him going to Rovers. You're not going yet? Have some more coffee. I'll serve it this time.'

'Can't, mate. Work to do.'

'What kind of work?'

Max told him.

'Christ!' said the chef with a glance in Ginger's direction. 'Hang on a minute. You're not here for the nuptial thingy?'

'Sorry.' Max clapped him on the shoulder. 'Great lunch, though. Thanks for asking us.'

Chapter Fifteen

Friday morning. Ten thirty a.m. 'Come in.'

Anna Makepeace walked briskly in through the front door, waving the large pewter dress ring on the third finger of her right hand and explained the reason for the visit to an abstracted Louise Shand.

'I wanted to say how sorry we are about Imogen's problems. I keep thinking about her. Wondering how she is.'

Mrs Shand still stood there with a blank expression on her face.

'You look tired. It must have been a strain for you as well.'

'I'm fine. Really.' Louise still remained distinctly distant, but managed a social smile and led Anna into the drawing room with fireplaces at either end, with imposing bookcases filled with china and ivories, a lion-skin rug and a collection of paintings on the wall above the very fine rosewood table.

'I say — that's rather good. The portrait. Is it you?'

'Done when I was eighteen.'

'Lucky you.'

'Yes . . . well.' Louise waved a hand towards the corner by the window. 'This is Tim Kidston. A friend of Imogen's.'

Kidston was a nice-looking young man with hair the colour of a red setter.

'I . . . just dropped by to ask how Imogen was.' He was clearly annoyed to be flushing.

'Me too.' Anna flashed her warmest smile first at the young man, then in the direction of Mrs Shand. 'She's to take her time about it, but we're all looking forward to seeing her back at work. Best way to take her mind off things. Don't you think?'

Kidston agreed. 'That's exactly what I said.'

'Once the shock has worn off.'

'Better than shutting herself away in her room.'

Louise Shand walked over to the fireplace and lit a cigarette. 'Try and tell my daughter that. I can't get her out of her room, let alone the house.'

'I'm working on that. I'm going to make her come out with me tonight. A film or something.' There was a raw keenness in the young man's hazel-flecked gaze.

Abruptly, Louise said, 'Make some coffee, Tim, would you? You know where everything is.'

Anna watched the door close behind him. One thing was certain. Imogen Shand would never be short of an admirer. They threw themselves at her feet and no wonder. The girl was a great beauty. Unlike her mother. Same blue eyes, same heart-shaped face, but the older woman's gaze was unreadable. Unresponsive.

It was like she was gazing at a window display instead of the contents of her own sitting room.

Of course, she'd had a hard time with Imogen this last year. Anna knew what that felt like. She'd had some hard moments of her own in the past. Rory, her oldest son, had died of a drugs overdose a few short years after coming down from Cambridge; what was it . . . almost four years ago? They didn't mention it much now. They remembered, but they didn't talk about it. Then there was the car crash that Oliver – her second boy – had been involved in the year after. But he was fine now, thank God, working in London and enjoying life.

'Pleasant young man,' Anna said, bringing herself back to the present.

'You wouldn't say that if you'd heard him last night.' Louise
lit another cigarette from the stub of the first. Began talking in a
rush. 'I made the mistake of getting out the malt. He got
absolutely plastered. He was going to kill Johnny bloody
Mulligan.'

Anna was curious. 'So how long has Tim known Imogen?'

'Years and years. His mother's an old friend of mine. I
suppose you could call him the boy next door. He had a teenage
crush on her.'

'Still has, by the look of it.'

'Yes . . . well. She went out with him for a while before she
met lover boy.'

'And?'

'And you're right. He's mad about her. Very protective.'

'Then maybe . . .'

A quick hunch of the shoulders. 'Who knows? It's much too
soon. Anyway, he works in Paris. Lives with some French girl.
Brought her over for the wedding. Came round here straight
from the church on Saturday to find Imogen and he's been in and
out ever since.'

'And the French girl?'

'Not happy. They had a row sitting out there in her car the
other night. Then she drove off. Haven't seen her since.'

'My God. It gets worse.'

'Doesn't it?'

The door opened. Tim Kidston's head poked round the side
of it. 'Anyone else want coffee while I'm at it?'

Anna Makepeace glanced at her watch, looked dismayed and
shook her head.

'Not for me, thanks. But I'd like a word with Imogen, if she'll
see me.'

Jan Finney looked at her watch. Ten thirty. Lucian would be in
the St Dunstan's minibus on his way to swimming. It was a good

school. Better than the hell hole that he attended before, the one she'd taken him away from. St Dunstan's had small classes, a caring attitude, lots of outings . . .

Like the time they'd all gone up to tea at the Beehive for Clara's birthday. Clara was worse than Lucian. Much worse. Couldn't talk. But she loved an occasion. Loved dressing up. She remembered how Kat had come swooping down on them, full of life, bubbling with fun. 'Have a hat,' she'd said, plonking a red baseball cap on Lucian's head. He'd thought her wonderful. And now . . .

Tears came into Jan's eyes. (It was happening all the time these days.)

Underneath, that vivid girl must have been so miserable. Jan knew what that felt like.

'Excuse me.'

The voice belonged to a dark woman with deeply-hooded brown eyes. She had been in the shop for a while, rabbiting through the confused heap of frocks and costumes on the portable rail by the cabin trunk. Fingering the lace mantles, the period wedding dresses, the veils and hats and dress suits . . .

'I'd like to see that brooch in the centre of your display stand.' The woman had a light voice. Educated.

'Certainly.' Jan located the brooch – a gold locket pendant, mid-Victorian – and extracted it from the other pretty things sparkling on the glass shelf.

'I'm looking for a birthday present for my sister.'

'Really?' Jan handed her the brooch. 'It's so pretty. But rather expensive, I'm afraid. The applied cherub's face is enamel and the wings are set with rose-cut diamonds.'

A nod and a cursory examination, then it was handed back. 'May I see some others?'

'Of course.'

But nothing seemed to suit. None of the brooches. There was something odd about this customer. You got them sometimes. Jan schooled herself to sound casual, but friendly. 'Maybe a bracelet, then? Try this one. It's nineteen forties. A little easier on the purse.'

The touch of cold skin. The safety clasp fastened. But it wasn't right. 'I'll think about it,' the woman said.

Celia Hannaford hurried down the steep, paving slabs of Bartlett Street, still feeling the cold stones of the bracelet around her thin wrist. She felt elated. Euphoric. Her thoughts seemed to be speeded up and racing against the clock

Must buy a *Chronicle*. Must get that book the lecturer recommended. What was it? Jerrold Northrop Moore. No, that was on Elgar. That was last term. Cantatas. The Linley family. That's it. And Alice told me to get some cheese. Or was it butter? Thoughts spinning round in her head like they were in a food mixer. It was because she hadn't slept. Well, not for ages. Toss and turn, mind buzzing with ideas.

And when she had slept, she'd dreamt that she had set off to go shopping and had finished up in church. Wrapping a long blanket thing around her skirt and fastening it with a vibrant blue poppy.

Inexplicable . . .

No, it wasn't. She'd been thinking about church the day before. St Bartholomew's. What she'd seen from the mirror above the organ. As on a distant TV screen, she saw it all again. The whack of the hand, the girl's shrill denunciation, the disorder that had followed.

Better than Jane Eyre. No one would ever forget it.

Wish I'd done that, Celia thought. I wouldn't have dared. But then, you didn't have the chance. It never got as far as the church door. He called it off six weeks before the wedding. Turned and walked away. Still, you could have done something. Too sensitive. Too morally timid, despite feeling hurt, rejected, angry, smarting, tearful. Humiliated at home and at work.

No act of revenge for Celia. Not then.

But now?

She was working on it.

Down through town Celia scurried (forgetting the shopping), down Milsom Street, right along Quiet Street, right again at Queen's Square and then up to a quiet back street behind Jolly's department store.

Big blue door with huge brass knob. First-floor flat. Lived here too long, said her inner voice. I know, but Alice won't move. I'll go one day if she doesn't. Celia fumbled with the key in the lock, drove open the door. Caught sight of herself in the sharp edge of the mirror in the hall, smiled at herself with perfect teeth. Well, almost.

'Celia? Is that you?'

Who else would it be? Silly old bag, Alice. Celia downloaded her bag, danced (well, almost) into the large and only sitting room. In the front and bigger half, between tall windows, stood the grand piano on which she had taken generations of children through their grade tests. Behind it the Edwardian cabinet stuffed with Staffordshire figures. Two easy chairs and a small sofa. Panelled double doors of a more gracious age led to the back room which had now been turned into a kitchen diner.

From which Alice emerged.

Looking disapproving. So what's new?

'You had a lesson half an hour ago. The little Grant girl. I had to send her away.'

So? Celia couldn't be bothered this morning with boring old pupils. More important fish to fry.

Her wrist still felt the imprint of the stones.

'You're sour today.'

'There are times,' Alice said, 'when I despair of you.'

'Me too,' said Celia, and went over to study the whole city beyond the Georgian windows.

* * *

Mulligan's wine bar was in an alley in the lower part of town, sandwiched between a hairdressing establishment with sofas in the window and a second-hand bookshop called Henry Beavis. At eight thirty p.m., Max and Ginger, trying to ignore the sound of fiddles and fipple flutes, tin whistles and mad harpists coming out of the sound system, were being introduced to a tall blond young man with a painfully posh accent.

'This is Rupert,' Caroline said, her face almost sunshiny for once. 'We're going to be married.'

Chapter Sixteen

—❖❖❖—

'Good God!' When Max had picked himself up from the floor, he offered them his congratulations. 'I hope you'll both be very happy.'

'Thanks.' Leaning forward, Rupert said in that grave, extraordinary voice, 'So you're Max. I've heard a great deal about you.'

'Sounds ominous,' Max told him.

'And this is . . . ah . . . Ginger. I'm afraid I've forgotten your real name.'

'Me too,' said Ginger. 'Pleased to meet you, Rupert. So when's the happy day?'

'Oh, not for ages.' Caroline's smile had now turned gracious. 'Loads of things to arrange. But I hope you'll both be there when we finally get around to it.' Not sure, Max said. His legs locked when he went anywhere near a church door.

Caroline didn't understand jokes. 'What would you like to drink?' she asked. 'Rupert is buying.'

Max thought he could take to Rupert. Well, apart from the cheery grin and the bulldog jaw and the yellow waistcoat and the MCC tie. But if he was going to pay his way . . .

Rupert worked in a rather grand interior design shop in Broad Street. He'd been there five years. Had just been promoted, hence the wedding plans.

'Oh, good,' said Ginger. 'I bought this old tub chair. Can't decide whether to redo it in linen or chintz.'

'Not chintz. Dear me, no.' Rupert paused in the middle of his pint. 'Chintz is out. Frightfully behind the times.'

'Oh, God,' said Max. 'I didn't realise.'

'Unless, of course, it's ironic,' Rupert added. 'Ironic chintz is fine.'

It was as well that Elizabeth's arrival provided a diversion. She talked to Rupert about Long Island mansions while Ginger dived out for an indecently long visit to the Ladies.

'Sorry,' she said later, after Caroline and Rupert had taken themselves off to another assignation. 'Fit of the giggles. Ironic chintz—' Max guffawed. Ginger went off into another shriek of laughter.

'He's a very nice young man,' Elizabeth said. 'A perfect English gentleman.'

'A perfect English berk.'

'But he's perfect for Caroline.'

'And what does that make Caroline?'

'I'm very fond of Caroline. She's . . .'

'A perfect lady,' said Ginger.

'Think she wears those pearls in bed?' Max asked.

'Leave Caroline alone,' Ginger said. 'He told Rupert to buy a dog instead of getting spliced. The licence is cheaper. And dogs are more reliable.'

Elizabeth shook her head.

'There was one odd thing . . . Apparently, Rupert knows Glory Fraser.'

'He does?'

'Mmm. She used to work in his shop.'

'Are you sure?'

'Positive. Can't be two black girls with a name like that. He said she was holding down three other jobs at the time.'

'When was this?'

'A couple of years ago.'

'Students have a hard time keeping the bank manager at bay.'

'They're not the only ones,' Max said.

'So did you talk to her today? Glory Fraser?'

Max told her about the interview and the superb lunch.

'You had lunch there? On the firm?'

'You told us to have a good nose.'

'I didn't have the dining room in mind.'

'You'd love it,' said Ginger. 'It's solid and elegant but wonderfully comfortable.'

No doubt . . .

'It was the chef's fault. He was very persuasive. Talked us into it,' Ginger said. 'You should have been there. Beautiful glass, crisp white napkins . . . proper grown-up food.'

For once Max agreed with her. 'It wasn't dog food.'

Saturday again. Two p.m. Elizabeth turned off the road into the Beehive car park. A clear wind was throwing scents around. Exquisitely soft grass and field smells mixed with a faint whiff of old-fashioned horse manure.

Anna Makepeace was waiting for her, as promised; a small, slender woman in a brown jersey top and wearing round her neck a blue silk scarf.

Elizabeth said, 'It was good of you to call me. Your husband didn't seem keen on us taking a look round the place.'

The slightest of hesitations. 'He was upset. He thought it an invasion of Kat's privacy. But I told him, there's Rose to think of, too.'

'Torn loyalties . . .'

'It's been difficult. Very difficult. We know them all so well. Rose worked both here and at the hotel. And Kat was in and out. I didn't bump into her very often, but Aidan adored her. In a fatherly way, you understand.'

Now why did she have to point that out? 'And you didn't mind?'

'Good heavens, no. She was a nice girl. Not one to break up marriages.'

Only weddings, Elizabeth thought.

'Kat was like a daughter to him. She made him laugh and God knows that gift is rare enough these days. He's very upset about this awful thing.'

A nice woman, Elizabeth thought. Completely genuine. The memsahib voice was the only thing that jarred on the sensibilities. Made you feel slightly intimidated.

Anna Makepeace continued, 'He tore her off a strip for doing that stupid thing at the church. Understandable, I suppose. You wouldn't want your daughter going through that. But then there's Imogen. We're fond of her, too.'

'The whole thing must have been a shock for you.'

'Worse for Aidan, actually. As I said, he was fond of Kat. He's tough. Has to be in his profession, but he's completely different at home. Bit of a pussy-cat, actually.' She got back down to business. 'I'm rather busy this morning. How long will you need?'

'I'll be as quick as I can. Say ten . . . fifteen minutes?'

'Fine. Only I'm on my way down to town. I'll show you upstairs to the private quarters and do a spot of gardening while I wait.'

She led the way through the eerily quiet tearooms and spotless kitchen to a precipitously curved staircase that took you up to a first-floor landing. Three stripped pine doors opened from it.

'The middle one's the bedroom and the one round the corner the bathroom. This is the sitting room.'

She pushed open the door. The room was circular, pretty and fresh-looking with arched windows overlooking the garden and across to Cheyneys. Old-fashioned oil lamps in the deep-cut sills, the original black-leaded fire grate and one or two good watercolours (one of the Abbey Yard) on plain, white walls.

'I should warn you, there isn't much left in the way of personal papers. The police took loads of stuff from the bureau.'

'Par for the course. She rented this place from you?'

'That's right.'

'Furnished?'

'Unfurnished.'

'Right.' So the stuff is hers, not yours. Elizabeth moved across to the nearest window, admiring the garden. 'Love the herb beds.'

'They need weeding. Soon goes to rack and ruin if it's not looked after.'

Murder, it is fair to say, is not normally considered a good thing. But an investigation of the said crime has its perks. Guilty perks, Elizabeth told herself as Anna Makepeace clattered back down the uncarpeted stairs. But perks, nonetheless.

It is not disagreeable to take a good, slow look round someone else's house.

Granted, there was a touch of discomfort in that the girl – woman? – who until a few short days back had lived here was now dead and gone. But Elizabeth had trained herself to switch off personal feelings and get on with the job.

She was as happy as a monkey in a monkey tree trying to figure out, with long deliberation and forethought, a difficult puzzle. Wrong word, she told herself. Puzzles can be cold affairs. At figuring out a puzzling character, then, from all the scraps and details that – often haphazardly – present themselves.

So where to start?

With Kat's occupation; which will determine much of what she was.

What do we know? That she successfully set up these tearooms. That a business needs capital. (Elizabeth knew this from her own hard-earned experience.) So where, given Kat's tender years, had that capital come from? A friendly bank manager? From her divorce settlement? Or, from Aidan Makepeace, who had admitted lending her money.

Whatever, the place had done well. We have a successful business woman on our hands. Forceful. Feisty. Could be snotty. Easy to imagine her clashing with the lady who was now tearing handfuls of bindweed out of the flower bed underneath the window and flinging them, with admirably fine aim, into a red plastic bucket.

Anna Makepeace. Another successful and determined business woman.

Elizabeth lifted the lid of the old schoolroom desk – knotted pine, beautifully restored – that stood in the alcove next to her. It contained nothing of any interest: a stack of new brown A4 envelopes, two bunches of felt-tipped pens anchored together with an elastic band, a pile of menus (black Gothic script on cream card) and some price lists for some nearby organic farm that supplied her with home-made jams and pickles. Elizabeth put them all back in their original order. On a shelf above the desk there was a *Chambers Dictionary*, a pottery letter rack empty except for a mail-order clothing brochure, a presentation pack of postcards that had come free with *Homes and Antiques* magazine and a brand-new Jiffy bag.

Nothing down the back of the apricot-coloured sofa. Nothing, except two oriental blue spice jars and some other nice bits of old china, on the open shelves on either side of fireplace.

A stone cat and a basket of dried flowers in the hearth. A CD player and a quite unexceptional collection of discs on a low table next to it. Odd that it was all so meticulously clean and well-ordered, when you considered the emotional storms that had raged through the place just a few short days ago. Had someone – the police or the Makepeaces – straightened it all up?

Surely?

Elizabeth moved to the bedroom, but there was still no sign of a living, breathing woman's presence in that hushed and immensely tidy chamber. There was a marble washstand – Edwardian? – with a flowered jug and basin. A double bed. (How the devil had they got that up the corkscrew staircase?) A yellow dressing gown on the brass hook behind the stripped-pine door. A Lloyd loom basket chair, a blanket box holding bed linen and a low bookcase with serried rows of videotapes.

Pretty Woman. Sense and Sensibility. Wallace and Gromit. The Piano. Secrets and Lies. Movies had obviously taken the place of a bedtime read. Except that . . . there, lying on the bedside table, was a single paperback. *The Little Book of Children's Names.*

A maroon Waterstone's bookmark inserted at Angel: Angela: Angelica: Angus.

And, on the page before: *Aidan. Old Irish diminutive of aid, 'fire'; the name of a seventh-century Irish monk of Lindisfarne, the apostle of Northumberland, which appears in Old English as Aethan. Revived by the Tractarians in the nineteenth century.*

Interesting. Might be pure coincidence, of course. She'd only just bought the book and hadn't got beyond the A's.

The wardrobe was still packed with clothes and shoes, but there was nothing (save a comb, two used tissues and a leaking ballpoint) in any of the pockets. The dressing table held pots of cream, perfume bottles, a silver-backed mirror and, in the drawers, the usual piles of underwear. The Lilliputian bathroom yielded only an inordinate number of fluffed up bath towels and fancy bath foams. And there was nothing on the cramped landing except a table with magazines and the telephone.

Elizabeth would probably have abandoned the search there and then, would undoubtedly have walked out of the place taking with her nothing but a full mental inventory of its contents — except for a weakness that she'd always had for browsing through other people's cookery books.

She happened to stop in the quiet, almost death-like kitchen on her way to the front porch.

It was a title labelled *Country House Cakes* on a green-painted shelf by the plate rack, that caught her eye. She reached for it almost automatically and as she did so, her fingers dislodged a thin box perched on top of the book.

A box that held more treasures. Recipes cut from magazines,

recipes scribbled on scraps of paper, on used envelopes, print-outs from the Internet. Before she knew it, Elizabeth was having a comfortable old browse.

Which was how she came across the pale blue envelope. Extremely small. On the back of it was scribbled:

> *Chocolate Chip Shortcake*
> *2 eggs*
> *6 oz chocolate chips*
> *2 tsp vanilla . . .*

But here it ended abruptly. Maybe to continue on the slip of paper inside the envelope? Elizabeth slipped the sheet out of the envelope and unfolded it: but there was only a brief, pencilled note.

Meet me tonight at 7. Usual place. Ash.

Chapter Seventeen

Elizabeth felt a tingle at the base of her spine. Of course, it didn't have to be *that* Ashley. But it was an uncommon name. She stood there for a moment, then slipped the paper back into the envelope and the envelope into her pocket.

As she walked out through the tearooms, Anna Makepeace was coming in through the front porch. Mrs Makepeace was looking tousled, having just caught her hair in the chain from the old lantern that graced the roof of the porch. 'Bloody thing!' she said fiercely. 'Chap who hung it there wants shooting. You're all done?'

'All done. Thanks for letting me look round the place.'

'Anything useful?'

'Not really.'

'You'll let us know if there's anything else we can do?'

'Of course.'

'Someone told me you keep a patchwork shop down in town. Bit of an odd combination, isn't it? Detective work and quilting?'

'Some might think so. But you reach the point somewhere around sixty when you don't care any more. You decide to just go ahead and weird out.'

Mrs Makepeace threw back her head and laughed. 'Sounds tempting. I must try it when I reach that particular birthday.'

Which will be when? Elizabeth wondered. Ten years? Give or

take a year or two. Must find out some time. Have a longer chat, if it can be engineered. No particular hurry, but there's something about you that intrigues me. Yes, something indefinably interesting.

Where had Kat been going on the night she died? Who had she visited early on the Saturday evening? As she drove back down the steep hill towards Bath, Elizabeth asked herself the question over and over. Somebody had to know. Somebody must have seen her on this very road, heading down to town for an assignation that was to be the last of her short – but eventful – life.

She slipped the car down into third. On her right, the clouds threw long shadows over the green valley – almost alpine in depth and roundness – that stretched away north of the city towards Gloucestershire and the Cotswolds. It was a view that seldom failed to move her. A mellow, timeless landscape dotted with stone-built farmhouses – just a hint of honey to soften their colour – and round-topped chestnut trees and nut-shell cottages. But for once her eyes drifted abstractedly over the scenery as she drove on automatic pilot.

Why had Kat Gregg driven down to town shortly before her death?

If we knew that, a lot of threads might work themselves loose.

The cottage she was heading for lay some hundred yards or so down the hill from the Beehive Tearooms. Elizabeth almost missed the turning, on the left-hand side, up a steep incline.

The cottage had mullioned windows and a grey slate roof. It seemed to be propping up a lopsided out-house that had definitely seen better days. Once a couple of farm cottages, Elizabeth conjectured, but now it had gone up in the world. The Benson sisters – known to Aidan Makepeace as the

Twinnies – had added a wing and thrown a conservatory out at the back.

They were keen gardeners, that was for sure. The spindly hedge all round the cottage had been grubbed out and a deep herbaceous border planted. No doubt it would be quite something at the height of summer, but on a gloomy day in October, all that lingered was a glorious, whole-hearted (and very English) medley of greens.

The Twinnies were planting out bulbs in the corner bed under the chimney stack. Easy now to see why they were so termed. Dressed identically in navy-blue jumpers, green trousers and matching knitted hats, they stuck their trowels in the ground and drew themselves up to their full height (which was considerable) when Elizabeth let herself in through the wicket gate.

'Miss Benson?' (Smiling carefully at both of them in turn.) 'Elizabeth Blair. I'm a private detective.'

They didn't seem overly surprised. 'Aidan said you might be down. You'll want to know if we saw anything that Saturday?'

'Hole in one,' Elizabeth said cheerfully.

'You'd better come in. I'm Hope and she's Vanessa, by the way. You won't tell us apart. No one ever does . . . so I wouldn't bother trying.'

They were as old-fashioned as a couple of deck chairs in summer. Elizabeth admired the beams in the hall. 'Father used to crack his head on them,' Hope-or-Vanessa informed her.

'So how long have you lived here?'

'Born here, both of us. Our earliest memory is of Father dragging a branch of that tree up the slope to the shippen. He used to farm then. When he retired, he sold most of the land. But we still know every field and every contour.'

At the age of thirteen, they'd started work as downstairs maids in the big house. Cheyneys Manor, as it was in those days. Owned by the Cleve family by then, only they'd gone bankrupt trying to keep the place in some state of repair.

'We used to walk home, once a week, for a bite with Mother

and Father,' Vanessa-or-Hope said. 'A hunk of salt bacon and a crust of bread. Or rabbit stew. Father was a dab hand with his gun. A crack shot. It was hard work up at the Manor. Some employers treated you worse than their dogs. But we were lucky. We had a good relationship with Lady Cleve. There was a strict hierarchy in the servants' quarters, but we were treated fair.'

'Neither of you ever married?' Elizabeth was curious.

'Married? No! Nessy had a chap once, but she wasn't going to marry him and leave me on my own. Oh, no, no.'

'You don't regret the decision?'

'Not for one minute.' Vanessa said, 'What's the worth of a chap compared to a good sister? No, when the Manor was sold, we retired and came home to look after Father. He was heart-broken when Mother died. What year was that, Hope? Eighty-two?'

'So how,' Elizabeth asked, 'do you get along with the Makepeaces?'

'Very well, on the whole. We have our little disputes, as any neighbours do. But nothing major.'

'We heard that you didn't care for the extra cars parked outside the Beehive?'

'So we didn't. Bit of an eyesore and we told her so. Complained to the Council, too. But nothing changed, so we had to get on with it. We did hope at one time that Mrs Makepeace might convert it into a souvenir shop. The lease was almost up and there was a rumour flying around.'

'Really?'

'The guests would walk to it across the park. We thought that a good idea. Do away with tbe cars parked outside, do you see?'

Elizabeth saw. And made a mental note. 'So how did you get on with Miss Gregg apart from the trouble about the park?'

'Didn't see her, except for when she passed in her little car.'

'Which was?'

'An old brown Saab.'

'You know the number?'

'We know all the numbers, dear. We're out there in the garden all the time and we don't miss much.'

I bet you don't! Elizabeth thought. What was it Miss Marple had said? Gardening is as good as a smokescreen . . .

'And you can see the Beehive car park from here?'

'Yes. Quite clearly.'

'Tell me — did you happen to see who was parked there on the Saturday Miss Gregg was murdered?'

'Certainly. It was full up, as usual, with customers' cars until about . . . let's see now . . . until about a quarter to one. And then, I said to Nessy, that's odd, they're shutting up shop.'

'So the car park emptied?'

'Yes. Except for Aidan's car. Well, he told us he brought her home. And Bethany's . . . the girl who works there as a waitress. But she went home at about one o'clock. We thought she must be ill. Miss Gregg.'

'So . . .' Elizabeth felt a tingle at the base of her spine. 'Can you tell me if there were any cars parked there during the course of the afternoon? Or later?'

They could. And they did.

But the most interesting thing they saved until last. They had seen Katharine Gregg set off down the hill in her battered old Saab at around seven thirty p.m. on the fatal night. With a couple of fat black polythene bags on the back seat.

'And I said to Ness, "She's not ill. She's been at the spring cleaning again."'

Chapter Eighteen

———◦◦◦◦◦———

Just before four thirty that same afternoon, Elizabeth finally managed to corner Marcus Finney at his shop near the Antiques Centre. Gleaming glass cases arranged all round him in order of height, the large-patterned rug under his highly polished shoes and the captain's chair from which he rose.

He fancied himself, that was for sure. Tall, sandy-haired, smooth, he had the bearing of a pompous member of the clergy. Always smiling, but his eyes never quite met your own.

Elizabeth handed him her card.

The smile disappeared for an instant. 'What's this about?'

Elizabeth gave him the background. 'I understand you were at the scene of the crime shortly after Miss Gregg was murdered?'

'That's right. I'd called back at the shop to meet a client.'

'On a Saturday evening?'

A shrug. 'Never turn down business, that's my motto. This chap couldn't make it during the day, so I arranged to open up for him in the evening. Waste of time, as it happens, because he didn't turn up.'

'Can you give me the name of the client?'

'I didn't actually get his name. He said he was on holiday, so I assumed he was just passing through.'

'Which hotel was he staying at?'

'Didn't say.' Finney spread his hands. 'Anyway, I hung

around in the shop until ten to eight and then I thought, damn you, and locked up. I was in a filthy mood, I can tell you. And it was a filthy night. The skies opened just as I left the shop. I have a lock-up garage in Alfred Buildings. You can't leave it in the street any more or they clamp you and tow you away. Anyway, I got soaked running up Bartlett Street, I let myself into the garage and was about to unlock the car when I heard the shot outside.'

'And?'

'Nothing at first. I decided it must be a car backfiring. I mean, you don't expect that kind of thing to happen. In Birmingham or London maybe, but not here in Bath. But when the second shot cracked out, I stuck my head out. Pretty stupid, I suppose, but . . .'

'How far away were you from Miss Gregg at this point?'

'Twenty yards or so.'

'So what happened next?'

'This car took off from across the road. Terrific squealing of tyres.'

'You didn't get the number?'

'Sorry. As I said, it was tipping down with rain and almost dark.'

'So what did you do next?'

'Well, this chap came running out of one of the houses. He was working late and just happened to look out of the office window and saw her go down. He ran over to help her. So I went across. It seemed like something out of a horror movie. There she was lying under the lamp-post in a pool of blood, her car keys next to her.'

'You didn't recognise the victim?'

'Nope.'

'So you didn't know Katharine Gregg?'

'No. But I've learned since that she'd had a busy day as well.'

Something immaculately nasty about that smirk, Elizabeth decided. A weakness about the mouth. A self-applauding indulgence.

'You didn't touch the body at all?'

'You must be joking!'

'Not even to give First Aid?'

'First Aid? She was beyond that. The other chap had established that before he ran back to his office to phone the police.' A pause. He was thinking, no, calculating. 'You asked if I knew her.'

'Yes.'

'I didn't know her, but I knew of her.'

A subtle difference. Elizabeth waited.

'My wife knew her. Well, faintly. There was this Antiques Fair up at Cheyneys a few months back. We had a stall there. They're always worth doing, these things. People pick up your card, remember you, look up the shop.'

'You were saying . . . your wife knew Miss Gregg.'

'She met her, yes. After the Antiques Fair, she took the boy to tea at the Beehive.'

'The boy?'

'Her . . . our son.' Something keenly felt for a moment. A moment of careful reckoning. But then he went back to Kat. 'According to my wife, she was big, busty and brash. Easy to imagine, after behaving like she did. I have to say that one feels a modicum of sympathy for the young man for getting his own back.'

'You think Johnny Mulligan shot her?'

'It's what the police think, otherwise they wouldn't have arrested him.'

'But you didn't see him that night?'

'I told you. I didn't see anybody.'

Elizabeth nodded. 'Are you familiar with anyone else up at the hotel?'

'I have a nodding acquaintance with the Makepeaces.'

'And?'

'She's pleasant enough. He's . . .' A pause to find the exact word. 'Rather full of himself. Charms the ladies. You know . . .'

'I'm afraid I don't.'

'Likes the ladies. I did hear . . .'

'You heard what?'

'Oh, just common gossip. Better not say.'

'You may as well, now that you've started.'

'Well, I did hear he was fond of the odd dalliance.'

'With Kat Gregg?'

'That I couldn't possibly tell you. But it might be worth your while to do a spot of digging.'

Another sly smirk. Irritating man. Malicious, she shouldn't wonder.

'Do you know any of the staff up at Cheyneys?'

'Sorry.' But then he changed his mind. 'I tell a lie. I use the health club at Cheyneys. That's how I heard about the Antiques Fair. Picked up the Orangery programme one night in the café. I must say, they have an amazing range of activities.'

'Your wife and son . . . do they use the health club?'

'Good God, no.' His face suddenly shut up like a clam.

'One last thing, Mr Finney. What number is your garage?'

'The first one you come to at the Bartlett Street end. Look – I have to stop you here. Appointment with a client, I'm afraid. So if that's all . . .?'

'Shifty so-and-so,' said Elizabeth, as she phoned Max to say she'd meet him the following day for Sunday lunch. 'Wouldn't trust him an inch.'

'Anything in particular?'

'Can't quite pin it down. He dislikes Aidan Makepeace, though he'll only admit to a nodding acquaintance. I think we should talk to the other guy at the scene of the crime. The one who rang the police. And we should definitely dig a bit deeper into Mr Finney's background. His shop, local gossip about him. I'd like to meet his wife. Something odd about his home life, I fancy.'

Chapter Nineteen

'I'll tell you something else for free,' Elizabeth told Max. 'I don't trust the best man either.'

Sunday. One ten p.m. The Old Green Bush just round the corner from Martha Washington. Elizabeth sat studying the specials board on the wall in the corner above Max's head. There was:

> SAUSAGE AND SPECIAL MASH
> CHICKEN AND CAULIFLOWER BAKE
> BACON AND STILTON JACKETS
> THREE CHEESE SALAD

It would be either the Jackets or the Three Cheese.

Decisions . . . decisions.

The place was filling up fast, but that didn't take much doing. Six tiny tables in a room no bigger than the captain's cabin in the *Mary Rose*. The eighteenth-century wooden panelling and the collection of chairs that looked as if it had escaped from some attic only added to the illusion.

She'd arranged to meet Ashley Lewis immediately after her visit to Finney's shop. He'd suggested they meet at Mulligan's. There was a side door, painted green, big brass knocker. Ring the bell and he'd be there at five thirty to let her in.

Which he was.

A fair young man, twenty-five perhaps, wearing a grey t-shirt and linen combat trousers. Freckles. See-through, pale blue eyes. Alert expression on an unformed face.

Elizabeth said, 'I'd like to know where you were on the night Kat Gregg was shot dead.'

'That's easy. I picked Johnny up from his mother's place at about five thirty and drove him up to my parents' place in the Cotswolds.'

'Where exactly?'

'It's a little village called Guiting Trimble.'

'So what time did you arrive there?'

'Six forty or thereabouts.'

'Would your parents confirm this?'

'Certainly would.'

'This will need to stand up in a court of law, you understand.'

'No problem there. My father's a country solicitor. He's hardly likely to lie to the police.'

'And your parents were with you all evening?'

'Well . . .'

'Well what?'

'They were with me. Johnny had been drinking all afternoon. I think it's fair to say he got astoundingly pissed. With good reason, wouldn't you say? All Dad did was give us a beer when we arrived. I sort of suggested Johnny had had enough, but he wouldn't listen. Anyway, that was the one that finished him off, so to speak. He collapsed in the sitting room and Dad and I had to carry him up to bed.'

'What time was this?'

'Hard to say exactly. Seven ten. Seven fifteen? Not much later.'

'But he could have got back to Bath with a fast car?'

'Not in the state he was in, believe you me.'

'So he stayed in bed until when?'

'Until ten the following morning, when he came downstairs looking a bit sheepish.'

But Elizabeth was only just getting started. 'So how much did you know about Johnny's relationship with Kat Gregg?'

He sat there on a bar stool, legs jiggling. Uncomfortable? Certainly restless, over-active. 'I . . . knew it was going on.'

'For how long?'

'How long had I known? Or how long had it been going on?'

'Both.' Don't get funny with me, buster.

'OK. He'd been seeing her – on and off – for a few months.'

'On and off?'

'Don't ask for times and dates. I never asked. Let's just say it was sporadic.'

'His mother said it was just the once. That's what Johnny told her.'

'Yeah, well, he would, wouldn't he. Mothers sort of disapprove of things like that.'

Elizabeth kept on gazing at him.

'Look – I'm not condoning what he did, but he's my best mate. I'm not going to appoint myself judge and jury. Right? We've been friends for years.'

'How many years?'

'Since we were about sixteen. As a matter of fact, I went out with Imogen before he did.'

Now there's an interesting fact.

'But she took one look at Johnny and that was that.'

'Love at first sight?'

'Something like that. Johnny could charm the birds off the trees. But he thought a lot of Imogen. More than any other woman.'

'He had a funny way of showing it. Seeing other women behind her back.'

'Didn't mean anything. It was just a bit of fun.'

'Your idea of fun must be different to mine.'

'Yeah . . . well.'

Elizabeth got the impression that he was laughing at her. Sneaky little toe-rag. 'So why bother to get married if he wanted to play around with other women.'

He shrugged. 'Wanted it all, I suppose.'

Yes, well. Lots of men do, Elizabeth thought.

'He liked a gamble. Irish blood. Love beautifully, leave quickly. That was what he told me one night. That's how he got away with it. He liked his jollies. You know?'

Oh, yes, Elizabeth thought, I know. Young men like you two, they keep things in a personal filing cabinet that women know nothing about.

'He'd say black was white, if it suited him. If he wanted a girl. If he was in that kind of mood. Oh, he was loyal enough to his mates, but not to women. Not even to Imogen.'

A slight pause. 'And how well did you know Miss Gregg?' Elizabeth asked.

He fiddled around with the beer mat on the bar in front of him. 'I'd met her a few times.'

'Where?'

'Here . . . occasionally. Or out clubbing. This is a small city. You bump into each other.'

'You didn't perhaps have a relationship with her yourself?'

'Who the hell's been telling you that?'

'Nobody. It was just a thought.'

'Well, you can think again. The only time I met her was when I was with Johnny.'

'So you never had a date with her?'

'Certainly not.'

'Sure?'

'Absolutely.' The door behind him was open, revealing the wine bar with its potted palms, shamrocks and a graphic representation of a Celtic serpent. Lewis's eyes were now a clear, shining blue. Defiance? Aggression? Or a mixture of the two.

'That's fascinating. Because I found this in her kitchen. You might take a moment to read it.'

He looked a bit heated when he read the note.

'What was that about your friend saying black was white if it suited him?'

Lewis sought now to recover himself and attempted, at least, a compelling explanation. 'It's not how it seems. I did ask her to meet me one night. Just the once. That was all.'

'The note says: *Usual place*. That would imply more than one meeting.'

'Not necessarily. I meant this place. Mulligan's. She knew that.'

Unconvincing. But she let it pass. 'So why did you want to meet her?'

'I . . . I wanted her to leave Johnny alone.'

'A sudden outbreak of altruism? What brought that on?'

'I was fond of Imogen.'

'You were still stuck on her, perhaps?'

'No. But it wasn't fair on her. And I knew he'd never refuse a gift horse . . . you might as well talk to that wall. But I thought maybe if I talked to her, I could appeal to her conscience. Kat Gregg, I mean. It had been going on too long.'

'But her conscience remained untouched?'

'That's right. You heard what she did on Saturday.'

'That night you met . . . you didn't threaten her by any chance?'

'You never met Kat. She wasn't the type to take threats.'

'How long ago was this?'

'Three months ago . . . at a guess.'

And could you believe him? Elizabeth still had no idea. She sat there trying to choose between the Stilton jackets and the three cheese salad.

'I'll just order mine then,' Max said. 'If this is going to take all day.'

'No. No, I'll have the jackets.'

'You always have the three cheese.'

'Oh, for God's sake, Max — just get on and order it.'

'The essence of good manners and friendliness,' Max was heard to say as he went off to the bar to order.

*   *   *

As Elizabeth took the last mouthful of her three cheese salad, she let out a blissful sigh. 'That was wonderful! I shall need to look at the insides of my eyelids for a while this afternoon.'

'Sign of old age. So what did you make of the chap who found the body?'

'Marcus Finney? He was scared. That I'm certain of.' She sat there for a moment, considering. 'What I keep wondering, Max, is what the Gregg woman was doing down there in the first place, at eight o'clock on a filthy wet night? Just a block away from Finney's shop. She must have been parked there for some reason.'

'There are a couple of restaurants nearby.'

'So she's dining out on her own to celebrate what she'd accomplished that day? I don't think so somehow. And the other things is, what happened to the black poly bags the Twinnies said were in the back of her car?'

'They'd gone by the time the police got there. Andy said.'

'So she'd dumped them somewhere?'

'Or they were pinched?'

'Lord knows. Tell me, assuming that it was Mulligan who killed her, why didn't he just lie in wait for her at the Beehive? Safer up there, hidden by trees and darkness, surely? Why follow her down to town? Which is presumably what he did.'

'I'd agree with you there. OK, so it was a lousy night, but anybody could have come along.'

'And did. Our friend, Finney. My guess is that Mulligan followed her down to town and just before Finney arrived on the scene, Johnny and Kat had another barney in the street. His watch strap broke or was yanked off. Her fingerprints were on it. Andy said.'

'OK. They came to fisticuffs — not for the first time that day. Kat's a spirited girl. She gets the better of him. Mulligan dashes over to his car, gets the gun out and shoots her twice from across the road. This architect chap comes running out, closely followed by Finney. And Mulligan drives off . . .'

'Andy said there were fibres from Mulligan's clothes on her

body.' Max's Detective Sergeant Andy Cooper from the local CID was a useful kind of drinking mate. 'And the forensic chap – Doctor Bulleid . . .'

'You are joking? Doctor Bleed?'

'B-U-L-L-E-I-D.' He spelled it out for her. 'He found traces of Mulligan's skin under her fingernails. But Mulligan swears it was from a fight they had that afternoon at the Beehive.'

'The watch could have fallen off then, I suppose. But how would it have got to the gutter in Alfred Buildings?'

'Someone took advantage of the scene in church that morning? Saw the ideal opportunity to get rid of her and put the blame on Mulligan?'

'That's what Mulligan said. I don't know whether to believe him.' Elizabeth sat there studying the photograph of Kat Gregg that she'd drawn from the folder in her lap. Late twenties. Attractive, if not pretty like Imogen Shand. Dyed blonde hair. Mascara so thick that her eyelashes looked almost scrunchy. Green eyes, good bones.

Big bones.

This woman is volatile. She upsets people. Makes enemies. Especially over the last month or two. The laughs and the larks have, of late, been less forthcoming.

So if Johnny Mulligan didn't kill her, then who? 'Finney could have done it,' she said suddenly. 'He was on the spot.'

'Motive?'

'Let's see now . . . He's a bit of an old lech. I'd bet on it. He's admitted that his wife knew Kat. Suppose he did too. Suppose, just for the sake of argument, that he'd come on to her and been rejected, so he shot her, then called the police and invented the story of the drive-by killer.'

'Thin, to say the least. Anyway, somebody else saw the car drive away. The bloke who called the police. We should see him. Find out what he knows.'

The boy was being objective for once. Unfortunately.

'The best man, then. Ashley Lewis, who tried to warn Kat off three months before the wedding. Or so he says. He lives in walking distance of Alfred Buildings. He has a house in Julian Road. I asked.'

'He was at his parents' house that night.'

'He could just about have got back here by eight. If he drove like the clappers.'

'Why would Lewis want to kill her?'

'Loyalty to his mate, Mulligan. Or . . .' And this made more sense. 'He's stuck on Imogen. Johnny more or less took her away from him. He admitted as much. And there's this look on his face when he talks about her.'

Max thought about it and shook his head. 'Can't see it. Mulligan's the one with the rock-solid motive. Andy thinks he's as guilty as hell. And he comes from Northern Ireland, where guns are not unknown.'

'No – his father's Irish. Johnny's never been over there except for family visits.'

'Could have contacts, though, who'd provide him with a gun.'

'Granted. But let's face it, Max. We're being paid to clear Mulligan's name.' She picked up her bag and got to her feet. 'What do you say we walk up and take a look at the scene of the crime?'

'Now?'

'Walk off your lunch.'

'Don't need to.'

'No, but I do.'

Chapter Twenty

A windy afternoon. Narrow passages that feel like the backstage area of the city. There is a certain theatrical feel to them. The action is going on elsewhere, in the auditorium way below in the Abbey Yard, but it would not be out of the way, in such corners where the architecture resembles a splendid pantomime back-cloth (porticoed doors for Prince Charming to burst out of), to catch a glimpse of the odd player in white stockings, full make-up and simulated brocade making his way back to the Green Room . . .

Bartlett Street. At first, a flattish alley with a deep, slabbed pavement on the right-hand side. A row of small shops, also on the right: a café, a hairdresser's, an upholstery shop. Then the shops give way to the Antiques Centre (known locally as Bart's Bazaar) and the hill suddenly gets steeper. Finney's shop is on the right, at the very top of the rise.

They stopped outside it for a breather. Elizabeth needed one. Cobbles and slabs. They were hard on the bunions.

'Closed,' Max said, peering at the notice on the door.

'It's Sunday.'

'Shops open on Sundays these days.'

'Not here, they don't.'

Up again and through another passage into Alfred Street. Assembly Rooms just in front of them. And the sun came out.

The street became unnaturally light. It looked more than ever like a glistening stage set.

'An epiphany . . .' Elizabeth said, stopping to gaze in admiration. 'I love this city.'

'A what?'

'Tis a gift to be simple, she thought. 'An epiphany. A special moment that will stay in your mind forever. You must have had them.'

'Like the time I first set eyes on Jess.'

His ex-girlfriend.

'Or like the moment you saw through her little wiles and dumped her.'

'Yeah . . . well.'

'Epiphanies . . .' Elizabeth said again, 'Less common as you get older. The sexual moments, at any rate. I have news for you. Sex doesn't last.'

He laughed. He thought it was a joke. 'So what other kinds of epiph . . . Of these things are there?'

He was very young. 'Oh, you can get just as much pleasure out of the ordinary things.'

Max's face said he didn't believe her.

'A walk in the country, a painting, an hour spent with a friend.' Or a great quilt. Like the one waiting at home for the border to be added. A bold rose pattern; red, yellow, pink . . . pretty near as loud as they come.

Like me, I suppose.

'Look at me,' she said. 'Jim's dead and gone. I live on my own. My kids are all the way across the Atlantic, but I have my moments.' Her steady green eyes regarded him. 'However . . . don't let me put you off sex.'

As if.

'Remind me not to get old,' Max said. He saw her face. 'Well, older.'

Such tact. She chuckled. 'Friends. Friendship. That's what lasts. Not the instant, "Phwooar, look at that" sexual kind of thing, but liking someone's company, finding someone who's easy to be with.'

'Ever think of buying a pulpit?'

'You can mock. One day, my boy, you'll remember this conversation and say that old girl, steadily sailing an unruffled course through life, knew a thing or two.'

'Unruffled?' A snort from Max.

OK, not always unruffled. But up and down less. Thank the good Lord.

Alfred Street was behind them. They turned the corner into Alfred Buildings. There, on the right, just as Finney had said, was the row of garages. The first one – the scruffy one with the white-painted door – Finney's, if she'd got it right.

Elizabeth stood there on the corner gazing at it. A perfectly ordinary metal up-and-over garage. Shabby, baldly sombre, did nothing for the neighbourhood, architecturally speaking. An eyesore, in fact. A single lamp-post, still marked off with police tape and surrounded by a makeshift tent marked the spot where the girl had died.

She went over and tried the garage door. Locked.

'What were you hoping to find?' Max asked.

'I don't know. What kind of car Finney drove. How much he could see from inside the door. What kind of stuff he keeps stashed away in there . . .'

Something . . . anything.

'Pity it's Sunday. We could have dropped in on the other guy, the architect. What's his name? Andy gave it you.'

'Christopher Hunter. First floor of Number Seven.'

'That'll be a job for another day.'

It never stopped. The tramping round, the telephone calls, the interviews . . . three-quarters of them yielding nothing of any use. Detective work is like seed, Elizabeth thought as they made their way back down the hill. For every quarter ounce you get, you have to sift a bushel of chaff.

*   *   *

The visit to Imogen Shand was a spur-of-the-moment thing. It's OK; I'll deal with the business of the commiserations and condolences and all that tricksy stuff, Elizabeth told Max. It won't matter if you get a bit red around the ears now and then.

'Detectives?' The girl looked panicky. Flowing gold-russet hair. A sweet face, in spite of (or perhaps because of) the flushed cheeks and the puffiness around the forget-me-not blue eyes.

Stale old cliché, but exact in this case.

Lucky that Louise Shand was out. As was Tim Kidston. He'd taken his mother to visit an ancient aunt in her nursing home. For once, Elizabeth thought, things were running their way. 'We're working for Rose Mulligan. She's trying to prove your fiancé didn't kill Katharine Gregg.'

'Ex-fiancé.' Imogen sat there twisting at the finger that until very recently had worn a sapphire engagement ring.

'Whatever. I have to ask you rather an uncomfortable question. Do you think Johnny killed her?'

She looked distressed. 'I . . . can't answer that question.'

'Why not?' Elizabeth asked the question as gently as she could.

'Because I'm too involved.'

An understatement and a half, Elizabeth decided.

'I can't think straight.' There was a quaver in her voice. 'I can't believe any of this has happened.'

'Life's not always like it is in the movies . . .'

It's a dirty old world sometimes.

A nod of the fair head. 'I just found that out.'

'It's a shock to the system.'

'Inside me . . . it's all such a mess.' Tears spilling over now. She scrubbed them away, glancing across at Max, who was wearing his sympathetic face. 'I'm mad at Johnny for doing this to me and mad at myself for being so gullible. I blame my mother for being right about Johnny and I blame myself for not believing what she saw from the beginning.'

'And, of course, you're mad at Katharine Gregg?'

'I'm madder at Johnny for betraying me.'

'So how well did you know Miss Gregg?'

'Hardly at all. Glory was quite friendly with her but I hadn't seen her for years until . . .'

'Until . . .?'

'Until Saturday morning.'

'When she burst in on you?'

'Yes. At first I couldn't take it in.'

'What she told you about her affair with Johnny was a complete surprise?'

'Absolutely.'

'You had no idea they had been carrying on?'

'I told you, didn't I?' There was a sharp break in her voice.

'It's just that I find that a bit difficult to believe. Women usually know.'

'Well, I didn't, so you'll just have to believe me.' Imogen took a deep, steadying breath. Her fresh-washed blue eyes came up to meet Elizabeth's. 'I didn't know about it until my wedding morning. I didn't suspect a thing. Maybe I'm naïve, but in my book, if you love somebody, you make them a gift of your trust.'

In an ideal world. So long as you don't pick a man like Johnny Mulligan.

'Could you tell me how you feel now about Katharine Gregg?'

She sat there chewing her lip.

'Shall I tell you what I think? I think that perhaps a little bit of you was glad when you heard she was dead. After what she did to you last Saturday, that would be perfectly normal.'

A pallor now on the childlike face. 'You're right. I was glad for a second or two. Then I thought—'

Elizabeth waited.

Her voice was almost inaudible. 'Then I got scared for Johnny.'

'So you *do* think him capable of murder?'

'If you'd heard him hammering on the door when my mother

wouldn't let him in—' An uncomfortable moment hung in the air. Imogen said, 'Yes. I can't deny it.'

'So have you seen him since the police released him on bail?'

'No. And I don't want to.' But she changed her mind. 'That's not true. We lived together for a long time. Of course I want to see him . . . but I won't. Not ever.'

Ever is a long time, Elizabeth thought. 'You didn't go up to the Beehive on Saturday afternoon?'

'No, I didn't.' Her manner was more composed. 'Glory wanted to, but I begged her not to.'

'Any particular reason?'

'I knew them both too well. Glory and Kat. I was afraid—'

'Yes?'

'If you must know, I was afraid they'd half kill each other. They both have tempers.'

Interesting.

'I told her not to get involved.'

'I see.' Elizabeth tried to make her voice sound casual. 'Did the police ask about your whereabouts last Saturday night?'

'Not in so many—' Imogen stopped in mid-sentence, clearly shocked. 'You don't think I killed Kat?'

'You have the best motive in the world, my dear.'

'But that's ridiculous! I was crying my eyes out here on Saturday night.'

'Any witnesses?'

'Yes. My mother. And Tim.'

'Tim?'

'Tim Kidston. My . . . He was going to give me away.'

'Does this young man have an address?'

'I . . . he's . . . well, he's staying here at the moment.'

'Really?' Elizabeth did not alter the tone of her voice.

'He's a very old friend and he came over from Paris for the wedding and he wouldn't hear of going back until he knew I was OK . . .'

'I see.' Elizabeth nodded. 'You told me how you feel about your ex-fiancé. What about his friend, Ashley Lewis?'

'Ash? What about him?'

Elizabeth appeared to weigh her words. 'I suppose basically I wanted to ask if he ever carried a torch for you?'

'Ash?'

'Uh-huh.'

'Don't be silly.' The girl's eyes still seemed as clear as glass. No side to her at all. She couldn't hide a single emotion. Or could she?

'I suppose he's told you he went out with me first. He always trots that one out. It's just a joke. A game they played . . . pretending to fight over me.'

'So Ashley Lewis isn't jealous of your ex-fiancé?'

'Of course not. They're best mates. Have been since the year dot.'

'One more thing. Do you know a man called Marcus Finney?'

'I know he's an antiques dealer. I helped arrange the Antiques Fair in the Orangery. But I don't know him personally.'

'Bit hard on her, weren't you?' Max said, as they walked away from Louise Shand's front door.

'It's our job, Max. You should know that. Never let yourself be deceived by a pretty face.'

'Even so—'

'Actually, I liked the child.'

'Could have fooled me.' Max was charging on ahead. 'Odd trio, though. Glory, Kat and Imogen . . .'

Elizabeth knew what he meant. Two go-getters, tough, sophisticated girls, and the beautifully naïve Imogen.

'Fascinating, isn't it?' she asked Max.

'What's that?'

'The friendships – the undercurrents.' The bonds being

formed and betrayed; the ever-present past; the endless calibration of power between people.

Wonderfully interesting . . . this job. And they paid you for it.

Chapter Twenty-One

Louise Shand parked her car in a very small space in Pulteney Gardens and watched them walk away from the house.

It was a windy, restless-feeling day. Louise (small and finicky – chestnut hair tidied back – hard to charm a smile out of her) picked up her mobile and dialled a number. 'It's me,' she said.

The voice on the other end knew who 'me' was. 'What's wrong?'

'They've been here again. I saw her let them out. I'm worried sick. God knows what she's said. It's just that I can't be with her all the time.'

'Calm down,' the voice said.

Male or female?

That would be telling.

'Calm down. Your daughter's a chip off the old block. Stronger than you think.'

Jesus, she thought, I hope so.

Across town, in the tiny churchyard adjacent to St Bartholomew's, the Reverend Timms said, 'That detective woman – what *was* her name?' Absurd that it had disappeared down some black hole. These days his memory was no better than it should be. 'Animated woman. Remember? Rather attractive, I thought.'

Warm green eyes. Bright lips. Magenta. No . . . poppy.

'For her age.' Brian Thursley moved his gaze to a patch of timothy grass that needed strimming.

'Will of her own, I remember thinking. She told me her name but I'm dashed if I can remember it.'

'I'll give you a clue if you like.' Thursley liked the intellectual challenges of the quizword in his favourite tabloid. 'Something to do with Downing Street.'

'That sycamore's on the turn.' Shifting clouds behind it, pewter and iron-grey. 'Brown,' said the Reverend Timms, who liked to tease old Thursley. 'Mrs Brown. That's it.'

'Not him! T'other one.' Thursley's long, angular body swooped to gather a thistle. 'You thinking of asking her to supper then?'

'Good Lord, no. Past all that. You know me. Confirmed bachelor.'

'Bambi—'

'Sorry?'

'Bambi. I'll tell you no more than that.'

'Ah, now I'm with you!' The gentleman parson let his face assume an expression of triumphant delight. 'Cook. Mrs Cook. There's something I should have told her. Something to do with the aborted nuptials . . .'

Eight ten p.m. that evening. Dottie Marchant sat up in bed with a book in her lap. She was exceedingly bad-tempered. 'How am I? I'm eighty-five years old and I'm bored with it all. When I got up this morning, I felt lousy. I still feel lousy.'

'Can I do anything?'

'Shouldn't think so for one moment. Just enjoy being young while you can.'

Young? Elizabeth thought.

Dottie said, 'The trouble is, you wake up in the morning and see all the same things. Nothing is changing any more.'

'I didn't think you English liked change.'

Dottie ignored the remark. 'It's too frustrating for words. What I need is a new body. This one's like my old Morris Minor. Broken down and you can't get new parts for it. I'm going to seed. I list to port when I walk. I'm nursing-home material.'

'Surely not . . .' Elizabeth heard herself murmur.

'I'm at the last bus stop before the terminus,' Dottie said. 'And it feels frightful. Wish I could go back fifty years. Well, thirty would do.'

When Elizabeth got back indoors, she twice rang the newspaper office where her daughter worked, only to be told that Kate was in Chicago for a couple of days interviewing some guy about a health scam.

This was nothing new. Kate was often hard to get hold of.

And moms do not belong in the office. Nothing wrong with that, Elizabeth told herself. Kate is thirty-three years old and is a busy lady. As someone once wisely pointed out to me, what's the big deal about them having a life of their own?

It's just . . . I don't know.

Well, God damn it, sometimes I do feel hurt that her telephone calls are so irregular. When I was her age, I saw my mother every week. She was like my best friend.

Different times, baby.

Forget it. Think about something else.

Anything else . . .

That article, for instance – the one she'd been looking for – no, delving for, for weeks now. The one that would turn itself, suitably blown up, preferably in calligraphy (Caroline's speciality), into an intriguing little piece to place between the folds of the Double Wedding quilt in the shop window. An article from *Eastern Montana Quilting Magazine* for November 1974:

Elizabeth put the kettle on, fished the article out of the scrap bag where she'd put it for safe keeping and settled down for a read:

The Double Wedding Ring.

This great American classic, popular from the nineteenth century on, may have been taken from an old motif found in the Old World in Egypt, Syria, Greece, or Rome. Some examples were even dug up in Pompeii. The design has many other names: The Rainbow; Around the World; King Tut; Endless Chain.

Another source for the design might have been the gimmel ring (from the Latin *gemelli* – twins): a ring composed of two, three or more interlocking loops fanning open from a pivot at the base. When shut, the hoops slide together so perfectly that only a single ring can be seen. Those of more complex design were thought of as puzzles, sometimes purposely designed to be difficult to reassemble when taken apart.

The most popular form of the gimmel ring was two separate loops that could be totally separated. During the period of the engagement, one loop was worn by the man and the other by the woman. At the time of the marriage, the two rings fitted back together again to become a wedding ring for the woman. The ring was often decorated with a clasped-hands motif. The hands would interlock when reassembled. Sometimes there was an inscription, visible only when the loops separated. '*Quod Deus coniunxit homo non separat.*'

Whom God has joined together let no man put asunder.

Martin Luther married Catherine Bora in 1525 with such an inscribed gimmel ring.

The gimmel ring probably came to America with Germanic settlers in Pennsylvania in the late seventeenth and early nineteenth centuries; settlers looking for rich farmland to form agrarian communities. Germanic settlers were conservative and Old World customs survived there.

The Double Wedding Ring was very popular in the 1930s when it was offered by every quilt-related publisher from coast to coast. By the early '30s, there were thousands of packs for sale with pre-cut fabrics. By 1949, county fairs had reclassified their quilt displays to include a special one for the Double Wedding Ring.

The phone shrilled and the kettle whistled at one and the same time. 'Damn!' said Elizabeth, who had been looking forward to her hot chocolate.

Max's voice said, 'I got hold of Christopher Hunter. The architect. I rang him at home. He corroborates everything Finney said. There's only one thing that's odd. He says that Kat's umbrella disappeared while he was back in the office calling the police.'

'Her umbrella disappeared?'

'Yeah. She was running to her car under it when she was shot. It was definitely there when he tried to help her, because the wind had wedged it between her car and the next one.'

'I guess the wind blew it away.'

'He told the police and they searched but didn't find it. Oh, and I rang the Lewises. Ashley's parents. She's very posh. The mother. Anyway, she confirmed Ashley's story. Johnny was out like a light. Ashley's car, the one they'd driven up in, remained parked in the front drive and Ashley was with them all evening.'

'Then Mulligan has a rock-solid alibi?'

'The police still have strong circumstantial evidence.'

'I guess. So what are you up to tomorrow?'

'A spot of Neighbourhood Watch for Mr Mold, I thought. Oh, and I've got to see the Gas Board woman about that fraud case. So, I thought I'd leave the Mulligan case in your capable hands . . .'

'Hold on—'

But he'd rung off.

Elizabeth made herself a hot chocolate and cut herself a new slice from the sunflower seed loaf in the bin by the window. The darkness outside was thick and dank. An owl hooted in the field at the back of the cottage.

She dragged the scrap bag over to the fireside. There was nothing better for driving off the glooms than an hour or two with the needle. For the last couple of months she'd been piecing a corner of a yellow Sunburst. Strong colours. A big old mess (and you made a mess while you were cutting) of vibrant yellows with a star and a couple of Nine Patches, a sunflower, a corn cob or two and I don't know what all . . . All the pieces fitting into one great big puzzle.

Not an attempted duplication of a corn cob.

Not an observation, but an approximation of the radiance of harvest.

An important distinction.

'I'll leave the Mulligan case in your capable hands.' In other words, Max was stumped. So am I, for that matter. As she matched up colours and sorted them, figuring and working with the cotton prints, Elizabeth's mind circled round the main characters in the Mulligan case. Johnny, who was of an age to want a pure, innocent little bride. Imogen, pure and innocent enough not to know what he was getting up to.

Katharine Gregg, the Shands, Marcus Finney . . .

Half a dozen interlocking lives . . .

It was like putting together the loops of the Double Wedding Ring. Sometimes you had no idea where to start.

Chapter Twenty-Two

Monday morning. Jan Finney was seeing Lucian off in the school minibus when she noticed the woman loitering by the front gate of Number 25. A woman that she recognised. Slight, middle-aged . . . brown jacket, pink scarf wrapped round her throat.

The woman who had tried on the bracelet.

She wasn't mistaken, because it wasn't the first time. She was there yesterday. Go on, say it. Admit it. And on Tuesday morning, in the same jacket but a blue scarf instead of the pink.

They were being watched. Jan was sure of it.

She closed the gate behind her and went back into the house, shutting out a regular autumn smell of damp dust and Michaelmas daisies. The sitting-room window was open a fraction. She closed that too and as she did so, the woman moved. Crossed over to stand under the plane tree on this side of the street, only twenty yards away. Who the hell is she? What do I do? Ring somebody? But who? Not Marcus. No safety there. The police? Not today. Not yet.

Now the woman was walking slowly along the pavement towards the front gate. Short, dark hair. Her feet encased in brown boots. Something peculiar about her. Had been in the shop. A mildly sinister figure.

It was eight forty-five a.m.

Then — Jan's heart leapt suddenly into her mouth — the

woman had speeded up. Had reached the front gate. Was opening it . . .

Jan moved sharply back and walked into the hard edge of the Queen Anne desk. Swore profusely. Next came a soft click from the letter box in the hall, but by the time Jan got out there to fling open the front door, the woman had vanished.

Something had been shoved through the letter box, however. Jan bent down and picked it up from the rough bit of carpet that they wiped their shoes on.

A photograph – 6" by 6" – that had been enlarged on a cheap photocopier.

The photograph of an attractive little boy laughing into the camera.

Nine thirty a.m. Max dug out another cube of chewing gum and watched interestedly as the boy climbed out of the battered van with what looked like a mattress in the back.

Faulkland Way. Number Twelve. He'd been watching it for almost an hour now and, quite frankly, the place intrigued him. There was a mother (tie-dye skirts and big earrings), a father (Nehru shirt and a motorbike parked behind the laburnum), plus a ratty old dog and four (or was it five?) teenage children. The Molds would love that! Loud parties, loud music, balls coming over the fence or worse.

But (and this was a big 'but') they seemed a nice crowd, the three lanky boys and the tiny girl who bobbed round behind them. And every window in the house was full of interesting objects. Pots and Victorian dogs and teddy bears and pots of red geraniums.

There were even window boxes. That had to be good. Unless, of course, they were awash with cannabis. Max popped the gum in his mouth and began to chew. Elizabeth hated him chewing, but Elizabeth wasn't here. Anyway, he hadn't had any breakfast.

The boy climbed back in again, heaving what looked like a box of rubbish behind him. A spot of rain fell on the windscreen. It was darkening up and beginning to look like a storm was brewing.

'Hi!'

Max jumped out of his skin. Somehow the older boy had crept up on him from the rear. This face was peering in. Teenage. Lively. 'I'm Bill. We wondered why you were watching us. If you don't mind my asking?'

'Feel free.' Max pointed to his clipboard. Exercised his ingenuity. 'Doing a survey.'

'Of what?'

'Traffic,' Max extemporised. 'Road bumps.'

'There isn't any. Traffic.'

'That's what I shall be telling the Council. You don't need them. Bumps. Waste of their valuable resources. I like your jalopy.'

'We bought it from a pig farmer. A bit crappy, but it does the job.'

'What job's that then?'

'My father has a second-hand bookshop in Walcot Street. He also sells LPs and railway stuff.'

That explained everything. Walcot Street was a wonderful hotch-potch of hippy and craft shops and junk emporiums. Harmless arty-farties, Max thought.

'Also, there are rather a lot of us kids. Two of Mum's, two of Dad's and one together. So the van gets us all around.'

'I had an old van,' Max remembered, 'when I were a lad. Cost me thirty quid. Great for pulling the girls.'

'This one isn't.' The lad grinned. 'Pongs of pigs. See you.'

'See you,' said Max.

Two of Mum's and two of Dad's and one together. Sounds fun, he thought. The balance sheet was in credit so far as he was concerned. But he wasn't at all sure that the Molds would approve.

*   *   *

Ten thirty a.m. Elizabeth said, 'Mrs Finney?'

The woman who had opened the door looked nervous. She wore a grey jumper and washed-out jeans. Curly brown hair, with grey flecks. Not drab exactly. Almost pretty or would once have been. But her face looked drawn, the eyes slightly puffed.

Good cheekbones.

Pity about the livid bruise on the right-hand one.

'Yes?'

'I'm Elizabeth Blair. I'm a private detective.' Among other things. 'I wondered if I could have a quick word?'

'What's it about?'

Elizabeth explained. 'I just wondered if you had any idea why Miss Gregg should have been down in Alfred Buildings that night. Not far from your husband's shop?'

'None at all. I'm sorry.'

'Your husband didn't appear to know Kat Gregg, but he said you did. Is that right? He says you met her at the Beehive? Apparently you described the lady as –' out came her notebook – 'as "big, busty and brash." '

'I never said anything of the sort!' Elizabeth saw the look of astonishment on the other woman's face. She looked flabbergasted. And angry. 'Kat's . . . Kat was a lovely girl. Full of fun. Full of energy.' Her lips suddenly trembled and her eyes brimmed with unshed tears. 'I'm sorry. I can't—'

'No, I'm sorry. You're upset. Look – would it be easier if we discuss this inside?'

The house was well-furnished, but somehow anonymous. Cream walls, a cane chair or two, a couple of easy chairs covered in green-and-cream plaid and one or two good pieces of furniture.

But it didn't feel like a home. Why was that? Some subtle sense of . . . unhappiness. Could you say that about a room? Was it being fanciful?

Elizabeth took one of the chairs and they started again. Jan Finney didn't know the identity of the mysterious customer who had stood her husband up on the night of the murder. Yes, she had met Kat the weekend of the Antiques Fair soon after they'd come back to Bath to live. Where did they live before? Southampton. And then Dorchester. Yes, she knew the Makepeaces. Slightly. Had chatted briefly to Anna at the Antiques Fair.

'And Glory Fraser? She's a part-time receptionist at the hotel. Do you know her?'

'Yes, of course. Nice girl. Very lively. Actually, I knew her before I went up to Cheyneys. Glory used to help out at Lucian's school. Saint Dunstan's. Voluntary work, mainly. Mostly observing. She's interested in mental health. Wants to specialise in that field, I believe, after she qualifies.'

The Mulligans? Imogen Shand?

Nothing. Zilch, except what she'd read in the papers, of course.

Elizabeth said, 'But you liked Kat a lot? Tell me about her.'

'Like my husband said, I took Lucian over there for tea. He had his friend with him — Clara. Clara's worse than Lucian. She can't talk. She looks . . . well, it's pretty noticeable that she's handicapped. Sometimes people stare or shy away. But Kat was wonderful with them . . . a natural. She made them laugh. Gave Lucian this silly paper hat and said he could come and help her bake cakes some time. He loves helping in the kitchen. And you know what? She didn't forget. She rang him up and fixed for him to come up one Sunday. Just him and her. He never stopped talking about it. She really cared. She even came along to help at his school fête because he asked her to. And she brought stuff for our jumble sales and came to concerts and raised money by putting a collecting box on the hall table at the Beehive.'

Mrs Finney turned to look at Elizabeth. 'She didn't have to do any of it, but she did and I loved her for it. You have no idea — it's so hard sometimes.' A hand fluttered over the bruise on her cheekbone. 'I haven't told Lucian yet. What happened to her. I know I'll have to, before he hears it from somebody else. They —

Downs children – do feel things, you know, the same as the rest of us. Some may not think it, but . . .'

Elizabeth nodded sympathetically. Felt constrained to ask one more time, 'But your husband never met Miss Gregg? That seems odd, considering—'

'Oh, he never comes to school events.' Once the words were out of her mouth, she looked as if she wanted to bite them back. 'You won't tell him I talked to you? He wouldn't like it.'

'No?'

'No.' The monosyllable spoke volumes.

'Any particular reason?' Elizabeth asked gently.

'No.'

'You're sure? Only it seems to me that something's bothering you.'

'No. Nothing.'

With skill borne of long practice, Elizabeth waited. The clock ticked. Sparrows twittered. The wind rattled at the window.

Elizabeth went on looking at Finney's wife and wondered how much longer she could hold it back. The hand fluttered again over the bruised cheekbone. Her lip trembled and she looked as if at any moment she would burst into tears.

'You can tell me, can't you? We're very discreet.'

Jan Finney got up. Paced nervously round the room, then blurted out, 'Actually – there's someone watching the house.'

Ginger looked up as Elizabeth walked into the office. 'Hi! You look weary.'

'I feel weary. Anything exciting?'

'Depends what you call exciting. Caroline's been telling us about her wedding plans. You'll never guess.'

'The rose garden at Buck House—'

'Not quite. Bath Abbey.'

'You're kidding?'

'No. Rupert's mother knows the Bishop of Bath and Wells.'

'Well, wouldn't you know? So apart from the Bishop, did anything exciting happen?'

'A Reverend Timms rang.'

They were having an ecclesiastical morning.

'He'd like to talk to you about Imogen Shand.'

Chapter Twenty-Three

Three p.m. Rose Mulligan said, 'So you've got one or two leads?'

'One or two ideas. There's a difference.'

'Anything's better than nothing.' Rose splayed fat fingers. When she spoke again, her voice was rather higher, agitated. 'I rang because I thought you ought to see these.'

Opening a drawer in the sideboard, she drew out a fat, brown envelope. Emptied the contents on to the table. 'Threatening letters. Mostly from women. Mind, this is strictly between you and me. The police haven't seen them.'

'Why not?'

'I thought they might hold it against Johnny, you know? And –' a rapid, furtive glance – 'several of them are from girls he contacted through the Lonely Hearts column.'

It got worse. 'But he wasn't?'

'Wasn't what?'

'A lonely heart . . .' Elizabeth's voice was dry.

'It's not like it sounds. He only did it the once.'

'Did what once?'

'Placed an advert in the Lonely Hearts column. It was a stag-night prank. Bit of a lark. Ashley got him drunk and bet him he wouldn't and the girl he met up with wasn't much of a lady by the sound of it.'

Don't tell me, Elizabeth thought. It's like our poor dear

President. She led him on and he didn't mean to do it and anyway, they didn't have real sex. He didn't inhale.

'I know it sounds bad, but . . .' Rose clutched at the glass of orange-coloured liquid in her pink-tipped hand and tried to justify her son's behaviour. 'He's . . . a good-looking boy and women throw themselves at him. It would take a stronger man than my Johnny to turn them all down.'

She'd forgive any of his sins, Elizabeth thought. But what does a mother do? She loves. Without rules. Unequivocally. We all do. I forgive JJ his hypochondria and his ditherings, Kate her sharp tongue and her off-handedness. And that's all there is to it. That's love for you. That's the meaning of life.

'These women who chase men like Johnny . . .' Rose sounded vicious now. 'These single, thirty-somethings.' A slight slurring of the 's's. Was she a little tipsy? 'They've no moral code, you know. They're fed up of being on their own and they're prepared to sleep with their best friend's husbands. They're desperate for a partner and they think the end justifies the means.' A shuddering sigh as she got herself back under control. 'But he loved Imogen. I know he did.' She stared down at her considerable stomach. Said heavily, 'You can't keep your kids on a lead like a dog. More's the pity.'

Elizabeth eyed the letters on the table. 'Which one's the Lonely Hearts girl?'

Rose extracted a pink envelope from the pile. 'One of the few that was signed,' she said.

You were deceiving two of them, you bloody pervert. And one of them expecting your child. I hope you rot in hell.
Jackie Townend.

Elizabeth said. 'Can I borrow the letters?'

A tired shrug. 'Help yourself.' Rose seemed utterly deflated, like a balloon that was slowly going down. She had got a few things off her considerable chest, but her face displayed a hopelessness which would get worse as the night went on.

Five p.m. Ginger and Max were deep into an existentialist conversation about crime and criminals. 'The thing is,' Ginger said, 'you should always have somebody you want to kill. Your mother-in-law. The bank manager. The boss at work.'

Max said, 'Thanks.'

'You're welcome. *Wanting* to kill somebody is perfectly normal. Healthy even. The thing is, most of us dream of it, but don't actually do it. The people who do it have gone past their breaking point.'

'So some people have a lower breaking point?'

'Exactly. Also there are varying depths of evil.'

'On a sliding scale?'

'Exactly. It's . . . well, take children. There's naughty, there's malicious and there's plain destructive.'

'And then there's plain sick,' said Elizabeth who had been listening with some enjoyment. The girl was bright. She made Max dig deeper into his grey matter – which had to be good for the boy.

'Psychotic, you mean. So which category does Johnny Mulligan fall into?'

'Not sure yet. I'll tell you that when I've got the answers to a number of questions.'

'Such as?' Max grabbed a Mars bar from the windowsill and peeled off the wrapper.

'OK. Question one. Who stole the umbrella that Kat was holding when she was shot? A blue- black-and-white-striped golfing umbrella – Bath rugby colours – according to Christopher Hunter. I called on him on my way back from Rose's. Of course, the umbrella *might* have blown away. Someone *might* have found it and pinched it. Along with a couple of black polythene bags, which weren't in the car when Hunter found her.

But then we come to question two. Why was Kat carrying an umbrella that didn't belong to her?'

'How do we know it didn't belong to her?'

'We don't, for certain. But I just spent a half hour calling her friends and family and they all say the same thing. She didn't possess such an item. Plus she's hated rugby ever since a friend of hers got a broken neck playing for his college side.'

'Says who?'

'Says her ex-husband. As far as he knew, she never went to a game. Of course, she might have had a conversion since her divorce. But it's unlikely. You see, she worked all day Saturday at the tearooms.'

'There are weekday games,' Max said.

Elizabeth shook her head. 'She hated the game of rugby. Everybody said so.'

'So she borrowed the umbrella. It was tipping down with rain and whoever she was visiting that night lent it to her.'

'Which brings us back to that old chestnut . . . question three. Who *was* she visiting.

Max took a bite out of the Mars bar. 'We should check which of our suspects follows Bath rugby.'

'Marcus Finney does. According to his wife, he does possess an umbrella in Bath colours, but when I asked to see it, it had mysteriously disappeared from the hall stand.'

'He took it to work with him.'

'It's not raining.'

'Then it's in his car. Did you call the man himself?'

'He's off buying, apparently. The gentleman's elusive . . . when it suits him, I rather think.' Elizabeth appeared slightly abstracted. 'Ashley Lewis follows Bath rugby. Oh – I nearly forgot.' She fished into the depths of her bag and tossed the letters Rose had given her on to the desk. 'Here's a nice little job for you. Johnny Mulligan's hate mail. It needs sorting and filing. Not that I can see at the moment where they'll lead us. But it'll keep you out of mischief.'

'Ginger can help,' Max said when he saw the size of the pile.

'Not today, I'm afraid.' Ginger glanced at her watch. 'You said I could leave early. I've got a date.'

'A date?'

'A date. Do we have a problem with that? As a matter of fact, it's somebody you know. Glyn Benson.'

'Glyn? I don't know anybody called Glyn.'

'Yes, you do. He's the chef from the hotel. He rang me up.'

'Here? At the office?'

'Is it forbidden?'

'No. But—'

'He talks a bit too much. Gossips. And he's a bit . . . well . . . northern.'

'Nothing wrong with that,' said Max.

'I mean, there's not much finesse. Not compared with Bath boys—'

She was winding Max up. Deliberately. Elizabeth could see that. She sat watching them, a glint of enjoyment in her green eyes.

'But I like him. He's quite good fun. We're going for a drink at the Merry Fiddler.'

'You're kidding?'

'Why? What's wrong with it?'

'You'll find out,' Max said darkly.

'Children, children. Here's another question for you. Quite an interesting one. Who's the woman presently watching the Finneys' house and sending him peculiar letters?'

'Saying what?'

She drew out the letter that Jan Finney had lent her.

Spilt milk, all of it. Might as well have brought it all out into the open years ago. All that measuring of other men against your memory. All for what? If life is a game, you won it.

> For he left his pretty boy,
> Father's sorrow, father's joy.

The Lord giveth and the Lord taketh away. Someone put the lights on, then off again immediately. Lucian. That's what he's called, isn't it? I see him in the park. Pay-back time. Oh, yes it is. Give me my money back or else. You owe me. You certainly owe me.

'Weird or what?' Max handed the letter to Ginger.

'Mrs Finney says her husband's had other letters, only she's not supposed to know that. She's scared someone's going to attack Lucian. She's also scared stiff of her husband. So, we've picked up some new business. She wants us to find out who this woman is . . .'

Max groaned. 'Not more work—'

'Don't knock it, sunshine. It keeps us solvent. Also, I have a hunch it might help us on the Mulligan case.'

'In what way?'

'Well, don't you find it odd, a coincidence, that the guy who isn't a million miles away from the scene of that poor girl's murder is also receiving threats?'

'Put that way—' Max sat there reflecting.

'So, here's one last question for you. What if – and it's a very big if – what if the person who shot Kat Gregg was really out to get Marcus Finney? It just crossed my mind. Kat may just have been in the wrong place at the wrong time . . .'

Chapter Twenty-Four

———◦◇◦———

Wednesday. Nine fifty-five a.m. Celia Hannaford pulls on her neat brown moccasins, walks with a sense of urgency over to the dressing-table drawer and fetches out the key to Father's old trunk. She feels heady, but tense. Her heart very cold.

Spots in his, a voice says. Cool fire in yours.

She lifts her head and gazes at herself in the mirror. Eyes look back at her; eyes that have lost their shine. Bare cheekbones, bare, bald stare, bare mouth, a little thin, now, around the edges. You look like an untrimmed Christmas tree; all the decorations, the pretty things put back in the box.

Beauty gone. What beauty? Never was any. That's why he never married you, even when you told him you were pregnant.

Pale eyes still stare back at her from the mirror. She thinks, I feel like the Lady of Shalott.

> *And moving thro' a mirror clear*
> *That hangs before her all the year,*
> *Shadows of the world appear.*

Her finger flicks at the key as she kneels to unlock the trunk for the first time in — how long? Twenty-nine years? The hinges squeak a little. There is dust on the tissue paper under the lid. Celia lifts and shakes. (Literally.) Drops the tissue on the floor and lifts out the wedding dress she stitched with her own fair (well, thin) hands in 1973. The silk is yellow now. Pale and decayed, a spot of mould on the shoulder. It feels papery.

Her mind goes spooling back over the years to a single summer.

She remembered meeting him as if it were yesterday. A handsome young man. A romantic risk taker.

> *The sun came dazzling thro' the leaves,*
> *And flamed upon the brazen greaves*
> *Of bold Sir Lancelot.*

'Celia?' Alice's voice echoes somewhere outside her head. 'You in there?'

Celia has often asked herself the same question. How can anyone find an answer to it?

Then the mirage dissolved. The storyline came to an abrupt end.

'Celia? You've only got five minutes.'

That's all I ever had. Five minutes . . . travelling to the land of heaven.

And hell since.

Celia crams the dress back into the trunk and shoves it hard underneath the bed. She drops her head for one moment on the softness of duck-down duvet. Is tempted by tears. But tears hurt your head, make you sweat. There's a better remedy. Celia heaves herself off her knees and makes for the vodka bottle she keeps hidden in the bottom of the wardrobe. Uncorks it, lifts it to her mouth with a hand that shakes.

'Celia?'

The vodka goes back into the wardrobe. Quick, before she catches you. And she almost does. The door opens. Alice stands there. 'Come on — slow-coach! Did you take your pills?'

Damn the pills. Vodka's better.

A vicious bite of shrillness. The doorbell. 'That's your pupil,' Alice says. 'Did you take your pills?'

'I'll take them tonight.'

'Celia—'

'I don't need them today.'

'For God's sake, Celia – when will you learn some sense?'

Never. Why should I? Who wants to be like you?

Five minutes later, Celia says to her ten o'clock pupil, 'Today we're going to have a treat. I'll play. You listen. Scarlatti.'

Alice hates tinkling Scarlatti. Alice also hates it when Celia is too drunk (or too high) to hit the right notes. But I've had enough of her trampling my thin life even flatter.

Alice can go hang.

At the exact moment when Celia Hannaford flies (rather ropily) into the Scarlatti, Imogen Shand is saying, 'I'm going to kill myself.'

'For heaven's sake—' Louise manages to keep her composure and pours her daughter a coffee.

It has been one of those mornings. The central-heating boiler is making ominous noises, she has a migraine coming on and that Blair woman rang to ask if she, Louise, was acquainted with Marcus Finney.

'Marcus who?' she had enquired.

'Finney. Marcus Finney. He's an antiques dealer.'

'It's news to me,' Louise said.

'Only I understand he's been receiving anonymous letters . . .'

'So? You think I wrote them?'

'Never occurred to me actually. You didn't, I take it?'

'Of course I didn't.' She was curious enough to ask, 'Threatening letters?'

'Not exactly. They seem to be from some woman whose child he may have fathered.'

'Well, don't look at me,' Louise said. 'One child's as much as I can contend with at the moment.'

The child in question is now sitting, head in hands, saying, 'There's nothing left for me to live for.'

'I've never heard anything so silly in all my life,' Louise says sharply.

'I shall go to the police then. I killed her. I feel so guilty.'

Louise raises her eyebrows for effect.

'I mean it.'

'Of course you do – now. But my darling, remember, you've got the rest of your life to think of.'

A sniffly sob. 'But I can't cope. I just can't cope.' Tears are pouring down Imogen's face.

'Yes, you can.' Louise lets her have her cry out. 'I'm here. Always will be. You know that.' A thoughtful silence. Then, 'You know, what you really need is to get away from all this. A good holiday.'

'I couldn't.'

'What nonsense. Of course you can. Actually, Tim suggested it. He'll take you over to Paris.'

'I couldn't,' Imogen said again; but this time with much less emphasis.

Maybe, Louise thought with a deep-felt sense of relief, maybe she'll just let herself be persuaded.

Alice Hannaford listens to the row (that was all you could call it) coming from the other room and purses her lips. Give me a good, soupy tune any day, she thinks, banging away at the dirty cooking bowls in the sink. But then, I know nothing. According to some people.

I'm a goose and not a swan. God, how many years ago did I hear Father say that? Celia's a swan and Alice a goose. Bloody tactless of him, but then he was. And I take after him, so we'll call it even.

Celia was always Father's favourite. Everybody's favourite, because of her looks and her musical talent. She moved people's souls in a way that my meals (and I'm a good cook) couldn't. Oh, they come and eat and enjoy, but no one ever says it feeds his soul.

Alice rests her hands on the heavy cooking bowl that sits encircled with soap bubbles and gazes out of the kitchen window at the chilly-looking street. Georgian windows are the best for looking out of. Large panes, interesting bits of swirl in the glass. In the alley below, a fish van disgorges its boxes of mussels and crabs. Pigeons wheel over the rooftops at the back of Milsom Street and a taxi crawls over the bumpy back lane behind Jolly's department store.

Swans glide, Alice thinks. Geese waddle. Awkward, ungraceful, bulging creatures. Foolish looking birds. Everyday creatures. Useful at Christmas, mind you. In fact, a more useful creature, all in all.

We can't all be poetical.

Anyway, geese make good watchdogs.

Alice has watched over Celia for as long as she could remember. Hissed if anyone looked about to attack. Sisters, she thinks. Fight non-stop, but attack one and see the other react! I can be as fierce as hell when there are predators around. Like . . .

She can't bring herself even to mention his name.

The cad, Father always called him. So long ago, but it seems like yesterday. The cad. All grand gestures and preened hair. Something Shakespearian about him. That's because he was so full of bombast, always good for a soliloquy – except that, like Hamlet, he knew where his audience was. He liked you to be listening in. Alice dragged the bowl (plus bubbles) out of the water and plonked it down hard on the draining board. Airy-fairy, I always called him. All mouth and no substance. But Celia could never see that. Not in a blue moon. Celia always makes an unerring beeline for the wrong sort. Not a ha' porth of common sense. All that Romeo and Juliet stuff. Hanging over a balcony rubbish. Always watching the clock for him . . . and him always letting her down. And he always had some excuse. He could do any mortal thing and she'd forgive him.

Alice swishes a tablespoon round in the water so fast that she catches the chain and pulls the plug out. Damnation! All that hot, soapy water guzzling away down the drain. She'd like to see *him* go down the drain. No loss! Absolutely no loss at all, but try and tell my sister that. No, she'd rather spend years and years mooning over him.

> 'And sometimes thro' the mirror blue
> The knights come riding two and two . . .'

Celia's voice from the kitchen doorway. The child is still sitting at the piano in the room behind her. Alice can see its little staring face and its wide-open mouth. There'll be no pupils left, at this rate. Several mothers have already removed them because of her funny fits.

'I've decided,' Celia says, 'to go to Lake Como on a coach trip. Donizetti and Verdi. You may come if you like.'

'Load of nonsense,' Alice says said gruffly. 'Hadn't you better get back to your scales?'

'I've finished for today. Declared it a holiday.'

'And what does Rebecca think of that?' Or her parents, for that matter.

'Oh, Rebecca's a wonderfully sensible and sensitive child. So sweet and calm and gentle.'

She might have been describing a child from a long time ago . . .

Alice suddenly feels a little wobbly, but she knows how to school her face. Learned that early in life. 'Pour yourself a coffee,' she says steadily. 'I'll see Rebecca out.'

Elizabeth, meanwhile, is having a good old curse because she's in danger of running out of the fabric she is using for the background of the Starburst. A butterscotch-yellow print that she'd brought over from Virginia and wouldn't be able to locate any more of.

This quilt is likely to be a long time in the making.

But then, quilts don't take notice of time. There was a pink-and-cream Rose of Sharon she remembered from a show down in South Carolina. A 'while-waiting' quilt, made by Nancy Frazier Greer while she waited for the return of her fiancé, Frank Peterson, who had gone to accompany a wagon on the Oregon Trail from Illinois in 1851. The nineteen-year-old Nancy said that quilting made the time go more quickly. Frank didn't return until nine years later. They were married on 15 August 1860.

How many girls would wait that long these days?

Elizabeth sits frowning at the starburst spread over her lap. I only want a quarter yard. Maddening. She ponders. Then thinks of something. That old scrap-bag of Ma's up in the attic. Perhaps there'll be something that vaguely matches.

But first she calls on Dottie, who managed to walk down to the post office that morning, but is still pretty crusty.

'That Aunger woman from the council houses was in there. Molly, or is it Maureen? A slummock with a backside a yard wide. Smelled to high heaven. They should never let her inside the door.'

Dottie shuffles over to the sideboard to fetch an extra cup. Pours Elizabeth some half-stewed tea. 'Then there was the chap who came and rang the bell this morning. Have you got a pair of clippers, he said, and I'll cut that back for you. Cut what back, I said, only he'd vanished. I went out to see where he'd gone and he was halfway up the garden wall snapping off a limb of my lilac that the wind had brought halfway down. Well, I mean, dear, what if he'd fallen off? He was seventy if a day. So I said to him, what am I going to do with the clippings when you've done it? The Council will take them, he said. The Council won't take them, I told him. Then I'll take them over there, he said. Over where? I asked. And do you know, he couldn't say. So I said you can't just dump things in the lane.

You'll be getting me into trouble . . . Robert White. That's his name. You know him, dear.'

'Do I?'

'Of course you do. They call him Chalky. Lives over by the pub. He's a what-do-you-call it?'

Elizabeth waits. She has learned to be patient.

'A . . . you know. Somebody who stuffs things.'

'A taxidermist?'

'That's it. That's what I told you. People bring him things.'

'Things?'

'Yes. Things that get knocked down in the road. Badgers. A deer's head once.'

'So how did he learn to do that?'

'To do what, dear?'

'Taxidermy.'

'Oh, he taught himself out of a book,' Dottie says impatiently. 'I told you that before too. They ought to stuff me and put me in a glass case,' she says suddenly. 'My life is a log-jam. Too many things. Too many memories. You want to clear them all out and start again. Send everything in the house to a rummage sale and bring back somebody else's. You know . . . ?'

And suddenly Elizabeth does know.

She stares down at her hands as if she's never seen them before. An idea has occurred to her which is so blindingly obvious that it almost makes her feel dizzy.

Good God! Why didn't I think of that before?

Chapter Twenty-Five

Eleven fifteen a.m. on a Wednesday morning. It seemed as good a time as any to call on the Reverend Timms.

The vicarage (Elizabeth had looked it up) was in a cobbled lane beside St Bartholomew's, a tall church built on the site of a former leper hospital in an unfashionable part of town not far from the Lower Bristol Road. Traffic lights at the top of the street that ran at right angles to it. A gate in a beech hedge ten yards down from where she parked the car.

The Reverend Timms opened the door himself. Behind him a snugly tiled hallway. Above his head, a fanlight in ecclesiastical style with cinquefoil tracery.

'Mrs Blair!'

'Nice of you to remember me.'

'Not at all. Come in. Come in!'

Elizabeth followed him through a door on the right-hand side of the hall and into an orderly, comfortable drawing room with a tea table and a writing table and missionary boxes and some rather fine water colours in modern frames.

Smells of silver polish, Elizabeth thought. And geraniums. Why? There are none.

'Sit down! Take that chair. The other one's lost its springs.' The Reverend Timms beamed down at her. He was a very tall man. Dark hair, receding fast. Dark eyes . . . looking at her with a sort of held-back impulsiveness. There was something about him . . . Trollope. That was it! *The bishop did not whistle; we believe that they lose the power of doing so on being consecrated; but he looked as if he would have done so but for his apron.*

'Tea?'

'No. That's fine. Really. I don't want to hold you up.'

'Rather like being held up, actually. Nice to have the odd visitor. It's a fairly solitary job, being a clergyman. You're very much on your own.'

'You're not married? Don't have a family?'

'I'm a widower. My wife died ten years ago.'

'I'm sorry.'

'So am I, but it doesn't do to brood on it. I keep busy. There are always good works to do, sermons to write. We have a lot of high-powered people here in Bath. You have to preach a good sermon. They don't suffer fools.'

'I'm sure.' Elizabeth smiled. 'I believe you wanted to see me, Reverend Timms?'

'Richard, please. Yes. Yes, I did want to see you.' Suddenly he'd gone pinkly self-conscious. 'There was something I should have told you the other night – the night of the lecture – and didn't. That darned electrics chap. Got called away and by the time I got back, you'd gone. But it's been troubling my conscience.'

He would have a very tender conscience. Elizabeth could see that.

'You were asking about the Mulligans. About the wedding that didn't take place.'

'You said you prepared Johnny and Imogen for the impending marriage.'

'I did. Over several weeks. What I didn't get a chance to tell you was that Miss Gregg – the girl who was murdered – telephoned me a couple of weeks before the wedding and asked if she could call round. She was troubled about something, but she wouldn't discuss it over the telephone.'

'And did she call round?'

'Yes. Yes, she did.'

'And what was the problem?'

'She told me about the baby she was expecting and she asked me not to marry them.'

'Imogen and Johnny?'

'That's right.'

'Yet you took no notice?'

'Of course I took notice. I was most perturbed.'

'But you decided to let the service go ahead?'

'Yes. After I'd talked to the young man about it and had been reassured.'

The Church talking to Beelzebub, Elizabeth thought. 'So how did he reassure you?'

'He said that Miss Gregg had a grudge against him and was making it up.'

'And you believed him?'

'In the end – and with some misgivings – yes.' Elizabeth said nothing and Richard Timms went on. 'He asked me not to say anything about it to Imogen. He didn't want her upset by the other girl's lies. That's what he said to me.'

'And?'

'And I thought he was wrong there. At the time, I went along with it, but after I'd discussed it with my curate, well, we decided that I would have to see the young lady. It was my duty as a priest.'

'So you went to see Imogen?'

'No. I asked her to call round at the Vicarage. She came round one evening. Let's see now. About a week before the wedding.'

'And you told her about Kat's visit to you?'

'Yes. I thought she should know.'

So Imogen had known about the affair; but had still decided to go ahead with the wedding.

That innocent-looking child lied to me, Elizabeth thought. Innocent, my foot! A voice said inside her head.

The dialling tone went on and on. Elizabeth cracked open a can of Diet Coke as she waited. Gazed out through the shop window at the greenish tones that were creeping in along the narrow alley. Olive-green in the windows of the music shop opposite with darker shadows on the murky roof tops. Something crouching about them. Made you feel discomposed.

These last few days, it had been colder. A draughty feel to the evenings.

Still ringing. Come on. Come on!

She lifted the can again. Filthy habit. Should fetch a glass. She put on her glasses to check the time. Twelve fifteen. Time for lunch. Should be somebody at home. I need to check this pie-in-the-sky and off-the-wall idea that popped into my head. I need to check it now, while it's still there. Ideas have a habit of walking these days. Sad, but true.

Ring . . . ring. Six more times and I'll give up.

Five . . . six.

The phone was almost back on the receiver when a voice (breathless, hurried) said, 'Hello?'

'Mrs Finney?'

'Yes.'

'It's Elizabeth Blair. I'm sorry to call you at this hour. Is your husband there?'

'No. No, he isn't.'

'Good. Then we can speak freely. Listen – I have an idea I want to try out on you.'

Bags . . . rubbish. Dottie had put the idea in her head. Had reminded her of something Aidan Makepeace had said about Kat Gregg: 'She had this thing about spring cleaning. She would suddenly have to clear the decks . . .'

'Yes?' Suspicion. Definitely.

'Well, I wondered . . . You mentioned jumble sales at Lucian's school. You said that Miss Gregg sometimes contributed.'

'Yes.'

'I just wondered if she sent – brought – any stuff down to you on the night she was murdered?'

Silence. She was thinking. At length. Hesitating. Was she still there? Yes, she was.

'I . . . I'm not sure.'

Elizabeth felt her heart leap. 'You mean there's a possibility?'

'I . . . I'd have to check.'

'Where? What was the usual procedure?'

'I . . . well, she would ring us.'

'And?'

'And I'd tell her to dump it in our garage.'

'The one in Alfred Buildings?'

'Yes.'

'And then what?'

'Then one of us would come along with a van just before the sale and pick it up.'

'The garage in Alfred Buildings acted as a collection centre?'

'I suppose so. It wasn't much of a collection centre. But people dumped things there. They'd either arrange to meet me there or pick up the keys from the shop.'

'And did you have a rummage sale coming up?'

'Yes. As a matter of fact we did. Do. On Saturday afternoon.'

'And Miss Gregg knew about it?'

'Yes. I sent her a leaflet with all the dates.'

'So did Miss Gregg call your house that Saturday to say she had some stuff for you?'

Another silence.

'Mrs Finney. It's very important. If you know anything—'

'I'm thinking. It's just that I can't honestly say.'

'Why can't you say? You must know if she rang that night.'

'That's just it. She *may* have rung . . . somebody did ring in the early evening.'

'But you didn't answer the phone?'

'Exactly. My husband picked it up.'

'What time was this?'

'I don't know.' Some sort of stifled emotion. 'Just before he went out again. Around six thirty.'

'And you think it might have been Miss Gregg?'

'I've told you. I don't know.'

'But you have reason to suspect?'

'I can't honestly say. It was a very brief conversation, but he did tell whoever was on the other end not to bother collecting the key. He'd leave the garage unlocked.'

'You didn't think to report this to the police?'

'No. Because I can't honestly say that it was her.' Rising tension.

'You didn't ask him?'

'No. I was . . . He was in a . . . It wasn't a good time.'

Elizabeth put the can down, very carefully, on the counter. 'So tell me . . . Assuming that Miss Gregg did leave some bags of stuff in your garage that night, what would have happened to it?'

'It'll still be there, I imagine.'

Elizabeth dropped into the armchair by the fireplace and said, more calmly than she felt, 'Could I take a look at those bags, do you think?'

Chapter Twenty-Six

One p.m. Martha Washington. The Mews was quiet; not a tourist in sight. A blustery wind and spots of rain had sent them scurrying into restaurants and cafés for lunch. Max plonked himself down on Caroline's chair. 'OK. Want to hear what I've been digging up about Finney and Makepeace?'

Finney and Makepeace. Sounded like a doddering pair of country lawyers.

'OK. You go first.' Elizabeth would save her own titbits for later. It wasn't often the boy looked this keen and ready to go.

'Marcus Finney. Born in Salisbury, sixth of July, nineteen forty-seven. Father something in the property business. Sent to Edgerley House, a minor boarding school near Malvern. Worked for a year or two in his father's property business, but appears to have left under a cloud. Some kind of embezzlement hinted at. Estranged from his parents. Appears to have run his own business for a while, in the Exeter area, buying and selling property, until that went bust. Bit of a gap, then he turns up in Dorchester, living in a rented house and running a bric-a-brac stall at the Wednesday market among other things. And then about a year ago, he seems to have come up in the world rather sharply. Must have hit gold somewhere, because he moved to Bath and bought rather a nice (you've seen it) Georgian terraced house. And what's more, he's got the funds to buy and stock the shop in Bartlett Street.'

'So what we need to know is how.'

'Knocked off goods?'

'Maybe.' Elizabeth preferred to reserve her judgement. 'You know what I'd like to do? Take a look round that shop of his.'

'Break in, you mean?'

'Slide in one dark night when nobody's looking.'

'Isn't that against the law?' Ginger dunked a shortbread finger into her mug of coffee.

Elizabeth said, 'My dear, don't ask. Then we can't tell you any great big whoppers.'

Max waited for this exchange to finish and then went on. 'While we're at it, we might as well take a look at Mrs Finney. Janette. A year younger than her husband and born here in Bath. Bath High School, nineteen fifty-nine to sixty-four. Worked in an accountants' office for a while, then travelled a bit. She seems to have met our friend Marcus while travelling in India. After that, their lives move more or less along the same track.'

'How do you get hold of all this stuff?' Ginger asked.

'Ways and means. Next . . . Aidan Makepeace. Born Cirencester, March the twentieth, nineteen forty-six. Father also a barrister. Mother a local Liberal councillor. Did a lot of charity work. Young Aidan grows up with a social conscience. He's sent to Marlborough then studies Law at Cambridge . . . became a prosperous barrister. A media barrister, I suppose you'd call him. Married Anna Barrington, who's half Italian and comes from a long line of restaurateurs. She's loaded in her own right. Bought Cheyneys Manor and turned it into a fine hotel – as traditional as a hunk of Cheddar. They have a house in Tuscany as well as a town house in Bath. They had two sons – Rory and Oliver. Rory, the oldest, died of a drugs overdose in his London flat aged twenty-one.'

'Sad,' Elizabeth said.

'Yeah. Happens, though. Oliver, the youngest boy, is a Detective Sergeant in the Metropolitan police.'

'That's interesting.'

'Mmn. I didn't tell you where Anna Makepeace went to school.' Here he shot a quick, sidelong glance in Elizabeth's direction.

'Is it relevant?'

'I think so. Bath High. Starting in September nineteen fifty-nine—'

'The same school as Jan Finney?' Elizabeth's manner changed.

'The very same year.'

'Really?' Elizabeth frowned.

School friends all over the shop.

She pumped the rocking chair back and forth. 'She didn't tell me that.'

'Want me to go on?'

'Don't ask dumb questions. So did you check on their movements last weekend?'

'Yes, I did. They had an old friend staying at the hotel. The Contessa di Stresa who owns a lot of land near their villa in Tuscany. They wined and dined her at the hotel. Loads of witnesses, including a young couple who had won a weekend in one of their special four-poster rooms at Cheyneys – and arrived there in a chauffeured limo. They were at the next table.'

'A villa in Tuscany . . .' Ginger said. 'Must be lovely.'

'Mozzies and Mafia,' Max said. He smiled his lopsided, aggravating smile. 'How'd your date go then?'

'You knew, didn't you?'

'Knew what?'

'That the Merry Fiddler had changed owners.'

'Didn't care for it?'

'Dirty tables and a slob of a landlord in a filthy t-shirt – why on earth didn't you say?'

'What would I know? I'm just a northern lad. No finesse . . .'

Ginger said, 'Well, it didn't matter. We went back to Glyn's place and he cooked supper. A light soufflé, apple and calvados

millefeuilles.' A long sigh. 'Lovely aftertaste. Not too over-
powering.'

'Sings and dances as well, does he?'

Possessive? Elizabeth asked herself. Thinking, this is interesting.

After the youngsters had cleared off for their lunch-break, she
started to unpack the box of quilts that the shipping firm had
delivered that morning. It was her favourite bit of the whole
business. Shoving a small knife that she kept for the purpose
into the soft bit of the wrapping tape. Hearing the soft crunch
as the blade bit. Tearing open the lid to find . . . who knows
what?

Jim Junior did the hunting back home in Virginia. The boy
grumbled and groused about it, but he had a good eye.

Usually.

Elizabeth lifted off the top layer of tissue.

What in hell's name was this? It made you shudder. Deranged
colours – orange and purple plaid squares with a border of poop
green and acid yellow – lumpy stuffing and only half the stitches
had made it through to the back.

Not to mention the bloodstain (must have stuck the needle
in her finger) in the wobbly centre block.

There was a name tag attached to it. DRUNKARD'S
PATH GOT LOST.

You're telling me!

The note from Jim Junior was pinned to the tag.

'This'll get you going,' he had written in his thin, backwards
sloping scrawl. *'It won the Worst Quilt in the World Contest in
Danielville, NC. They judged using the Three G System. If
the quilt didn't make you Gasp, Gag or Guffaw, it was out of
the running. Enjoy! Your loving son, JJ.'*

Oh, boy!

What are we going to do with you?

Elizabeth sat there, listening to the wind out in the alley. Puzzled over the question for a bit (as she had over not a few questions that day), and decided that rather than have hysterics, she would have a sandwich and a cup of Earl Grey.

She was halfway through the sandwich when the phone rang. It was Kate. 'Hi. It's me.'

'Hello, me.'

'Sorry I wasn't around. Work. You know.'

'I know.'

'You OK?'

'I'm fine. And you?'

'I'm OK.'

'And Saul?'

'Saul's great. He's a teddy bear.'

'So did you move in with him yet?'

'Yesterday.'

'Uh-huh. You'd better give me your new number.'

'I will. Only try not to call during the day. He's working on a new book and he hates the phone.'

We know that much about him.

'All-righty. We won't make ourselves a nuisance.'

'Mom — don't be like that.'

'Like what.'

'You know.'

Yes, I know. Don't flap, flip your lid, hit the panic button. Whatever you do, don't commit the cardinal sin and let out what you really feel.

'Sorry. So . . . what kind of books does your teddy bear write?'

'Biographies. And by the way, while we're about it, I might as well tell you now that he's older than me.'

'How much older?'

'Twenty-four years, actually. Well, twenty-five. Yes, I know that's old enough to be my father, but he's . . . well, he doesn't seem old. Not to me. Mom – you still there?'

'I'm still here.'

'You're mad again. I knew you would be.'

'You're assuming things again. As always.'

'And you're fibbing. I can tell. Look – Mom – if – when you speak to Saul, you won't take him apart, will you?'

'Take him apart?'

'Only he's a bit sensitive. You know? He won't like it if you grill him.'

'Grill him? Me?'

Whatever happened, Elizabeth thought, to the days when a young man (young, mind you!) presented himself formally to request the hand of your daughter. Or at least presented himself. For that matter, what happened to the ten-year-old Kate who used to gaze up at you with an infinitely sweet, gappy smile? The one who used to hug you to death every night before she went to bed.

'Mom? I've got to go. Busy schedule.'

Pin-sharp. As always. The phone clicked. She was gone.

I love her dearly.

Just as well, or I'd never put up with her.

Chapter Twenty-Seven

Max approached Finney's shop with great care, slipping carefully along the dark shadows of the passage at the rear of the premises. A neglected alley, bordered by high stone walls that shut you off from the world. It was ghostly, half unreal in the gathering darkness.

A soft rattling sound. He stopped, every nerve alert. Stood stock-still for a moment, listening. There it was again, nearer this time. A soft pad . . . pad over there by the blank wall. No doors or windows . . . no corners for anyone to hide in. So how could there be anyone following him? He waited, then moved again. Only to leap a mile. This spitting thing leapt down at him from the top of the wall.

A moggy.

That was all.

Max breathed a sigh of relief, gathered his wits about him, crept on another few yards. He turned the corner, peered into the dim recesses in front of him and made out the shape of a door. OK. This has to be it. Gloves on. Torch on. Nobody around. Safe enough. It took him a few minutes (not bad, considering that it was black as pitch and the lock was some rusty old museum piece) to get the door open. OK. So far, so good.

'You'll have three minutes,' Jan Finney had said, 'to switch off the alarm.' She'd given him all the necessary information to tackle it. 'I have to know what's going on. For Lucian's sake. I'm frightened for him and he has to be protected. But I can't give you the key. If Marcus found out — I'm sorry. I daren't.'

'Don't worry about it,' Max told her. 'We'll find something that'll tell us who your stalker is.' He said quickly, 'Of course, it would be easier if you asked your husband straight out.'

'You don't understand. I can't. It's . . . difficult.' Her face was as blank as a wall.

'OK. Forget it. We'll unearth something.'

'There's a locked drawer in the office desk. That's where he keeps things he doesn't want me to see. Are you sure you can get in without the key?'

'Sure.' He gave her a quick pat on the arm. 'This way, if I'm caught, you won't know a thing about it.'

But you won't get caught, he told himself as he thrust his hand above his head to find the alarm switch. There. That was done. Now he could relax.

Well, in a manner of speaking.

A short passageway stretched in front of him; on the right, a knee-high door obviously led down to the cellar; on the left, halfway down, a panelled door led into what seemed to be the office. Max moved cautiously towards it, feeling the wall as he went. Outside the door, he paused to listen . . . then pushed it open an inch or two. The room wasn't large and as he flashed the torch around it, Max saw that it was poorly furnished. A portable gas stove. A couple of faded rugs, a row of pegs with some old coats on them, a table covered in old newspapers and on it, a pile of dirty dusters and some silver polish.

There was a faint smell of cigarette smoke and stale whisky.

Then he spotted the sturdy old desk against the wall.

Max made his way over to it, propped the torch under his chin and tried the drawers, one by one. Envelopes, writing paper, a box of ballpoints. A calendar, packets of paper clips, rolls of labels, a stapler . . . a dog-eared *Miller's Guide*.

Not much that was interesting or of note.

The bottom drawer on the left-hand side was locked. Max took a small screwdriver from his jacket pocket.

A shove and a sharp snap.

Oh, dear. It's broken.

How sad.

Sad as the black bruise I saw on your wife's arm. Sad as her wincing when I patted her on it.

He caught hold of the brass handles and pulled the drawer right out. Laid it carefully on the leathered surface of the desk in front of him. The first thing he found was a roll of banknotes in a bank bag. Underneath it, a small white envelope containing a strip of photographic negatives. A bundle of letters fastened with a blue elastic band. Two jewellery boxes (containing one sapphire-and-diamond ring and one set with rubies). Wonder which lorry they fell off, Max thought. Then his fingers found a brown manila envelope, A4 sized. He slipped in a finger and drew out two photocopied newspaper articles. Max put them down on the desk and examined them in the full beam of the torch. The top one, dated 22 December, 1994, began:

BARRISTER'S SON IN DRUGS OVERDOSE

Rory Makepeace (25) a promising young City broker, was found dead of a heroin overdose in a flat in Islington early on Sunday morning. Mr Makepeace was thought to be staying with friends when the accident happened . . .

Max slipped the article to one side and turned to the second sheet, also photocopied from the *Bath Chronicle*, this time 21 December 1995:

Media Barrister in Car Crash

Oliver Makepeace (24), second son of Aidan Makepeace, the Bath barrister who regularly champions the underdog, was slightly injured in a car crash on the way home from a party at a friend's house on

Saturday night. Mr Makepeace was driving his son back from a friend's house in Bradford-on-Avon to their home in Bath, when he had a puncture and skidded into a wall. Oliver Makepeace was taken to the Royal United Hospital, where he was treated for a head wound. Oliver lives in London, where he works as a CID officer for the Metropolitan Police.

'Right,' Max whispered, shoving the sheets back into the envelope and stuffing the envelope, together with the pile of letters, into his jacket pocket. 'We'll see what Betsey makes of these.'

Shortly afterwards, he left the shop by the same door as he had entered.

Chapter Twenty-Eight

Max sat with his camera beside him on the bench. Whistling lightly. Bloody draughty places, park benches. A mist, like sea fog, hung over the trees.

He glanced at his watch. Ten fifteen a.m. Lucian (Max had tracked him from the house in Claremont Hill, not a hundred yards away) was sitting on a swing, staring down at the plastic yo-yo that he held in his hand. Dreaming.

'Don't worry,' Max had told Jan Finney. 'I'll look after him. How long does he usually stay in the park?'

'Twenty minutes. Half an hour. He likes to watch the other children. You will look after him?'

'Trust me. Lucian won't come to any harm. This woman . . . she was there yesterday, watching him? You're certain of that?'

'Yes. She followed us there. I saw her.'

Max could see her too. A woman in a pink jacket, standing almost idly by the baby swings, had come trailing into the park behind the boy. No, not trailing. Drifting. And yet that was wrong, too. OK, so get this right, Max. Something wistful about her. A hurt Bambi look. No, too old to be Bambi. How old? Late forties? Early fifties?

Lucian was now swinging industriously away. In his own world. Enjoying the unexpected day off school. (An in-service day, Jan Finney had said.) Unaware that the woman, after a rapid glance right and left, had sidled up behind him.

'That's a nice yo-yo,' Max heard her say in a bright voice. Cultured.

Lucian looked round.

'Can I see?' the woman asked.

Max lifted the camera and clicked the shutter. Shoved it away again underneath his jacket.

Lucian considered for a moment, then held out the yo-yo.

She took it and vigorously wrapped the string all round it. Wheeled it up and down a couple of times; then let it spin and hang. 'Won't go for me. Too heavy.' She wound the string round once more and shoved the yo-yo in her pocket.

Lucian didn't know what to do. He seemed a polite boy. 'It's not yours to keep,' he said.

'I know. Have a bon-bon,' the woman said, proffering something she'd dug out of her other pocket.

'No, thank you,' said Lucian, who had obviously been primed never to accept sweets from strangers.

'Oh, go on. It won't poison you.'

Again the boy shook his head.

A shrug, then she popped the sweet into her own mouth. 'Does your father ever come here with you?' she asked abruptly.

'No.' Lucian jumped off the swing with such a jerk that she was forced to step back from the spot where she had been standing. The empty swing jangled on its chains. Max lifted the camera and snapped again. Careful. One move too many and she would see what he was up to. Lucian ran off. Through the park gate and back up the road towards home. The woman started up the path behind him; but then she stopped, as if arrested by a thought. Turned her head (just her head) and glanced back in Max's direction.

A curiously intense glance out of her dark eyes.

He'd been rumbled.

But no, she was walking quickly down the path and over to a

tree seat on the far side of the park. Sitting down with a bump, she pulled a notebook out of her coat pocket. Then a pen. Began to scribble.

Caroline's neater-than-neat, dark head popped up from under the counter. 'The very person I was wanting,' said Elizabeth, who had just come down the stairs from the office. She reached into the pine chest that stood in the corner of the shop and, with a flourish, shook the Drunkard's Path Got Lost all over the floor.

'What do you think of this?'

Even Caroline looked stunned. Caroline, whose oval-shaped face was kept as smooth as a wet beach newly washed over by the tide.

'My latest acquisition,' Elizabeth said.

'Oh – right.'

We were back to the bare beach again. 'Thought I might give it to you for a wedding present. Whaddya think?'

'I'll . . . I'll ask Rupert,' Caroline said in her duchess-like tones. But faintly. Oh, so faintly.

'You do that,' Elizabeth told her. 'You see, he's into good design. I thought he might appreciate it.'

Eleven a.m. Elizabeth felt as if she'd been kept in after school. She stood alone in the classroom. Rather a pleasant classroom in ice-cream-parlour colours. Jugs of flowers in the windows, shelves full of books, jolly paintings and a model of . . . What was it? A Greek temple? The Forum in Rome?

'I'll be locking up in ten minutes.' The caretaker in the doorway.

'Okey-dokey.' If that wasn't a hint, she didn't know what was. Miserable old jerk. Slug-like walk and brown polyester slacks. Jan fixed it for me to come in, but he thinks I'm snooping.

Well, so you are. Get on with it. You've only got nine and a half minutes.

The rummage sale stuff was in the far corner, half hidden behind a long trestle table.

Two black poly bags, Elizabeth thought. That's what I'm looking for. That's what the Twinnies said. Tied up with string.

They've got good eyes, I'll give them that.

Not to mention long noses.

She got down on her knees to ferret under the table. Pulled out a couple of boxes of kids' clothes. Then some supermarket bags stuffed with toys and books. An old suitcase stuffed with clumpy shoes. Smelled a bit. But no sign of black polythene.

No – hang on. What's that at the back?

She dived under the table leg, fished under the piano leg and pulled out a black bag tied with white string. Bingo!

There was another one behind it, right back against the wall.

OK. Now for the knots. Somebody knew how to tie them. Somebody had once belonged to the Girl Guides. A last fiddle and a tug. And what do we have here? A glittery, backless frock, two silk shirts, a couple of sweaters (one Shetland), two pairs of shoes with stiletto heels and a man's jacket. Nothing in the pockets. Nothing to prove its ownership. Anything else? Not a lot. A navy swimsuit, two bras. Size 36 B? And two pairs of leggings, one paint-stained and one with a hole in the knee.

Hang on to the one with paint stains. You never know.

So, on to bag number two.

Goddamned knots again. Two of them. Not the Girl Guides. This was tied by an old sea-dog. Or else by somebody in one hell of a mood.

Tight?

You wouldn't believe it.

'You all done?' He was there again in the doorway.

'Not quite. I've got another—' Elizabeth lifted her wrist high in the air. Examined her watch. 'Another four and a half minutes.'

He looked daggers at her, but she turned her back and got on with the job. One more yank and the string was off. So, what have we here?

Three men's shirts, a pair of boxer shorts, a shaving kit and – underneath – the pair of men's trainers (size 11) and the black polo neck.

She couldn't quite believe it.

Her hunch had paid off.

A length of heavy white lace. Slowly, Elizabeth drew it from the bottom of the bag.

A bridal veil. Which, if she wasn't mistaken, belonged to Rose Mulligan.

Chapter Twenty-Nine

Max said, 'How did you know?'

'I didn't know. I took an educated guess.' Elizabeth spread the veil over the back of the office chair. 'OK. So you're Kat Gregg and you've had one hell of a day and Kat being Kat, she doesn't stay down for long. She decides to turn her back on it all. Clear Mulligan out of her life. So, late on Saturday afternoon, she fetches a couple of black polythene bags from the kitchen and she fills them with all the stuff Mulligan ever left at her house — everything connected with him — including Rose's veil. That's that, she thinks. She ties the bags tight and she dials Jan Finney's number. It's six thirty. Marcus answers and tells her to dump the stuff in his garage in Alfred Buildings. He'll leave it unlocked when he parks the car there at around ten to seven.'

'Right.' Max was beginning to look interested.

'We know what time she drove down to town. The Twinnies saw her go by at around seven thirty. So, at around, shall we say, ten minutes to eight, allowing for traffic and the like, she parks her car in Alfred Buildings and heaves the bags out of the car. That's when I'd guess Mulligan's watch may have landed in the gutter. There was a hole in one of the bags. Only a thought. Anyway, she dumps the bags in Finney's garage, as arranged. Now comes the interesting bit. Christopher Hunter was an enormous help.'

'How?'

'Well, he told me the exact time the downpour started that evening. Seven fifty-two. He knows this because he was about to pack up work and as he was checking the time on his computer, the rain started to thud down outside. And – this is where we move into the realms of speculation – but I've got a little theory I want to try out on you. It may just explain the loss of the umbrella. Suppose, just suppose, that Kat Gregg was still in Finney's garage when the downpour started and that she was still sheltering there when Finney arrived, complete with golfing umbrella, at around five minutes to eight. Think about it, Max. She's marooned. She needs an umbrella and he doesn't. After all, he's about to get into his car and drive off home. So, being the perfect gentleman for once in his life, he says, borrow this. Drop it back to the shop when you're passing.'

Max said, 'Finney goes into the garage under this very distinctive umbrella—'

'—and two minutes later, Kat comes running out under it. Take your mind back to that thought I had about Finney being the possible target.'

'You mean, whoever fired the shots thought she was Finney?'

'Makes sense, doesn't it? She's tall and Hunter told me she was wearing one of those nondescript, unisex raincoats. Now, this being the case, if you were Finney and you've got things to hide – a dodgy past, a spot of blackmailing and wife-beating, would you want the police asking what your fingerprints were doing on the murdered girl's umbrella? I think not. I think Finney panicked and picked up his umbrella while Hunter was off calling the police. He had at least several minutes in which to spirit it away somewhere. Now, nip out and fetch me a couple of cheese cobs, there's a dear. Use the petty cash. My grey cells are faint from lack of nourishment.'

*　　*　　*

While Max was out, she examined the newly developed photographs from the pack that he had dumped on her desk. Six of them, from the strip of negatives he'd filched from Finney's office. Number one. Aidan Makepeace and a tall, blonde girl coming out through the swing doors of what looked very much like a hotel. Yes, there was the sign on the far side of the steps. The Grand Marine.

Next? Aidan and Kat (for she was sure by now that the blonde was Kat) coming down the steps of the same hotel. Having a very nice little tête-à-tête, hands clasped together, heads almost touching. The third showed him hailing a taxi. Then there were two shots of a close embrace.

Anna Makepeace wouldn't care for that.

That was a fact.

The sixth photograph was of Glory Fraser, on a green chaise longue, wearing nothing but a pair of high-heeled green sandals.

She didn't look happy.

Elizabeth leaned back in the chair and snapped the blue band from the bundle of letters. Cream paper with a swan watermark. Good paper. Artistic. Same handwriting as the letter Jan Finney had shown her. Very beautiful handwriting with a strong whiff of calligraphy about it.

Elizabeth unfolded the first note. You couldn't call it a letter:

> *You're probably most shocked. I've frightened the wits out of you. Now that you know all the facts, what are we going to do about it? Such a delicate process. But your boy . . . your other boy . . . needs help.*

She took another one from the pile and read it:

> *Some distant relations sent him a little money. But I'm afraid that we need more. A hundred pounds goes nowhere. Shall we meet? Where would you suggest?*

There were six or seven others in the same vein. The most interesting of which read:

Tomorrow. Saturday? Remember when we used to meet on a Saturday night? He looks like you, you know . . . our boy. I've got to stop now, as someone's trying to get through to me. I'll wait for your call.

Her gaze fixed itself next on the photocopied sheets. Neither seemed to present grounds for blackmail. Rory Makepeace's death was tragic but the story was an all too common one these days. Unfortunately. And for the life of her, she couldn't see why Finney would keep an article about a relatively minor road accident. Care and concern for an old friend from schooldays? Somehow I don't think so. Something to take home and show the wife? But why photocopy it? Why not simply take home the newspaper?

'It doesn't make much sense,' she said when Max returned with the cobs.

'The letters make sense. Finney's being blackmailed. Somebody, some woman wants money out of him for a child he's fathered.'

Elizabeth gathered up the letters. 'The blackmailer blackmailed?'

'He's certainly got one hold on Makepeace. The affair he was obviously having with Kat Gregg.'

'You think that's sufficient grounds? You don't think that if he tried it, Makepeace would just tell him to sod off?'

'He wouldn't want his wife to know.'

'I don't know. There's a lot of it goes on these days. Is it such a big deal? A bit of hanky-panky? You got the other photographs? The ones you took in the park?'

'I'm collecting them this afternoon.'

'Right.' She nodded. 'One thing is for sure. We need to talk to Makepeace. We also need to talk to Little Miss Innocent. Imogen Shand.'

*   *   *

But it wasn't Imogen that she called an hour later. It was Marcus Finney's home number.

Jan Finney said, 'So did you find anything interesting in the rubbish bags?'

'As a matter if fact, I did.' Elizabeth filled her in. 'I'm afraid the police will have to be informed. They'll probably want to see your jumble sale bags. Sorry to deprive you of them, but it might be important.'

'That's OK. I quite understand. You won't tell my husband how you came by them?' She sounded petrified.

'I promised, didn't I?'

'And what about the other night. The shop——?'

'Max's little mission? Yes, that was interesting, too.' Elizabeth went through the contents of the letters. 'We're doing our utmost to find out who wrote them. There was something else in the locked drawer . . . a photocopied newspaper article that intrigued me. A piece about a car accident involving Aidan Makepeace and his younger son. You wouldn't have any idea why your husband would be interested in that?'

'None at all.' Her voice sounded anxious. 'Sorry. I can't help you there.'

'OK.' Elizabeth changed tack. 'Mrs Finney, something's bothering me. So I'll come right out and ask. Why didn't you tell me that you were at school with Anna Makepeace?'

'I . . . Didn't I?'

'Not so far as I remember. It seems that you've known Mrs Makepeace for thirty years or so?'

'Yes. No. That gives a false impression. I left the West Country when I was in my mid-twenties. Anna and I lost touch. But when we came back here to live . . . well, we met up again. At the Antiques Fair up at Cheyneys actually.'

'And you see each other how often?'

A hesitation. 'Now and then. When she's got time, of course.'

'So where do you see each other?'

'I . . . I've been up to Cheyneys to lunch with her once or twice. Or she comes here. Mostly I meet her at the hotel. She's been a—' Mrs Finney stopped suddenly. 'I'm rabbiting on. Do it too much. Is there anything else you want to know?'

'Out of curiosity . . . our little break-in the other night. Did your husband tell you about it?'

'Yes, yes, he did.'

'And did he report it to the police?'

'No. No, he didn't.'

Now that was interesting. 'Why not?'

'He said nothing was missing.'

'Really?'

'Just that the back door had been broken open and the front window smashed.'

'The front window?' Elizabeth didn't raise her voice. But she spoke with a contained surprise that gave the words some force.

'Yes. Someone put a brick through it that same night. I thought it must have been you.'

Elizabeth was now sitting on the edge of the chair, looking very alert. 'It most certainly wasn't. I'd like to speak with your husband when he comes in.'

'You will remember what I've said?' Even her voice was twitchy. 'Don't tell him you spoke to me. Please . . .'

'I'll remember. Don't worry. So what time do you expect him?'

'He should be here by six.'

'Could I reach him at the shop?'

'He's not there. I've tried. I'm sorry. I don't know where he is.'

Chapter Thirty

Max spent the next morning just mooching about, really, at the office. There was no point in trying to get hold of Aidan Makepeace. He was in chambers in London, or so his wife said on the telephone and you couldn't very well ask her (well, not yet anyway) if she knew that her famous husband had been having it off with Kat Gregg.

It was pissing down with rain. So he found all sorts of excuses to hole himself up in his own particular chambers above Martha Washington and spent a happy couple of hours nibbling away at a sausage sandwich (his breakfast), making lists, getting the Mold report (well, the start of it) into a new file on the computer, chasing up a couple of addresses for a missing teenager case that had been on the books for a couple of months and placing a couple of bets with William Hill.

It was comfortable in the dry with your feet up. He found himself whistling tunelessly.

'Busy?' Ginger asked at twelve forty with the merest hint of sarcasm.

'Thinking day,' said Max.

'Ah.' She was shrugging herself into her jacket (something velvety and gingerish to match her hair). 'All right in small doses . . . thinking.'

'Meaning?'

'Meaning don't wear yourself out. I'm off. Back at two.' She picked up her bag, flicked back her hair and left him to it.

Why do I let her get away with it? Max wondered. I suppose because she's so bloody good at her job. But I'm her boss, after all, and she has to take the piss. At best it's disrespectful. At worst, downright cheeky.

I'll have a word with her. This afternoon . . . as soon as she gets back.

Tell her to pack it in.

He made himself another coffee and helped himself to two chocolate biscuits from the tin. Plonked himself back down in his chair.

'So this is where you hide out!'

He was standing in the doorway. Checked shirt (pink and green), washed-out jeans, ebullient grin, letting his friendly eyes (reminded Max of his sister's dog) rove all over the office and waiting for a reaction. Rochdale's answer to Delia Smith.

'How's business? Crime thriving? I just popped in to see if anyone fancied a pint.'

Glyn Benson was still gazing briskly all round. The 'anyone' he had in mind obviously wasn't here.

'She's out,' said Max. 'You just missed her. She's meeting a friend for lunch.'

'Ah.'

Female, Max was going to add. Her mate from school. But then, for some reason, he decided not to bother.

Pushing aside his disappointment, Glyn said, 'Fancy a beer?'

Max rarely turned down an invite to the pub. 'I suppose I could manage half an hour.' He took his feet off the desk and reached for his jacket.

'Max – about the . . .' It was Elizabeth, half out of breath from hammering up the stairs. 'Oh, sorry. Didn't know you had a client.'

'He doesn't.' Glyn said, 'I just came to drag him off to the pub.'

'He doesn't need any dragging.'

'So I gather. You're the gung-ho Yankee lady from downstairs.'

'I've been called some things!'

'It's OK.' Glyn gave her a large grin. 'I like Yanks. They're always a laugh. And they leave huge tips.'

'This one doesn't,' said Elizabeth.

Max said, 'Mean as hell. I'll be half an hour.'

And the rest, Elizabeth thought.

'Another?' Glyn asked as the clock in the Saracen's Head struck two.

'No, thanks. Got to get back.'

Glyn ordered another pint for himself. His third. 'I've eased up on the sauce a bit lately,' he confided.

You could have fooled me, Max thought.

Glyn cleared his throat. 'You don't mind my asking . . . but is there anything . . . er . . . going on between you and Ginger?'

'Me and Ginger?'

'Yeah. You know. A relationship?'

'Don't be daft.' Max's startlingly blue eyes looked – well – startled.

'Only it just struck me that I ought to ask.'

'Look – I'm her boss. She's my secretary. That's all.'

'You're sure?'

'Positive!' Me and Ginger? Max thought. Bloody hell. What a thought!

'Only you don't butt in on a mate. Not where I come from. And she does talk about you a lot.'

'You mean, she moans.'

'Not really.'

'What then?'

'Oh, you know. Things that go on in the office. This and that.'

I will bloody have a word with her, Max thought. God knows what tittle-tattle she's been passing around.

'Well, just thought I'd ask. Clear the decks, so to speak.' Glyn took a long sip at his pint. He looked like a bloke who'd had a load taken off his mind. 'Look – I wouldn't tell everybody this. But I'm getting very wrapped up in this little girl. She's class. Top drawer. Know what I mean?'

Ginger? You can't have pulled much lately, Max thought. You could hardly call Ginger a pin-up. I suppose her eyes are all right. When she's sparking. And her legs. They're OK. But she's, well, hardly the stuff dreams are made of. Wake you out of them, more like.

That tongue of hers.

'You've only known her a week.'

'Sometimes that's all it takes.' Glyn stared down into his pint. 'That hair. Burnt copper. Beautiful. Ginger relish, I thought, when I first saw it.' He must have seen Max's expression. 'Don't mind me. I'm just a romantic fool.'

Max mumbled something about Ginger being a bit of a handful. Chat-wise.

'You mean her sense of humour? That's rare, too. Refreshing.'

You wait, Max thought. You'll find out.

'I think she's terrific. As soon as she smiled at me . . . well, I could be in here, I thought.'

In your dreams, thought Max.

Getting crusty for no real reason.

Three p.m. 'That letter to Banes . . .' Ginger came through the door of Martha Washington. 'Is it for today's post?'

'No. Tomorrow will do. There's something I want to enclose,' said Elizabeth.

'Right.'

'So where's Max?'

'Oh, he just rang in. He's getting hammered in the pub.'

Hammered? 'Beaten up?' Elizabeth asked.

'No. He's getting drunk.'

'Really?' A dry tone. Sometimes she thought the young lived on a different planet. Spoke Martian.

'That's pretty.' Ginger stood admiring the Starburst, spread over Elizabeth's lap.

'It passes the time.' Elizabeth fastened off a thread. 'We're quiet today, so I thought I'd pitch into it.' OK, so Max drinks, I quilt. We all need our fixes. 'So . . . how are you two getting along these days?'

'He was in a funny mood on the phone. Accused me of passing on office secrets.'

'Take no notice. Your friend was here. Did he tell you? The chef from Cheyneys.'

'Glyn?'

'That's the one. Max went out for a pint with him.'

'That's funny. He didn't say.' Ginger disappeared back upstairs.

Six thirty p.m. Elizabeth popped in to check on Dottie. The old girl was propped up in one corner of her moth-eaten sofa, reading. 'What's this?' Elizabeth peered through her specs at the cover. 'Poetry?'

'Mental exercise. "He that can love, unloved again, hath better store of love than brain . . ." '

Dottie recited. 'A lot of sense in that, don't you think?' She seemed better this evening. More her old self. 'I've had Mary Barrington in to see me. She had a bulb burst in the hearth when she lit the fire.'

'A bulb?'

'She must have chucked it in there by mistake with the old newspapers. Made her jump a mile. Bits all over the room . . . took her all day to clean it up.'

Dottie was not only much more cheerful, she was at the gossipy stage. 'Oh – and I must tell you this. Mary had a man die next to her in the bus in town.'

'Really?'

'Quite a natural sort of death. He just went to sleep. Give him a nudge, love, said the driver. They thought he'd nodded off. And so he had. Well, that took us on to undertakers. Kingsley Martin – do you know Kingsley? – well, he was telling Mary what a job they'd had locating the empty space left for Jack Tilzey in his first wife's grave. They had to put a line down. And of course we had all that rain last week. Ideal popping-in-the-ground weather, of course.'

Elizabeth's eyebrow must have gone sky high.

'Bulbs, dear. Must do my crocuses. Anyway Kingsley was telling Mary the whole grave is in danger of collapse. He's worried it'll give way during the interment and the mourners will disappear six feet down with poor old Jack.'

Graveyard talk. Old people had spells of it. Hope I don't get like that, Elizabeth thought.

'And then Mary was saying they've taken down the angels in the church.'

'Taken the angels down?'

'For restoration work. Those angels have been above the altar for as long as I can remember. Mother couldn't abide them. Victorian, you see. Bright red cheeks and yellow curls. Of course, overblown angels were the fashion back then, but Mother always said they looked like music-hall tarts. They'll be replaced, of course. They've only taken the top layer of plaster.'

Elizabeth was, for once, stuck for an answer.

'Now the angels in St Bartholomew's . . . they're in a different class. When I was in the Bach Choir, we did a concert at St Bartholomew's. Celia Thingummy did the solos. Can't remember names these days. Taught music at St Theresa's. Wonderful voice. Her mother was Anglo-Indian . . .'

'Hannaford?' Elizabeth asked. She sat up in her chair, suddenly very alert.

'That's it. Celia Hannaford.'

'Does she play the piano at the music lectures?'

'Music lectures? Wouldn't be surprised. Are you leaving? I was just going to ask you to make us a cup of tea.'

'I'll be back,' Elizabeth said. 'There's something I want to show you.'

She was back a few minutes later with the park photographs that Max (a very inebriated Max) had brought back from City Photo. 'Is this her?' she asked, a trifle ungrammatically.

Dottie peered at the photograph. 'Yes. That's Celia.'

Elizabeth could have kissed the old buzzard. Though she managed to restrain herself.

Chapter Thirty-One

At seven forty-five p.m. that evening, Max's mate, Andy said, 'This Ginger. Keen on her, are you?'

'Don't be a prat.' Max's head felt like something had trampled on it. Andy had turned up unexpectedly at his flat with a takeaway that smelled like curried dog. With heavy-lidded eyes, Max watched another dollop of it being forked (avidly) into Andy's mouth.

'You've talked about nothing else since I got here. She must be quite some bird.'

'She isn't. So shut it.'

'I'm not the one going on about her.'

'I said shut it.'

A hiatus. Irritation bubbled inside Max. Wish I'd never said anything. I didn't bloody say much anyway. You drop the odd remark to let off steam and you get verbal attacks. No wonder he felt so bloody narked, sharp, snappish. He decided to change the subject. 'So what's it like being a dad?' he asked.

'Great.'

'Only you haven't been out much lately.'

Andy looked embarrassed. He raked a hand through his stiff, yellowish hair. 'Bit difficult some nights.'

'Got you changing nappies, has she?'

'Got to do your bit.'

'Sad, if you ask me.'

'Well, nobody did, mate.'

'I mean, who am I supposed to drink with? Bloody Rochdale *pot-au-feu* merchants, that's who.'

'You could always come round. Share a jar with me and the babby.'

He had to be joking. Max wasn't going to get mixed up with nappies and such. 'Marcus Finney,' he said abruptly. 'Antiques dealer. One of the blokes who found Kat Gregg. Did you know he had a brick through his shop window?'

'When was this?'

'Last night.'

'Nobody mentioned it at the nick.'

'So why wouldn't he report it?'

'No idea.'

Max told him about the letters. 'Damned peculiar.'

'I didn't hear that. You ought to hand them in, you know. Could land yourself in trouble.'

Max seemed not to hear. He had something else on his mind. 'When you were looking for the missing umbrella, did anyone take a look round Finney's garage?'

'Not to my knowledge. I can find out for you.'

'Might be useful. And if you could look into that road accident for us. The Makepeace lad. Oliver.'

'We'll see what we can do. Anything else? Tell you what, this curry's good. Still, I suppose you're used to a better class of nosh these days. Now that you're hobnobbing with top chefs and such . . .'

Max shook his head. 'Sod off,' he said.

Rose Mulligan said, 'Hello. Is that the Samaritans?'

She flicked the ash from her cigarette (shouldn't have started again, the doctor had warned her against it) and poured herself another whisky from the bottle standing in the centre of the table.

'Please . . . is there any way you can help me? Yes, I know that's what you're there for. I'm an alcoholic. That's the first thing I have to tell you. A secret drinker. Only soft drinks when I'm out, but sometimes I'll drink a bottle of wine to find the courage to go out. Ask Johnny. Who's Johnny? He's my son. And he's in deep trouble. I was just thinking . . . I lose everything that ever means anything to me. My son . . . my husband.'

With shaking fingers, she picked up the photograph of Tom taken just after they were married. Handsome face, if burly. Broad chest, amply covered in dark hair. 'He worked bloody hard. Rough hands, rough tongue at times, but he had a warm heart. Never laid a finger on me or the children, even when we played him up.

'I was like a shadow then. Thin? You'd never believe it. Yes, I drank even then. Wouldn't admit it, mind you. But I drank because he womanised. And when I'd had a few . . . well, I had the knack of sticking a knife in his weak points. You know? Wish I hadn't, because he was basically such a sweet-tempered bloke. Like my Johnny. Went all quiet, he did, when I unleashed my tongue. He stuck it for twelve years. And then, one morning, he was gone before I was up. Worn out by it all. Never came back. Can't blame him really. I was devastated, of course. In danger of drowning for a while. Yes, more booze . . .

'The drink . . . you use it as a comfort blanket. You use it to blot out the misery inside your head. Maybe the boy picked up on it, young as he was. All the grief. It definitely affected him. Maybe that's why he goes for comfort to all these women.

'I tried to explain to him once, but he wouldn't listen. Drinking . . . it's an illness. A mental illness. I drank because of the problems I had in childhood. My father died when I was ten and my mother two years later in a road accident. I went to live with an aunt that I hated. It was mutual, I think. Anyway, I started drinking when I was fourteen. It gave me confidence and took the pain away. I've tried to stop . . . several times . . . but take the drink away and the problems come back. It's a vicious circle. I joined an alcohol support group. You've got to do a lot of work on yourself, they said. Try a new hobby, they said, as a substitute for the bottle. It worked for a while. I took up gardening and the choir, but they don't work for long.'

Rose's face twitched with emotion. Tied itself into a knot. For a second or two the words refused to come out, but then she got herself back under control.

'Yes. I'm still here. So, you try to master it. You tell yourself you'll only drink in the house. Or at a party. Then you'll stay on the right side of the line. The thing is, when you've had a couple of drinks, you don't realise you're crossing the line. When you're blotto, you can't even see it.'

She wiped her streaming eyes. Said in a whisper, 'That bloody line! It's so hard staying on the right side of it. Impossible lately. The first one I had this morning – the first hit – it made me sick. That's when you know you're in for a bad day. I used to try and hide it from Johnny, you know, when I was nauseous. I used to lock myself in the bathroom and pretend I was having a long soak. But he knew. He finds me vulgar and embarrassing. Oh, I know what he thinks of me.

'Do you have children? You do? Well, tell me something. Do you ever stop feeling responsible for them? For what they do? Or don't do? You don't think so? Well, thanks a lot! That really makes me feel better.' A long pause and a clinking sound as, wobbling slightly, she refilled her glass. 'Booze makes you feel better. Isn't that what they say? Well, it's not working very well at the moment. Shall I tell you something? Sometimes I just hate the smell of it. Alcohol. And I've always hated the taste. Isn't that ridiculous? Doesn't make sense. Does anything make sense? The other thing I hate is the things it makes you do. No, the things you can't remember you did. Do you know, I woke up a couple of days ago with a head like a banged drum and my hands all cut? How did that happen? God knows. I don't.

'Anyway, the reason I rang – one of the reasons – is that I've got a new problem. And I don't know who else to talk to. I'm in a real quandary. What I found this morning when I was cleaning . . . Do I do anything about it? Do I tell somebody? That bloody bossy American woman? God knows. I don't. Sorry, I didn't catch. Go more slowly? I'm not making sense? I'll let you into a secret. My life has never made any sense. Not much of it, anyway. What did I find? I'll tell you.' A long gulp from the glass. 'In a minute. But I need a straight answer. I know you lot. Hedge your bets. Sit on the fence and listen. Well, that's no good to me, I'll tell you now. I need you to be specif . . . speciff . . . I need you to come bloody out with it and say what you think . . .'

Nine p.m. Max said to Elizabeth on the phone, 'You want me to come to some old music lecture?'

'Tuesday night. You needn't stay for all of it.'

'I should hope not. Any particular reason?'

'I'll tell you when we get there.'

'Did you ring Imogen Shand?'

'I did. her mother informs me she's gone off to Paris with her friend, Tim Somebody or other.'

'All right for some. When will she be back?'

'Next week some time.'

'So . . . what's it about? This lecture?'

'It's about the Linleys. A famous musical family in eighteenth-century Bath.'

A deep groan. 'Do I have to?'

'I'd appreciate it. Do you good to have a little worship at the shrine of Saint Cecilia.'

'Saint Who?'

'Saint Cecilia. She's the patron saint of music. She was a holy young girl in ancient Rome who vowed always to stay a virgin and when her father ordered her to marry, she said she'd rather die than break her vow. So they boiled her in oil.'

'Nice.'

'But through her entire ordeal, she still sang hymns. They only stopped her singing by cutting her head off.'

'Wish somebody would cut my head off,' said Max. It was splitting. 'So what time's this do?'

'Seven thirty.' She thought a minute, then changed her mind. 'No, meet me outside Saint Batholomew's at seven twenty. It gets very full.'

Chapter Thirty-Two

There was, quite suddenly, this terrible fear of the clock. Celia had turned it to face the wall.

Not everyday time any more. That was it. That was why she was so afraid.

Peculiar time instead. Time measured in associations and memories.

Alice was communing with the television set over in the corner. Celia's ear kept picking up random snatches of a local news broadcast. Underneath the other soundtrack. The whispering. It was like – like when you lift a shell to your ear and you can hear the rustle of infinity, she told herself.

No, the voice told her.

The voice was one of the whisperers.

Celia knew what he looked like . . . this man. Like Mr Kirby, her first piano teacher, the one who used to rap your knuckles with a ruler every time you went wrong. A little fat man who pretended to be your friend, but wanted you to make mistakes.

You'll never get away with it, he was whispering now. *You'll attract attention to yourself. They're watching you. Taking pictures of you.*

'Celia? Is that you whispering?' Alice's voice. She had switched off the television and was coming over. Celia gave the top of the baby grand a flick with her handkerchief.

'Are you all right?'

Nothing to do with you. Mind your own business.

'I said, are you all right?' Alice sounded taut.

'Of course I'm all right. Stop fussing.'

'I only thought—'

'You're always thinking. You think too much.'

'One of us has to.'

Alice gave her a searching glance. 'Cup of coffee?'

'No. Haven't got time.'

'Why's that?'

'It's Tuesday.' Stupid! 'Lecture night.'

'Darling – is that wise?'

The voice said, *She sounds like Father. Don't do this. Don't do that. Don't let her stop you.*

He was right. The voices were always right.

Alice said, 'The thing is, I'm not sure if you're fit to go out.'

No reply.

'Celia? I'm talking to you.'

Celia took herself off to her own room and refused to answer.

It was important not to talk to those who wouldn't understand.

Celia had always had a fierce will of her own, though for a great many years, this had been kept under wraps. She walked quickly now, head down, hands in pockets, across King Street and turned into Queen's Square.

The sky was dark, but the city was never gloomy. Celia walked briskly (some might say hastily) over wide pavements, separating pedestrians (in the eighteenth century as now) from the dirt and danger of busy streets. Pavements which were white again now after the rain. Gentle terraces stretched down from the old city, pale gold in the evening sun. A gradual descent became a sudden steepness. She stopped underneath a dripping tree. Rooks jostled for space in the trees above her head. Small boys shouted, a long way off.

It reminded her of St Theresa's. Shouts in the playground. Those three girls. Kat, Glory and Imogen. Celia watched the birds and had strange thoughts – a stream of thoughts, running very fast – as if time had been speeded up.

He broke my heart.

The only one I've got. Last used in 1973.

The voice said: *You should have been more of a drama queen.* Would have made more sense.

Why did you waste so much of your life pining for him? For such a charming and convincing liar? But perhaps you had a lucky escape. Perhaps you should just forget him.

'I can't!' she said aloud, viciously. 'Not yet. Not until he's paid for what he did to me. And to our son.' She remembered his look of shame-faced, laughing apology whenever he took a cheque from her. 'I'll pay you back,' he always said. But never did.

He will, though.

There was sweat on her forehead and her throat burned.

A damp pigeon rambled out from the saturated grass at her feet. Head bobbing. Grey and white. Poking its neck out. 'Go away,' Celia said. It took no notice, just went on peering at her with one beady eye. Laughing at me, Celia thought. True and sharp, her toe caught it. Kicked it away . . . a fluttering mess.

There.

Serves you right, she said viciously. Serves you bloody well right.

Chapter Thirty-Three

St Bartholomew's Church House. Seven forty-five p.m. The place was packed. 'Is there anybody here under eighty?' Max hissed.

The lecturer's voice wandered on. He was a slim boy with curly brown hair and a surprising air of authority. 'Beau Nash brought the first small orchestra of six musicians to Bath and soon there was music at all the main places of assembly, even at breakfast time in Spring Gardens. The Abbey organist for thirty years or so until his death in seventeen sixty-six, was Thomas Chilcott.'

'Any relation to Gareth?' Max murmured.

'What?'

'The rugby prop.'

'Shush!' said Elizabeth, giving him an almighty glare.

'It was Chilcott who first taught music to Thomas Linley, who, with his gifted children, ruled over the musical life of this city for twenty years. Director of Music at the Assembly Rooms, Linley managed concerts, engaged the best-known performers of the day, and regularly conducted. He was a Handel enthusiast. Handel's music had been much neglected since the composer's death, and Linley restored it to popularity.'

'So where is she?' Max whispered.

'Who?'

'The woman in the park.'

'You tell me. Use your eyes instead of your tongue.'

'Thomas Linley's children were among the leading performers in his concerts. "A nest of nightingales," one critic called them. Good-looking musical prodigies, all of them. Thomas, the violinist, made a strong impression on Mozart while studying in Italy. Samuel was a talented oboist. Unhappily, both died young. Elizabeth and Mary were both singers. Elizabeth, the elder, was incomparably gifted. From early childhood, she had possessed a voice of perfect pitch and great sweetness . . .'

'Can't see her,' Max said, shuffling on the hard-bottomed chair.

'You haven't looked.'

'Yes, I have.'

'Sssh!' said the old dear in front of them, turning to remonstrate.

'Taught by her father, Elizabeth gave her first public performance at the age of twelve and from then on was in constant demand. There is an account, dated seventeen seventy, of her singing a Handel aria in Salisbury Cathedral. "I know that my Redeemer liveth". She was a slight girl, but her voice filled the nave with its pure clarity. And then . . . they called this a miracle . . . an epiphany . . .'

Max raised his eyebrows at Elizabeth.

'A tiny bullfinch found its way into the cathedral. Perched on the gallery over her head, it accompanied her with its warblings through a great part of the aria . . .'

Max continued to scan the room. And then, suddenly. 'I'm with you,' he hissed.

'I know you are,' Elizabeth whispered back.

'No. I've seen her.'

'Where?'

'At the front.'

'Where at the front?'

'The pianist.'

'Right! Good boy!'

The lecturer pressed a button and dimmed the lights. Two faces came up on the screen. Two delicate-looking girls posed in a woody glade. 'The Linley Sisters – Mary and Elizabeth – painted by Gainsborough. Elizabeth's beauty charmed Bath society as much as her musical talent. Reynolds painted her as Saint Cecilia . . .'

'You're sure now?' Elizabeth asked.

'Positive. The same jacket.' And the same twitchiness, he thought. The pianist sat there with a look of intense concentration on her face; fiddling and playing with an elastic band which she held between her fingers.

'Linley made a handsome living by exploiting his gifted children. He made them sell concert tickets in the street and Elizabeth could earn a thousand pounds a year with her singing. He even made plans for her to marry a rich elderly man called Long. Elizabeth dutifully gave in to her father, but the whole of Bath felt sorry for her. Samuel Foote, the comedian and playwright, quickly wrote *The Maid of Bath*, in which Miss Linnet, young and lovely, is betrothed to one Solomon Flint, "an old, fusty . . . water-drinking, milk-marring, amorous old hunks". The play, in which everyone recognised the characters, was a considerable success.

'It was only at the last minute, after the marriage settlement had been agreed, that the wretched girl begged to be released from the engagement. Long, to his credit, agreed. Incredibly, Linley threatened to take him to court, whereupon Long, who was obviously a very different person from Foote's caricature, generously agreed to settle three thousand pounds on Elizabeth and allowed her to keep the jewels which were to have been his wedding present to her.'

There's many a slip twixt the engagement and the wedding, Elizabeth thought.

Then as now.

'Right. Can I go now?' Max demanded.

'Not until the coffee break.'

'How long's that?'

'Three quarters of an hour.'

'How long?'

The old biddy in front grew apoplectic. A funny old thing with a grey pigtail wrapped in a coil at the back of her head and skewered with what looked like hat pins. 'Look here – if you're not going to listen, would you kindly leave?'

'If only,' muttered Max.

'If as a father Linley was less than admirable, he was still a first-rate musician and impresario and his son, Thomas Linley junior, was a brilliantly assured and forward-looking young composer whose early death in a boating accident on the fifth of August, seventeen seventy-eight was a tragedy for English music. Tonight we are going to hear his cantata, "In yonder grove", which was performed at his benefit concert at the Haymarket Theatre in March, seventeen seventy-three at which, we are told, his sister Elizabeth sang divinely . . .'

Max slumped back down in his seat. Elizabeth, the corners of her mouth twitching, closed her eyes all the better to listen.

At eight fifteen, she dug him in the ribs with her elbow. 'You can wake up now.'

'Thank God for that.' He sat up and stretched his arms.

'I take it you won't be buying the CD?'

'Pass. I'll tell you something, though.'

'What's that?'

'She can play the piano. Our park lady.'

'Definitely gifted.'

'Are we going to have a word with her?'

'You think it's the right moment?'

He shrugged.

'OK. We'll grab a coffee first.'

'You'll grab a coffee first. I'm off.'

216

Elizabeth didn't get a chance to argue.

He was out of there before you could say *Water Music*.

Released from culture, Max walked rapidly away from St Bartholomew's and took the first left turning to cut up through the narrow lane that led to the Charlotte Street car park.

It was dark in the alley, but it was out of the wind; the back of the church house was on his left; a pale block of yellow light from the street lamp on his right.

His shadow passed through it and it was dark again.

He had almost reached the top of the alley when he heard the footsteps. Running, urgent footsteps coming up behind him. Max turned, thinking to let whoever it was pass. But they didn't want to pass. Whoever it was had stopped. The next moment, he was being thwacked from behind with what felt like a truncheon.

He dived backwards in self-defence and hit the wall. A pummeling of fists hit him next. Small fists.

'You! You're following me!' a voice accused.

In the orange glow from the next street light, he saw a face. Not a smiley face. It belonged to the woman from the park. The piano lady.

'Is it your voice I keep hearing?' she demanded. 'Is it?'

Max hadn't a clue what she was talking about. And he wasn't going to stop around for a girlie chat. Dusting himself down, he decided to get out of there fast.

Chapter Thirty-Four

Ten a.m. the following morning. 'You didn't talk to her?' Elizabeth said.

'No. Did you?'

'How could I? She shot out of the place during the coffee break.'

'Don't I know it?' Gingerly, Max fingered the lump on the back of his head.

'The lecturer had to play tapes for the second half. He assumed she was ill.'

'So she is.' Max said. 'Bloody head case.'

Elizabeth sat there thinking as she sipped a fruit juice. 'I shall have to ring the Vicar. He'll know where she lives.' She had a sudden thought. 'Glory Fraser. Did you call her?'

'Yeah. She's away on a course until the weekend.'

Rose Mulligan said, 'So you found it?'

Elizabeth dropped the veil on the table. 'Yes. Yes, it was—'

'She'd sent it to a jumble sale?'

'It seems so. With a lot of other stuff she'd cleared out. Clothes. A man's clothes. Your son's, I rather think.'

'Johnny? Never! How do you know . . . how do any of us know how many men she had up there?' Rose was angry now.

'That's as may be. But I'd like him to take a look some time.'

'You're on to a loser there.' Rose said disgustedly, 'Well, as far as I'm concerned, you can keep the ruddy veil.'

'But—'

'Why would I want it? Too many bad memories attached.'

'But you got married in it. Perhaps you'll change your mind.'

'I shan't change my mind.' There was bitterness in her voice. 'It was a lousy marriage anyhow. Aren't they all?'

Max spread the photographs on the table in front of Aidan Makepeace. And waited.

'It's a hotel. Any hotel. In fact . . . they could have been taken here.'

'You think?'

'Certainly.'

'I don't think so,' said Max. He drew out the second photo. The one with the hotel name sign on.

They had the place to themselves. The waiter had come through once to ask if they needed anything further. Then went back to serve lunch at the other end of the hotel. The room went back to being very silent.

'Hmm.' Leaning back in his seat, Aidan Makepeace fiddled with the photograph, which he was no longer looking at. Max didn't say anything. A waiter in a white jacket went along the path outside the window. The clock in the corner went on ticking.

'OK. You've got me,' Aidan Makepeace said. 'But for God's sake, don't show this to my wife.'

Outside, a cold wind was blowing clouds across the October sky.

'I'd need the truth then. No more cock-and-bull stories.'

'OK. OK.' He looked tired. 'Kat and I . . . we had a bit of a thing. Two and a half . . . no, three years ago. It didn't last long.'

'How long?'

'A matter of weeks. This weekend . . .' He fingered the photograph that he was holding. '. . . in Brighton. Another somewhere in Sussex. Oh, and she stayed in my flat in London for the odd night. It was just a bit of fun, but we both knew it wouldn't last. We were better off as friends and that's how it finished up.'

Could you believe him? He's a barrister, remember. Slick of tongue. He spends a lot of his life standing up in court arguing his clients' interests.

'You weren't still sleeping with her?'

'Good God, no.'

'And the child she was expecting, it couldn't have been yours?'

'Assuredly not.'

'OK. I'd like to ask about your relationship with a man called Marcus Finney.'

'Finney?'

'Keeps an antiques shop in Bartlett Street.'

'Oh. Him.'

'So you do know him?'

'I wouldn't say that.'

'What would you say, then?'

'Why do you want to know?'

'Finney happens to be looming quite large in our investigations at the moment.'

Makepeace passed a hand over his thick, silver hair. 'I know of him in a roundabout sort of way. My wife knows his wife. They were at school together.' A pause. Then, 'I'll tell you what I know about Marcus Finney. He survives on brass neck. Brass neck and bullshit. And that's about it.'

'I gather you don't like the gentleman.'

'Finney's no gentleman, I assure you.'

'I gather he had a stall at your Antiques Fair.'

'Did he? I'm a busy man, Mr Shepard. I don't get much chance to hang around at my wife's business functions.'

'He also belongs to the your Health and Fitness centre.'

'My wife's Health and Fitness centre.'

'You don't use the facilities?'

'I have a swim on occasion. But not often. This is a very busy hotel. The chances of me bumping into acquaintances here are really quite minimal.'

'Did Finney know Miss Gregg?'

'Not to my knowledge.'

The waiter re-passed the window. A fine drizzle had started to fall.

'And on the night Miss Gregg died, you were dining here with your wife and a friend?'

'I've told your partner this already. I really don't see much point in going over it all again.'

Tetchy, Max thought. And a touch patronising. But maybe I would be under the same under the circumstances. He drew the cutting about the car accident out of his briefcase. Laid it on the table in front of Makepeace.

Who kept a perfectly blank face. 'You found it where? Finney had it? Extraordinary. No, I can't tell you why. It was a long time ago. A minor accident on a foul night. I'd been to fetch my son home from a friend's house. I took my eye off the road for a minute to check the clock and . . .'

'It *was* you driving the car?'

'Of course. I'm not in the habit of lying to the police.'

'Darling – I didn't know you were still here . . .' A new voice. Female. A small, stylish woman in a pale linen suit. Quality, Max thought. Suit and woman.

'I got caught.' Aidan had swept the incriminating photographs under his newspaper. 'This is Mr Shepherd. He's a private detective. My wife, Anna.'

'How do you do. I met your partner, Mrs Blair.'

She gave Max a charming smile.

'Great place you have here,' he told her.

'Good. I'm glad you approve. I like to try and preserve . . .

well, I always think of it as the spirit of the eighteenth century. Yes. That's about it. Forget the horrible, strident world out there.'

Nice if you can get it, Max thought.

'At a price,' he said.

'You're right. But isn't that true of everything?' She stood there gazing at him for a moment. 'So . . . what is it this time?'

'He's asking about Marcus Finney.'

'That horror.' A quick shudder. 'Strutting around the Orangery as if he owned it. I expect Aidan's told you that Jan and I were at school together. How she ever finished up with a peacock like him I'll never understand.'

'Peacock? If only that were all,' Makepeace murmured.

'Meaning?' Max asked.

'Never mind. Better not say.'

'Darling, you can't stop halfway through. Meaning . . .' she said to Max, '. . . that he knocks his wife around.'

'Allegedly.'

'Oh, come on, Aidan. That bruise on her arm the other day . . .'

'Wouldn't prove it in court. And she'd never testify against him.'

'Well, no. She's scared to death of him. That's why.'

Max was crossing the back terrace. The rain had stopped, but the lawns were still covered with fine pearls of moisture and there was a smell of wet rosemary. The sky was lighter.

There had been some kind of friction between Makepeace and his wife when Finney's name was mentioned. Something in the air. A strung tension. Why was that? he asked himself.

'So what's cooking?' Glyn's voice said behind him.

'I should be asking you that question.'

'So you should. Vanilla-roasted duck. Stir-fried sugar snap peas. Chilli ice cream.'

'Chilli ice cream?'

'You should try it, mate. You'd love it. Made some for Ginger last night. Did she tell you?'

'Busy morning. No time for gossip.'

'Right.' Glyn stuck his thumbs inside his chef's jacket. 'So, join us for a jar one night, why don't you?'

Max didn't think he had any nights free.

Not this week.

He drove back down to town with a scowl on his face. Any fool can cook, he thought. You don't need a brain. All you do is follow instructions. And bash a few things round in a saucepan.

Chapter Thirty-Five

The hairdressing salon was pretty quiet when Elizabeth walked into it that afternoon. There was an atmosphere of relaxation. Music bumping, idle chatter, a whiff of sweet lemon and coconut drifting between the window blinds and the potted palms and the giant vases stuffed with orange lilies.

Jackie Townend was a dark girl with nice brown eyes and a clear complexion. She sat upright, hands on the tall receptionist's stool, hands on plump (but pretty) thighs. She had been at a low ebb, she told Elizabeth, when she had answered the ad in the Lonely Hearts column. Just out of a lousy marriage, on the loose but not knowing what to do with all that freedom.

The advertisement had read:

> Hello, Ladies! Let's get together. Tall, well-repre-sented, athletic male—32, six foot two, enjoys music, country pubs, seeks lively, imaginative, wild-at-heart, very active lady. Scary Spice would be nice.

Yes, of course it had been a bit . . . well, racy. But fun as well and Jackie hadn't had much of that lately. Anyway, she'd arranged to meet Johnny Mulligan in a pub one lunchtime. Safe enough . . . lots of people around. And you could quickly disappear if he turned out to be some freaky type in an anorak.

When Johnny introduced himself to her . . . well, she couldn't believe her luck.

At first.

They'd been out together three times (yes, she had slept with him) when she found out, quite by accident, that he was living with somebody. That he was about to get married. How had she found out? From a friend of a friend who was a regular at his wine bar. What then? Why, she'd confronted him. He'd had the grace to look uncomfortable for a couple of moments. And then it had come out that he'd done it for a bet.

Men have all the choices in life, Jackie said.

'And do you know, all the time I was in that wine bar having a go at him, his mate was killing himself laughing,' Jackie said indignantly. 'He thought it a right hoot. So I laced into him as well. And do you know what he said to me? That bloody Ash somebody or other with the poncy voice?'

'No idea,' said Elizabeth. 'Tell me.'

'He said . . .' And here Jackie flushed a little at the memory. 'He said you'd be surprised how many girls are out there waiting for a quick shag. I felt . . . Well, I can't tell you how I felt. I wanted to curl up in a corner and die.'

'Nasty,' said Max when Elizabeth got back to the office.

'Uncalled for. Cruel. Bears out my original feelings about our Mr Lewis. I'd think we should tackle him again some time.' She glanced at her watch – four thirty p.m. 'I'm calling at the Vicarage on my way home for Celia Hannaford's address. Fancy dropping in on her with me?'

'Provided you go first,' Max said.

'Don't worry. I'll ride shotgun.'

'Miss Hannaford's address? It isn't in the book?' Richard Timms scratched his chin. 'I've got it somewhere. Yes, It's probably in my little red book under St Swithin's.'

'St Swithin's, South Harptree?'

'No, the Church of St Swithin at the eastern end of the Paragon. Walcot parish church. Celia used to organise concerts there. And Jane Austen's parents were married there, you know, in seventeen sixty-four. The entry can be read in an earlier parish register.' He quoted it by heart: ' "Geo Austen, Bachelor of the Parish of Steventon, County of Hampshire to Cassandra Leigh, Spinster. Married by licence this 26 April by me — Thos Powys Minister in the presence of James Leigh Perrot and Jane Leigh." ' Mrs Austen's brother and sister, he explained. 'The old church was pulled down between seventeen seventy-four and seventeen seventy-seven and the present one — neo-classical — built on the foundations. Mr Austen was buried there when he died in Bath in eighteen hundred and five. His grave is in the crypt. Ah — yes — here we are. Hannaford, Celia. I'll jot it down for you. Er . . . any particular reason for your wishing to speak to her?'

Elizabeth was circumspect. She mumbled something about needing a pianist for the South Harptree Christmas concert.

Disgusting to tell fibs to a vicar.

Especially this one. He oozed integrity.

However, needs must where the devil drives.

Time flits on. As it does. Evening came. A gloomy evening, followed by a night that was uncommonly dark. While Elizabeth threw together something for dinner (an omelette filled with yesterday's cold sausage and one or two spring onions), she propped a slim, red volume (borrowed from the Linley lecturer's book box) against the ridge at the back of the hob and dipped in while she chopped and whisked, as was her habit:

Richard Brinsley Sheridan, having finished his schooling at Harrow, joined his family in Bath in

1771. He fell in love with Elizabeth Linley and eloped with her to Lille, where Elizabeth stayed in a convent, from where, a month later, her father came to fetch her home. In the meantime, Sheridan had declared his love and they had apparently been secretly married. There is no proof of this, however.

It is important to state at this point that an elopement was an infallible means of compromising a lady in such a case, and a certain way of ensuring marriage if she were respectable. In other words, it was a shrewd move on Sheridan's part, which in the end, would finally end her father's opposition to the match and win him the game. Unscrupulous tactics which would have been condemned in a less attractive personality, but all his life young Richard would use his charm and talent for getting his own way.

Nothing changes, Elizabeth thought.

It still goes on.

The phone began to bleep in the other room. She wiped her hands and went to answer it.

'Mrs Blair. It's Saul Nicholson. I . . . well, Kate's just moved in with me.'

A pause. Elizabeth's brain reacted, but her body was a good few minutes behind. 'So I gather.'

'Yes . . . well.' A long silence. 'This is kind of tricksy . . .'

'You might say.'

'I gather . . . well, Kate says you don't exactly approve of our relationship.'

Good PR, Kate. Well done.

'I don't know the first thing about your relationship with my daughter, Mr Nicholson, so I can hardly disapprove.

Let's just say that it came at me from an unexpected angle.'

He laughed. 'A sense of humour. I like that. I did tell Kate it might be best to break the news gently.'

'You did? Let me ask you something. How long have you known my daughter?'

'Six months. Maybe seven.'

'Then you'll know by now that Kate never does anything gently. When she was seventeen years old, she took it on herself to announce, while we were visiting the quilt show at the Turkey Creek County Fair, that she'd lost her virginity to some boy who took her to the high-school dance. It was quite a moment. Jim says it shut me up for a whole week.'

'Jim?'

'My late husband. He was a big, calm man.'

'Kate doesn't take after him then.' There was humour in the voice at the other end of the phone.

'She certainly doesn't.' Elizabeth stood there trying to imagine what Saul Nicholson looked like. Big and gangly, she decided, with a bird's nest beard. A sort of American version of Lytton Strachey. What should she say next? May as well come straight to the point. 'Were you . . . are you . . . married, Mr Nicholson? Do you have children?'

'I'm divorced. And I have three kids – boys – who are all away at college.'

'I see.'

'No, you don't. Not really. But feel free to call me and talk any time you want. Contrary to what Kate told you, I'm quite sociable. I hope we can become friends.'

I'll reserve judgement on that, Elizabeth thought as she put the phone down. But, he sounds affable. A teddy bear. Wasn't that what Kate said?

We'll see.

Give it time.

She had barely put the phone down when it rang again. It was Max. 'Just thought you might like to know. Some bloke fishing down by the canal caught more than he expected. A body. A man's body. He's just been identified as Marcus Finney.'

Chapter Thirty-Six

Three p.m. the following afternoon. Max's size twelve feet came hammering down the corkscrew of oak stairs from his office. So young, Elizabeth thought enviously. So full of bounding energy. 'Good gracious! Where's the fire?' she exclaimed as he shoved open the shop door.

A tall, spindly female customer stepped, sharpish, out of his way as he strode to the counter.

'I've just been on the phone to Andy. Finney was shot before he went into the canal. And the bullets are from the same gun that killed Kat Gregg. A rusty thirty-eight Smith and Wesson.'

The spindly female, ears twitching, held a quilt end (the Double Axe Head) with solemn care, as if to examine the stitching.

'Forensic says he was killed between seven thirty and eight and that he was still alive, but fatally wounded when he went into the water.'

'Max, dear. There's a time and a place.'

Spindle-shanks had taken fright. Heading for the door, she caught her cuff button in the Double Axe label and yanked quilt, stand and the whole shebang into a collapsed heap.

'Do drop by again,' Elizabeth called after her. 'We're not normally—'

But she had fled.

'Thanks a bunch,' Elizabeth said to Max. 'You're a great guy to have around the place.'

'There's something else.'

'What's that?'

'The police found a Bath rugby umbrella with two sets of prints on – Kat's and Finney's – when they searched his house. It was in the attic hidden under an old carpet. You're brilliant, Betsey. I wouldn't say this about any other Yank, but you're a bloody marvel.'

Elizabeth said, 'Get out of here before you embarrass yourself. And before you frighten away any more of my customers.'

Seven forty that evening. Max dodged the baby's sticky fist, wondered what that brown stuff was on its podgy fingers and picked up the can of Fosters that Andy had searched out for him.

'What's it called?' he said, as the baby stared back at him.

'He. He's a boy. Rollo.'

'Like the chocolates?'

'No. Rollo as in Rollo the Strong, who sailed for Ireland . . . or was it Finland with . . . was it Eric the Brave?'

'Search me,' Max said.

'One of those Eriks, anyway. Ask Lyn. She'll tell you. She reads all these things.'

Lyn was out at her art class. Hence the boys' night in. 'That accident,' Andy said suddenly. 'The one involving the Make-peace lad. He'd had a skinful, but he wasn't driving the car so there's nothing much to report.'

'Any witnesses?'

'Just some old dear who lived in the flat across the road. But she didn't see much. Had her reading glasses on instead of her distance ones.'

'Better give me her address anyhow. There's got to be some reason Finney kept that cutting. Is he supposed to be doing that?'

The baby – Rollo (daft name) – was shoving what looked like a glass bead into its mouth.

'Come here, my babs—' After a prolonged struggle which involved upending the child and hitting him on the back, Andy fished the bead from his son's mouth. 'Want to help bath him?'

Max didn't know. 'Finney's body. Who found it?'

'Some bloke fishing. Thought he'd caught a whopper, but couldn't work out why it wasn't moving. So he fixed the rod to his fishing basket and waded in to find out. The hook had got itself caught up in Finney's cuff button. When he pulled at the line, this arm came up out of the water . . .'

The baby had now shuffled itself inside an enormous card-board box that was laid on its side next to the bookcase. He pushed back one of the flaps and stuck his head round. Gave Max a gummy grin.

'Home-made Wendy house,' Andy explained. 'The new telly came in it. Lyn's idea. Cheaper than the Hamley's model. He thinks it's great.'

Max could see that. The baby was pushing the flap to and fro, shaking its head and saying, 'Ab-bab.' It seemed to be waiting for a reply.

'He wants you to play Peep-Bo. Go on – have a go while I run the bath.'

When Andy came down again, five minutes later, the baby and Max were old mates. Andy said, 'By the way. Mulligan's best man, Ashley Lewis. He's got a police record. Did a youth custody sentence when he was sixteen. Broke into some local business premises with a mate.'

'Interesting.'

'Isn't it?' Andy picked up the babby and swung him about a bit. 'Right – bath time.' He said to Rollo, 'Then Uncle Max might cook us a bit of supper. He's been getting tips, you know, from his friendly Masterchef . . .'

Max said something very rude. Well, relatively rude. There

was, after all, a baby listening. But the idea must have stuck in his mind, because . . .

. . . when Elizabeth rang later that evening, he said, 'How would you like to come round for dinner at my place next week? You and Ginger?'

'At your place?'

'What's wrong with that?'

'I've seen your kitchen, remember.'

'So?'

'So you'd need to fumigate.'

'It's not too bad at the moment, actually.'

'Max, dear boy — let me get this straight. Are you planning to cook?'

'I thought so. Yeah.'

A bit of a silence. Then, 'I wouldn't,' she said.

Which was like a red rag to a bull.

'Has this got anything to do with that Glyn guy?' Elizabeth asked next.

'Nothing at all. I just fancied cooking.' He thought he heard a snort at the other end. Then she said, 'OK. Fine by me. But if I were you, I'd do something plain. Or else buy from Mr Marks. Smoked salmon. A quiche and salad. Look — what I called about was Celia Hannaford. How would eleven o'clock tomorrow morning do you?'

'Fine,' said Max. 'You'd better give me the address.'

Chapter Thirty-Seven

Alice Hannaford opened the door to them. She was a square, determined-looking woman in a green tartan skirt. She stared at them, frowning, while Elizabeth explained the reason for their visit.

'Letters?' Alice said. 'Attacks on your young colleague? I have no idea what you're talking about.'

'I'm sorry, but we have hard evidence. I wonder if we might come in. I don't like discussing this kind of thing on the doorstep.'

'No, you most certainly cannot come in. I'm very busy. I have a—'

'Who's that, Alice? Who is it?' A voice came ringing out from the room behind her.

'No one. Nothing of any importance.' Desperately, Miss Hannaford tried to shut the door on them. But Elizabeth's foot was prepared for that. It stuck itself, almost instinctively, in the way.

'There is someone. I'm not deaf.' Celia Hannaford appeared suddenly by the console table that stood at the back of the entrance hall. Her face had been almost cheerful, but as soon as she saw Max, it changed. 'You!' she said, one hand coming up as if in self-defence. 'You're here again. Following me . . .'

'No. No, really.' Max tried to calm her down.

'You think I'm guilty, I suppose, but I can assure you you're quite wrong. I have all sorts of things that will prove it. Do you want to see? Do you want to see his letters? I still have them.' Celia gave a short, very high-pitched laugh. 'I didn't throw them away. Alice wanted me to.'

'Did you write back to him, Miss Hannaford?' Elizabeth had to ask her.

'Yes. Yes, of course I did. Why shouldn't I? Is there any reason?'

'Come along, Celia.' Alice Hannaford had hold of her arm. 'You're not well. I don't think—'

'I'm quite well.' Celia's eyes continued to stare at them. 'I know why you're here. He's dead, isn't he? They found him in the canal. Well, I'm glad. He was such a – a – I hated him so much . . .' And then, quite suddenly, she collapsed in a heap against the wall, her whole body racked. She began to wail. It was the most unnerving sound.

Alice Hannaford's voice, sharp as a blade, said to Elizabeth, 'Help me. Help me get her back upstairs.'

In the first-floor flat, they got her on to the sofa that stood to one side of the grand piano. Alice Hannaford fetched some pills, made her sister take one. Celia shuddered as it went down.

'It's all right,' Alice said soothingly. 'You're all right. It'll make you feel better.'

'I did write him letters,' Celia said in a voice that shook. 'I couldn't help it. I had to tell him. He had a right to know that Edward was his son.'

Alice gave a deep sigh. 'No, darling. Edward wasn't that man's son.'

'He was, I tell you.' Celia's slim hands twisted and writhed. Extreme agitation in her voice now. 'I had to tell him. He didn't know, you see. And the voice said—'

'Celia – that man wasn't Alistair.'

'He *was* Alistair. I know he was.'

'Alistair died ten years ago. You know that. We talked about it.'

'No. Alistair died two days ago. I read it in the paper. Somebody shot him.'

'That was Marcus Finney. Someone else entirely.'

'It was Alistair – I know it was! I used to go round to the shop and talk to him.' Celia was very flushed, almost incoherent.

'Did you put a brick through his shop window?' Elizabeth asked gently.

Celia wouldn't look at her. 'He wasn't very nice to me that day. He asked if I'd been writing him letters and then he swore at me. I suppose I should have known. He dropped me once before, you know.'

'I know, dear.' Alice had given up the attempt to reason.

'Look – I bought this from his shop.' Celia made a sudden dash for the china cabinet. She scrabbled with the key, opened the door and grabbed a group of Staffordshire figurines. Held them up, saying desperately, 'See this one? The baby in the cradle. I told him it looked like Edward and he agreed with me.'

'I'm sure he did.' Alice's voice was dry. She said to Elizabeth and Max, 'Come into the kitchen. I'll make us a cup of coffee.'

'No milk for me,' Celia said. 'I'll just put this back then. You do believe me?'

'I believe you.' Alice's face suddenly looked drawn. Exhausted. They followed her out of a door at the back of the sitting room.

The flat grew more cluttered the further back you went. Boxes of stuff stacked on all surfaces. Alice led the way through into a long, tall kitchen with a view down over the street below.

For a moment, she stood there as still as stone. Cold, seemingly unmoved. Then she dragged herself over to the kettle and filled it before turning to say in a heavy voice, 'Celia's a manic depressive. She has spells of bizarre behaviour. She lost her job at St Theresa's because of her illness. Of course, they called it voluntary redundancy, but it's a euphemism. Now she just gives lessons at home. But even that's dwindling. The children are getting scared of her.'

'I see,' said Elizabeth. Suddenly it made more sense.

'I'll tell you this in confidence. Eighteen years ago, she . . . she had an affair with a married man. She lent him a lot of money – money our father left her. Money which she never got back and which she now misses. A sum large enough to have provided a cushion against the genteel poverty we now live in. There's something else. She had a child by him. A son. For the last few months she has believed very strongly that Marcus Finney was the man who got her pregnant and deserted her.'

'But he wasn't?'

'Of course he wasn't. Oh, there's a surface likeness. He has the same colouring as Alistair Kent, the baby's real father. But Alistair's dead. He died of leukaemia ten years ago. I know that for a fact.'

'And the child?'

'He's dead, too.' Alice stood there in the middle of the kitchen, hanging on to the kettle for all she was worth. 'Edward. We idolised that little boy. He died in the road out at the front when he was just three years old. You know how they are at that age? All energy and curiosity. Can't wait for anything. Can't sit still for a single moment.' She hugged the kettle to her as if it were a child. 'One morning – a Wednesday – I'll never forget it as long as I live. We were setting out for the shops and suddenly he spotted a horse and carriage trotting down the hill. One of those contraptions they keep for the tourists. In a split second – I couldn't stop him – he tore his hand out of mine and dashed into the road to see the horse. Right under the wheels of a car. He didn't stand a chance.'

'God, how awful. I'm so sorry.'

'I thought it would kill her, too. Celia. The shock of it. It almost killed me, I can tell you. Edward . . . it was difficult at the beginning, but he was everything to us.' Alice's voice had turned to a rough croak. For a moment, she couldn't speak. Then wiping the side of her eye, she reached up to the calendar above the fridge. Drew from behind it a snapshot of a child with unruly fair hair and a playful smile.

She passed the photograph to Elizabeth. 'He was such a sweet child. As harmless as a robin. I like to look at him sometimes, when I'm working, but it upsets Celia . . . unbalances her . . . so I have to hide it.'

Her air of detachment was gone now. The lines of her rather gaunt face had grown softer and there was raw pain in the hazel eyes. Looking as though she was about to burst into tears, Alice Hannaford went on: 'Sometimes I can't bear to look at him either. I loved him so much. He was so innocent, you know? It shone out of him. I used to go in every morning and there he would be, grinning at me from his cot . . .'

Elizabeth stood there in pitying silence. At last, she managed to say, 'How . . . how did your sister meet Marcus Finney? How did it all begin?'

'How? We went up to the Antiques Fair at Cheyneys back in the spring. The end of April. I'd picked something up from Finney's stall. Can't remember what. A cup, I think. And I turned to Celia to say how pretty it was and there she was, staring at the man with this look on her face. Rapt. "He looks like Alistair," she said when I'd managed to move her on. Of course, I pooh-poohed it, but there was a likeness. I suppose Alistair would have looked much the same had he lived to middle age. Anyway, she didn't say much more at the time, but she'd sneaked one of his cards and she kept visiting his shop. Buying little bits of things. Bits of Staffordshire. Alistair had once given her a shepherdess figure, you see – a fairing – and somehow she got it into her head that he was still alive and had opened an antiques shop. I know it sounds absurd—'

'It's a brain disorder?'

'Exactly. The experts don't know what makes people shift from a harmless interest in another person to a full-scale obsession.'

'Is it curable?' Elizabeth asked.

'It can be controlled . . . stabilised, if she takes her medicine. But she's very naughty. Sometimes she won't take it or pretends she has when she hasn't. And then her mood will swing quite quickly. One minute she's as high as a kite . . . restless, impulsive, uncontrollably energetic. Then when it burns itself out, she'll go down like a lead balloon. She's empty, sad . . . suicidal even. There are bouts of normal mood in between, but she'll tip over quite quickly. It's very frightening. And wearing. I have to watch her all the time. Sometimes I feel like a hostage. Trapped. I know she's been sending Finney photographs of Edward . . . of her child. I caught her putting them into an envelope she'd addressed to him.'

'I'm sorry to ask this. But do you think her capable of killing him?'

'Don't be silly. She doesn't even possess a gun.' But Alice's face had blanched.

A sound in the doorway. Celia. She'd been standing there listening . . . for how long?

'I keep buying things from him,' she said, 'but he doesn't care for me any more. I don't suppose he ever did.' She began to weep. Fat tears rolled down her cheeks.

Rachel weeping for her children. Child. One was pain enough.

'Of course he did.'

'No. He didn't. And he's turned into a bit of a windbag. Did you know that? I'll tell you something else. He shouts a lot at his boy. His other boy. There's something wrong with him, you know. Lucian. He didn't care for the boy and he didn't care for me.'

Alice crossed the room to her sister's side. Put an arm around her. 'He cared for you a great deal. Alistair, I mean. Not that man. Come on. Come along. I want you to lie down. Tomorrow we'll have the doctor in.'

She looked across at Elizabeth.

'She's had enough for one day.'

'Of course. Thank you for talking to me. Let me know if there's anything I can do for you.'

Some hope, Elizabeth thought. Some problems you can't do much for. Miracles apart.

Chapter Thirty-Eight

When Jan Finney heard Anna's hysterical (for once) voice on the other end of the phone, she felt nothing. In the end, she had to put it down.

'Trouble?' said Lucian, gazing at his mother with becalmed blue eyes. 'Mrs Freeman says I can go to France camping. Can I take my tape recorder? And my rucksack?'

Jan fumbled at the buttons on Lucian's blue checked shirt. 'You can. But it's not until next June.'

'Next June.'

Jan was at a loss to know how to explain time to him. Lucian had no conception of it. But maybe at times like this, it was a good thing.

Live in the present. Free as a bird.

Feel again . . .

The curious thing was that she no longer seemed to have any emotions.

'Right,' she said. 'Weetabix time. Then it's off to school. You'll like that.'

Eleven a.m. Caroline came out of the kitchen with two mugs of coffee and a plate of shortbread biscuits. 'The Glory you were talking about on the phone just now. Is that the girl who used to work for Rupert?'

'Glory Fraser. Yes.' Elizabeth had been talking to the girl's grandmother (jolly old type, by the sound of it) trying to find out exactly what day Glory would be back from her course. 'Why do you ask?'

'It's just that we were talking about her the other day. I can't remember why, but Rupert said she seemed to be in some kind of trouble just after she started working for him.'

'What kind of trouble?'

'She wouldn't say. All he knows is that she was crying a lot.'

'Did she have money problems?'

'No idea. Sorry. Rupert did say she was always broke. He arranged a lift to Bristol every day for her because she couldn't afford the bus fares.'

She doesn't seem broke now, Elizabeth thought. So what's changed? She took a sip of her coffee. 'By the way,' she said, 'did you tell Rupert about the quilt I showed you? The one that might be your wedding present.'

It was undoubtedly naughty of her. At your age, you should know better. Tormenting the child.

'The quilt?' Caroline's voice had gone up a notch or two, but she kept her cool. 'As a matter of fact, I did. He said . . .' She was playing for time. 'He said he'd have to come along and take a look at it some time.'

That'll be fun, Elizabeth thought.

Must make sure Max is here. Let's stir the beans a little.

Max, at that exact moment, had just decided that Imogen Shand was unpaintable, No one, however deft with the brush, would be able to capture that exquisite grace, her luminous skin. The half-shy, half-inquisitive look she gave him before subsiding grace-fully in a rustle of silk (long, blue skirt) into the corner table by the window. Even the blurry blue shadows under those eyes added to her beauty.

'Thanks for finding time for me, Miss Shand.' A titanium

flash of charm. 'I thought coffee in town might be easier than . . .' He stopped to find a suitably tactful way of putting it.

'Than talking in front of my mother?' She threw him the most lovely smile. 'You're probably right. I'm sorry about the delay.'

'You were in Paris?'

'Yes.'

'With a friend?'

'Yes. With an old friend. Why do you ask?' A spontaneous question, but a bit too quick off the mark? Max wondered. Too ingenous? Over-eager?

'No reason,' Max said smoothly. 'I expect it was good to get away?'

'Yes. Yes, it was.' Imogen averted her gaze. 'So what did you want to see me about?'

'We just wanted you to confirm something for us.'

'What's that?'

'You did say you knew nothing of your fiancé's affair with Kat Gregg before she showed up on your wedding morning?'

'Yes. That's what I said.'

'And still say?'

'Yes.'

'I think I should tell you at this stage that my colleague, Mrs Blair, had quite a long conversation with the Reverend Timms.'

Her face suddenly grew flushed.

'Who informed us that he told you before the wedding that Miss Gregg was pregnant and that she claimed the father was your fiancé.'

Silence.

'So what you've just told me was nowhere near the truth. You did know about the affair?'

'All right.' All the colour had left her face. She was as white as a sheet. 'Yes, I did.'

'So how long had you known?'

'Before he — Reverend Timms — told me.'

'Really?'

'Yes.'

'So how did you find out?'

'I . . . I was standing at the top of the stairs one morning and I saw Johnny hiding a letter. I saw him scoop it up and hide it in his pocket.'

'So how long ago was this?'

'A few months. I don't remember.'

'So what did you do? About the letter?'

'I . . . Well, that night I went through his pockets and found the letter and read it. It was from her. Kat. She was angry because he hadn't been to see her.'

'Did you tackle him about it?'

'Of course. I . . . he told me it was all on her side. That she'd got a crush on him, but that he'd never given her any encouragement.'

'And you believed him?'

'Yes. In the end. He can be very persuasive.' She had control of herself again. 'I knew that women liked him. Other women. I knew he sometimes played around. I just thought that it would be different after we were married. I thought I could cure him. I was wrong.'

'Your mother said you had a row with Johnny a few weeks back. That you came home to her house in tears.'

'That was the day I found the letter. I was upset.'

'But you weren't anywhere near Alfred Buildings the night Kat Gregg was murdered?'

'No. I was at home in bed. Flat out.'

'At seven thirty in the evening?'

The blue eyes came up to meet his own. 'You know what kind of a day I'd had.'

Max felt as mean as hell, but the questioning had to go on. He waited.

'I'd been crying all day and I was dead tired, but I still couldn't sleep. So I took one of my mother's sleeping pills. And I wish I hadn't.'

'Why's that?'

A hesitation. 'Because I'd arranged to meet Kat. And I didn't make it.'

'You arranged to meet her? Why?'

'I had to talk to her. I knew she must be feeling lousy. I needed to know certain things and talking to her seemed better than sitting around doing nothing. In agony. So I rang her.'

'Did you tell the police this?'

'No. No. I was scared to. My mother said I couldn't have done anything. There was no need to get involved.'

'So what time did you arrange to meet Miss Gregg?'

'At eight fifteen. She was reluctant at first. Then she said she'd meet me at my friend's flat in town.'

'Your friend's name?'

Max noted the name and address.

'We daren't go to a café or bar. The press were sniffing round. I just feel so guilty. If I hadn't asked her to come down to town, she might still be alive.'

Max shook his head. 'You can't say that. She'd had a clear-out.' He thought twice about saying what Kat had cleared from her house. 'She'd probably have gone down to Alfred Buildings anyway.' He made himself ask the next question. 'You must have heard about the second murder? An antiques dealer called Marcus Finney?'

'Yes.' She waited.

'He died on Tuesday. Where were you that night?'

'I was in Paris with Tim. I only got back last night.'

Which could presumably be proved? But Max was inclined to believe her anyway. She looked so despondent. In some obscure way, it made him feel depressed. But we all go through it, Max thought, at some time or other. It's just that hers was a very public humiliation.

Poor kid.

*   *   *

The Vicarage door opened. Celia Hannaford smiled nervously. 'It's probably not a convenient time,' she said.

If Richard Timms was surprised to see her there on a Friday lunchtime, he didn't show it. The Vicarage door was always open to his parishioners. Sometimes he cursed the fact, but never in public and never without feeling he'd failed in his chosen vocation.

'Celia!' he said jovially. 'What a pleasure. Come in. Come in. What can I do for you?'

Chapter Thirty-Nine

Guiting Trimble was a village which hadn't changed much in centuries. Sunlit fields (well, today, at least), Cotswold roofs, a church, a pub, a telephone box (red) and a dozen houses at the most.

The Lewis house faced the sixteenth-century church from a small grove of beech trees. Wooden gates, broad lawns, a sundial by the French windows. Mrs Lewis was fair with fine, untidy hair. As Max had said, she was very posh. She made morning coffee, corroborated Ashley's story about the evening Kat had died. There was no way Johnny or her son could have been in Bath that evening. She had been worried about Johnny's state of health (and mind). As her son had been. They'd looked in on the sleeping (sleeping? Zonked out) bridegroom every twenty minutes or so.

However, Elizabeth gained some useful background knowledge about the family. Dear Ashley was not an intellectual. His father had wanted him to join the family legal practice, but that had proved impossible. Ashley hadn't even made it to college. One of his sisters had joined the practice instead.

Yes, of course they were disappointed that their boy hadn't made the grade.

But he had other talents. What were they?

'You'd have to know him to answer that question,' Alison Lewis said, her smile fading rapidly.

The approved school? The boy had got into bad company. That was the trouble with living out in the sticks. He had picked up with some village louts, people with whom he should never have been mixing. But he had learned his lesson. 'Another biscuit?' Mrs Lewis enquired sweetly of Elizabeth. 'Have you seen our stocks? They're in the middle of the green?'

Had the lady had her way, Elizabeth would have been in them.

Life had been very easy for Ashley Lewis, that much was clear to see. Too easy and too pleasant, perhaps. Public school . . . spoiled young man among a batch of sisters. He'd never had to try too hard, Elizabeth thought as she drove out of the village. It made for a weaker character. People were inclined to give him what he wanted and he'd got used to it.

Driving back through Gloucestershire, she compiled a mental dossier on him in her head. Aged thirty-eight, but looks twenty-five. Older than Johnny. Makes out to be the follower, but what if he's actually the leader? Leading Mulligan astray? Yes. That dare on the stag night.

OK, so what if Finney had been blackmailing Ashley as well? For what? No idea, but there were mean little vices under the smooth exterior. A dishonest streak. That much had been proved. He most certainly had been – was – jealous of Johnny's looks and charisma with women. Sick, perhaps, of having to live in Mulligan's slipstream. Of picking up Johnny's rejects.

Now what would that do to you?

I don't know, but I'm certainly going to find out.

Next port of call. Anna Makepeace. It was time to carry out a slightly unpleasant task that Max had baulked at. As she showed Anna the photographs of her husband and Kat Gregg, Elizabeth was prepared to feel vaguely sorry for the woman. But there was little reaction.

Disappointing, that.

'If you were hoping to surprise me,' Mrs Makepeace said, passing the photographs back to her, 'I'm afraid you'll be disappointed.'

She was managing to keep a very clear head. But perhaps you would expect that from the owner of a hotel like Cheyneys. Too well-bred, too dignified, too darned in charge of herself to let her innermost feelings out to a stranger. Particularly to a private eye.

Not to mention a Yank.

'You see, my husband told me about the little fling he had with Miss Gregg. Soon after he ended it, actually.'

'You didn't mention that before.'

'Why should I? It's my business and Aidan's.'

So you can just bog off, her expression said. Entirely at ease with herself and everything that went on in her world.

Well, that was how it seemed . . .

One thirty p.m. The phone went. Elizabeth picked it up. 'Martha Washington. Can I help you?'

'I very much hope so.' Richard Timms was on the other end. 'I've just had a visit from Celia. Miss Hannaford, who, I must say, was in quite a state.'

'Really?'

'Yes . . . really. May I ask a question? Have you . . . or your young assistant—'

'Partner.'

'Partner, then. Has either of you been — what's the word? — bothering — no, hassling Miss Hannaford?'

'Of course not.' Elizabeth was annoyed that he should think so. 'What do you think I am? We went to visit her, that's all.'

'About your concert at St Swithin's?'

Silence. Elizabeth felt mortified. 'Listen — I can explain—'

'Don't explain to me. Explain to Alice Hannaford. She's as worried about Celia as I am.'

'I'm sorry about that, but I can assure you—' Elizabeth stopped in mid-sentence. 'Would you mind my asking? Why exactly did Celia – Miss Hannaford – come to see you?'

'Why would any of my flock come? Spiritual guidance. I'm afraid I can't say more than that.' He put the phone down on her. That hurt. Damn it, Elizabeth thought, he needn't have made me feel like cheap white trash.

When the phone rang again two minutes later, she was convinced it was the Reverend calling back to apologise. It wasn't. Rose Mulligan's voice said, 'Mrs Blair?' She sounded slurred. 'Mrs Blair. I'm sorry to have to say this, but we've . . . I've decided we won't be needing your services any more.'

As simple as that.

No attempt at an explanation. 'So if you would care to forward your account . . .'

For the second time that day, the line went dead on Elizabeth.

Chapter Forty

Elizabeth went home for a late lunch. She'd had enough of the Shepard Agency for one day. The darker corners of modern life were not always to her taste, though she spent half of her life investigating them. Why do it then? she asked herself, when you could be taking it easy just minding your own business and running a quilt shop.

Which is enough in itself. The bills, the business rates, the tax inspectors, the customers. I mean, it's not as if you need the money. And at your age, you should be slowing down a little. Watching your blood pressure, which probably shot sky high while Richard Timms was reading you his little lecture. Did you ever think he was right? Maybe we were hassling Celia.

And maybe that's what vicars are for. To put us right when we're walking up the wrong path. The thing is, you have to go where you can in this business – right or wrong. The alleys ahead are shrinking like last year's long Johns.

Maybe I'll just quit. Quit and quilt.

Poor old dear.

Two p.m. She put on some soothing music, but the soft beat reminded her of Kat Gregg. It was like the heartbeat of an unborn child. She switched it off. I won't go back this afternoon, she thought. I'll just stay here in peace and quiet and quilt. But for once, that didn't work either. She took out the Starburst, cut herself a few good old-timey-looking prints, but her bad temper must have affected her needle hand. The block all went crooked. Made you feel seasick. And then, as she sat pulling the stitches all out again, her mind would keep harking back to the Mulligan case.

The two would run along together.

Because detecting and quilting . . . they're very similar. You collect piles of material and put it together to make your own unique pattern. You get an idea and tinker with it; you adapt, you vary, you interpret, using whatever you've got, big or small. It takes ingenuity as well as artistry.

Even the intentional flaw you're supposed to put into a quilt, bowing to the popular belief that only God makes something perfect (tell that one to the Reverend Timms). Even that. Most of the characters Max and I come across have flaws, too. Powerful, interesting aberrations that brings your mind back to them again and again.

Anna Makepeace has no flaws that I can see. She must have . . . somewhere. That lady intrigues me. She raised Johnny's bail money. Has she also been helping Rose pay our bills? Maybe she's behind Rose's decision to call us off the case.

Something to hide?

Scared of us getting too close? I wonder . . .

With each new answer came a new question. That was the problem.

Half an hour before, Celia Hannaford had parked her car in the road outside St Dunstan's School – Lucian's school – as she had done several times before in the last few weeks. She rather enjoyed watching children at play. Perpetual motion, she thought. They were like little birds flying round and round the playground. And if a little bird flew too far . . .

For the moment, she stifled the thought.

The car was airless. She wound down the window. Then,

smiling gently to herself, opened the door and got out. It was at that point that she spotted Lucian. He was over by the climbing frame, slightly apart from the other children.

Celia hesitated, then made up her mind. Nodding and smiling in Lucian's direction, as if extraordinarily pleased to have found him so quickly, she walked into the playground. It was all right. The girl who was keeping an eye on them was occupied with a child who had fallen down at the far end of the yard.

'Hello,' she said to Lucian. 'Remember me? I'm your friend from the park.'

'Hello,' said Lucian. 'Where's my yo-yo?'

She hadn't expected that, but instantly shuffling the question into the vague plan she held in her head, she brought out a winning card. 'It's in the car,' she said. 'Want to come and get it?'

'All right.' Unaware of the sudden exhilaration that was filling Celia's heart, Lucian shoved his hands in his pockets and followed her out through the gate.

It was quite easy really.

No one seemed to notice.

By the time they reached the car, Lucian was telling her about the book his mother had helped him choose from the library. 'It's about Roman things. Ships. And swords. I wanted to bring it to school, but she said I couldn't.'

'Why not?'

'It might get broken.'

'Torn?'

'Yes.'

'I don't think you'd tear it. Want to fetch it? I could take you.'

Lucian stood there for a second or two gazing at her. Then he gave her his slow, friendly smile. 'All right,' he said. 'I'll get my coat.'

'No need for that. It's warm in the car.' She opened the door for him and Lucian climbed in.

Chapter Forty-One

Three p.m. Ginger was stowing some envelopes away in a drawer when Max walked into the office.

'I need a favour,' he said. 'Phoebe's packed up on me.'

'Phoebe?'

'My car.'

'Oh, that old thing. Can't say I'm surprised.'

He let it pass. Put on his most dazzling smile. 'I just wondered if I could borrow yours for the afternoon?'

'Sorry. I'm only insured for one driver.'

'You could drive me.'

She wasn't keen. 'I'm low on petrol.'

'I'm not going far.'

'How far's not far?'

'Outskirts of town. Glory Fraser's place.'

Reluctantly, she said, 'I suppose so. But I can't be hanging around.'

'Why not?'

'Because I'm seeing somebody later.'

'Delia Smith, I suppose?'

'What's wrong with you? Glyn's nice. I thought you liked him.'

'I can take him or leave him,' said Max. 'Right. Get your keys.

Shut up shop. Seeing that Betsey has declined to give us the pleasure of her company . . .'

Naomi Tilbert shunted her weight from side to side as she led Max and Ginger into the small front room of her council house in Highland Road and waved them towards the Dralon-covered sofa that filled the space in front of the bay window. 'Sit down. Sit down. Friends of Glory, are you? She won't be long now. She just running an errand for me. Your legs got more life than mine, I tell her.'

Mrs Tilbert was a big, bustling West Indian lady with a gleaming smile and a runaway tongue. In three minutes flat, she had told Max and Ginger about the shop (groceries and a little tailoring on the side) her father used to keep back home in Jamaica, about the time she had worked in a Brixton laundry to keep a roof over her head after her first husband dropped dead of a brain haemorrhage and about the old dog she had once kept that chased snakes in summer.

'Not rabbits. Not anything you could put in the pot and eat. But snakes!' Out came an explosive laugh. 'Sooner or later, I tell him, you'll bite off more than you can chew. And he did. Found him one morning stiff as a board in the porch. But you don't want to hear about that. I just baked a cake. Can I fetch you a slice while you wait?'

Max said, 'That would be—'

'I expect my girl told you she's studying at the university? She's a clever girl. A sweet girl! She's my sunshine. Works all hours God sends. I tell her, you got to ease off now. But she always knows best. Can't tell her a blessed thing. Always the same from a tiny child.'

Settling into her theme, Mrs Tilbert went on to tell them how proud she was of her grand-daughter. That Glory had never made a big issue of her father walking out on them or her mother spending so much time away from home. She was a strong girl. A good girl. Never had to be lectured about anything.

Except maybe getting into the odd rumpus at school.

'Rumpus?' Max said.

'Only about one thing ever. If they say anything about the colour of her skin.' Mrs Tilbert hugged her stomach and elaborated. 'Take no notice of such foolishness, I tell her. You take no notice, girl! But I'll let you into a secret: nobody ever get away with insulting my Glory. She always knows how to fight her corner. Yes, indeed!'

Max waited a second or two. Then:

'It's an unusual name . . . Glory.'

'My choosing. As soon as I saw her, I said, 'Glory Alleluia! And my daughter, she say . . . that's a nice name. Glory.'

In his head, Max was sorting through all the questions he needed to ask. The first was, 'Must be difficult for a medical student these days? Financially, I mean?'

'You're right there! Forever worrying about owing the bank manager, she was.'

'Was?'

'Oh, things are better these days. She works up at the hotel, you know.'

'So how many hours does she do up there?'

'Less now than she used to, thank the Lord. Falling asleep at lectures, she was. Sugar, I say. You slow down or you'll be sick. But Mrs Makepeace sees how it is. She has been very good to that girl. She looks after her. My girl makes friends wherever she go. But she'll pay that lady back one day. Like she says she'll pay her old Gran back . . .'

A door slammed out in the hall. Someone called out, 'I'm back.'

'In here, sugar.'

After a brief interval, Glory appeared in the doorway. Abundant hair all bunched and scrunched back in a silk scarf. Long legs and high buttocks encased in tight black trousers. She stopped short on seeing Max and Ginger.

Glory's eyebrows lifted.

'Some friends of yours come to see you.'

'All right, Gran. Thanks. Make us a pot of tea if you like.'

After the old lady had gone and shut the door behind her, Glory stood gazing at them with a look of annoyance on her face. 'So what the hell are you doing here? And what did you tell my Gran?'

'Didn't tell her anything,' Max said cheerfully. 'Couldn't get a word in edgeways, as a matter of fact.'

'Good. So next time you want to see me, do it at the hotel. I don't want Gran worried.'

Glory has a temper. She's volatile. Likely to erupt, just as much as her friend, Kat. A pretty pair.

'Why should she be worried?'

She came right back at him. 'I mean I don't want her bothered . . . by you or your carroty assistant. This business about Kat. Gran knew her. She was upset about it and she suffers from angina. Right?'

'Right,' said Max. She was rather alarming in this mood. The warm, funny Glory had turned nasty. He hadn't expected that.

'So what is it? What do you want?' She stood there tensed, as if expecting trouble.

How to go about it? A quick bash in the nose to catch her outright? Or the stepping stone method. One little question leading to another? Max decided on the former. He brought out the photograph and placed it on the table in front of her.

She snatched it up at once, with a glance towards the door. 'Where did you get that?'

Max told her.

Silence. She was obviously going through her options.

'I think you'd better tell me about your relationship with Marcus Finney.'

'There wasn't one.' No hesitation this time. The answer came back as quick as a flash.

'Really?'

'Really. He . . . I bumped into him occasionally at the health club. We saw each other once or twice. That's all.'

'He took the occasional photograph?'

There was a dark flush under the coffee-coloured skin. 'Look. It was nothing.'

'Nothing?' Max stared her out.

'OK, so I drank too much whisky one night. OK, so he took a photograph. It's none of your business. And for God's sake, don't tell my grandmother.'

Max was struck by the panic in her voice. 'You know that Finney's dead?'

'Yes. I heard it on the news.'

'Were you shocked?'

'I suppose so.'

'You suppose so. Is that all? A friend of yours is murdered—'

'He's no friend of mine.' She shook her head to emphasise the point.

Max looked sceptical. 'I'd like to know where you were last Tuesday night. The night Finney was killed.'

'I was in a seminar in Exeter. Ask anybody. OK?'

'OK. And the night Kat Gregg was murdered?'

'I was at my boyfriend's flat in Bristol.'

Max nodded. 'That's what he said when I rang him.'

'So?'

'Besotted, is he?'

'I wouldn't say that.'

'Stupid then?'

'Hardly. He happens to be a junior doctor at the BRI.'

Max said nothing. There was silence, except for the tick of the clock, the flicker of the gas fire.

'So we have to move on to a conspiracy theory.' Max picked an imaginary hair off the knee of his trousers. 'The Twinnies,' he said. 'They live just down the hill from the Beehive. Gooseberry-green jumpers – hand-knitted – and hats to match. That was what they were wearing yesterday when I called on them.'

'What on earth are you talking about?'

'They offered me a glass of elderberry wine. Nice old dears. A touch on the batty side, but nothing wrong with their eyes.'

She looked flustered for the first time. And well she might.

Max said, 'They saw you at the Beehive that Saturday night. The night Kat was killed.'

'Not me. I wasn't up there.' Arrogant. Off-hand.

'You were. They saw you.'

'Must have been someone else.'

'No. No, it was you and they're prepared to confirm that to the police if necessary. You didn't actually go in, because Kat pulled out of the car parking area about two minutes before you arrived. You must have just missed her. I'll let you tell me what happened next.'

She took a breath and then swallowed it again. Seemed to weigh up her options, before making a wry face and rejecting all of them.

'All right,' she said at last. 'You've got me.' There was a short pause, then suddenly, without any warning, she changed her story. On leaving the Shands' house at about three in the afternoon, she'd come home and got changed out of her wedding gear. Tried to get down to some studying, but couldn't get Kat out of her mind. After all, they'd been sort of friends once and though what Kat had done to Immy was unpardonable, she'd done it because she was suffering.

Gran had said so, over and over.

Glory was in a fix. Fond of Kat and of Immy.

At five thirty, Ed – her boyfriend – had rung to ask her to meet him for a drink, but she hadn't been in the mood. She'd called Aidan – Mr Makepeace – who had told her what a state Kat was in. So she decided to go up there. Only to miss Kat by two minutes.

'I saw her pull out of the car park and drive off down the hill. I waved a hand to attract her attention, but she didn't see me. So

I turned round outside the Beehive and I followed her back down to town. At the bottom of Lansdown Hill, she indicated that she was going to turn right into Alfred Street. I was about to follow her, but this prat stalled his car dead in front of me and there was no way I could get round him. I had to wait there until he got going again, by which time I'd decided there was no way I'd catch Kat up. I'd have to go home and try again later.'

Max had sat listening throughout her explanation. He said abruptly, 'You expect me to believe that?'

'Please yourself. It's the truth.'

'Oh, come on — so why didn't you come clean before?'

'I was scared. Didn't want to get involved.' She saw his face. 'You don't believe me. Then I'll tell you something that might prove I'm telling the truth. As I was stuck there in the traffic behind this guy, a car I recognised came up the hill and turned into Alfred Street right behind Kat.'

'Who was that?'

'Ashley Lewis. I saw his face quite clearly.'

Chapter Forty-Two

'Carroty!' Ginger said, as they climbed back into her car.

'Sorry about that. You get flak in this job.'

'Telling me. Fun, though, isn't it?' she said, slamming the door behind her and strapping herself into the driver's seat. 'Nosing around. Interfering in other people's lives. Do you think she was right about Ashley Lewis? Kat had an affair with him?'

'She didn't actually call it that.'

A drunken shag was the phrase Glory had used when she came out to see them off. Not a girl to mince her words, Max thought.

'So why didn't she tell anybody this before? The police, for instance?'

Max shrugged. 'Didn't want to admit to being on the scene?' It was a brown, sodden afternoon. Dark soon. Ginger's hair burned bright in the smothering gloom. He had this sudden urge to put out a hand and touch it.

Bloody fool, he thought, as she turned the key in the ignition.

The engine kicked into life.

Lazy, crazy thought.

Glory Magdalena Fraser watched them drive away from the house. Then went back in and shut the door with a little smile on her face. Something was amusing her. Some illicit thought. Pity there was no one she could share it with.

Elizabeth, at that moment, was making herself a pot of tea and wondering what she should use to back the Starburst. She had once given a talk in which she had argued that the back of a quilt is almost as interesting as the showy bits. All those down-home, back-of-the-cupboard things they tacked on to the back: flour sacks, sugar sacks, feed sacks; salt and tobacco bags, washed, bleached and dyed, then pieced in simple, large block patterns; wool trousers, old blankets, worn-out sheets.

Then there were the textile mills, especially in the South, that made available cheap, or sometimes free, material for backing. The Chatham Manufacturing Company of Elkin in Yadkin County, North Carolina, exchanging woven goods for wool with local farmers. The Alamance Factory in NC in 1837 installing four box looms to produce their alamance plaid. And the home dyes: maple bark, black walnut, Pokeberry, sumac and even red clay.

Social history, all of it.

Quite fascinating. Like the back views of people's lives . . .

Elizabeth got out a cup, shut the cupboard door and wondered what lay underneath the outer shell that was Anna Makepeace. For of course, there was more than one of her. (Was it Proust who had talked about 'the many gentlemen of whom I am comprised . . .'?) The inner Anna, deep down underneath. What would she make of a husband who cheated on her? What would she do about it?

She wouldn't be blown away by it, I'm sure of that.

She's a strong woman. A very grounded person. Definitely of the earth. She works hard, she earns respect from people, she can handle any situation. She's not a coward. She would probably stand up and say her piece. Elizabeth lifted the pot and began to pour. If I were Anna Makepeace and I suspected him of playing around, what would I do? What might I do?

Bale out? Not really. Too many family ties, too many business interests, too many years together. She wouldn't do anything stupid.

Would she?

At a guess, she would want to protect Aidan from his own weaknesses.

She would . . . And here, Elizabeth put the teapot down hard on the top.

I know what I'd do.

I know what I'd do. Good God – why didn't I think of that before?

Max wasn't thinking about Proust. He was thinking about asking Ginger if she fancied supper at his flat.

Not a date.

After all, Elizabeth would be there. Just a bit of nosh with friends. Could he say that? Yeah . . . go on. Get it over with.

He sat staring at the traffic lights, which were on red. Sat there apparently lost in thought. When to ask her? Now? Or later, when they got back to the office? Now would be best really. It was getting dark. Well, dusky. She wouldn't be able to see his face. On the other side of Ginger, away to the right, the lights of Bath were dotted around all over the valley.

He opened his mouth, then shut it again.

He didn't even know why he was asking her.

To prove a point. That was it.

What point?

Max didn't know exactly, but some point had to be made. Some point of pride . . . of keeping one's own end up. He cleared his throat.

'Got a cold?' Ginger asked.

The lights turned green.

'No. Why?'

'Take some garlic. Squash it up and put it in a mayonnaise sandwich. Heads it off. Works every time.'

They drove on down the hill. Max turned his head from time to time towards the stone terraces on either side and the tall shapes of the trees. He could feel his lips again forming the words. Putting them together. I was wondering if . . . Would you like to . . . ? How about . . . ?

'You all right?' Ginger asked.

'Yeah. I'm fine. Why?'

'You just seem a bit odd.'

'Thanks a lot,' said Max. He bloody wasn't going to ask her now. 'Petrol's low,' he said, peering assiduously at the gauge.

'I did tell you that. And you didn't give me any warning. I won't object if you fill it up for me. It's the end of the month and I'm broke.'

They stopped at the all-night garage on the London Road. 'I'll do it,' Max said, leaping from the car almost as soon as she'd switched off the engine. He was very conscious that he'd been in danger of losing some sort of status, that Ginger had been getting the upper hand.

The upper hand in what? He didn't know.

Like a man getting himself back in training for a race, he swung his arms back over his head, loosening the muscles of his neck. Then reached out a hand to unscrew the petrol cap. As he did so, he turned his gaze towards the lit window of the garage shop. For one moment, he thought he was seeing things.

Couldn't possibly be.

But it was.

Celia Hannaford . . .

Was she following him? Had she turned the tables? It wasn't Celia. Must be somebody that looked like her. Max caught hold of the pump and shoved it into the open cap. Heard the thing start pumping and stood there watching as the woman paid her bill.

It was, though. Surely?

The woman was emerging now from the lit doorway and crossing the forecourt towards the blue Fiesta on the other side of the pumps. And . . .

God almighty. Who was that with her in the passenger seat? Lucian? It couldn't be.

But it was. Bloody hell!

Max pulled the nozzle out of the cap and went to shove it back in the pump. He'd meant to put in more, but this had changed everything. Celia Hannaford was climbing back into the driving seat. Max stood there as if transfixed.

And then two things happened at once. Celia Hannaford started the engine and Ginger's voice spoke sharply from behind him. 'Max? What the hell do you think you're playing at?'

'What?' His eyes – and half his brain – were still on the Fiesta.

'You idiot! You used the wrong pump. You put diesel in. It runs on petrol!'

Sod it! thought Max.

Bugger it! Bugger! Bugger! Bugger!

Chapter Forty-Three

Celia put a tape on. Bach. She felt like dowsing herself in music. 'Do you like it?' she asked Lucian.

'Yes.'

She turned her head to look at him. 'Yes . . . but what?'

'But I'm hungry.'

'I'm afraid I don't have anything. No . . . hang on. There's a bar of chocolate in the glove compartment.'

Lucian didn't respond.

'In front of you. Pull that handle.'

Politely, Lucian did as he was told.

'Go on, then. Take it out.'

He reached out a hand and took hold of the Crunchie bar.

'It's OK. You can eat it.'

'Would you like some?' Lucian asked politely.

'No, thank you.'

Celia turned the volume up and began to sing along with the tape. She heard her own voice echoing back as if from a great distance. What she wanted to do was sing her heart out. Yes, that would do. In the back of the car were all the letters Alistair had ever written her, tied up in blue ribbon. And the figurines. Together with a tartan travelling rug and a small red ring box. The one he had given her. Empty now, like me, she thought. Sad and hopeless.

She drove on. In which direction? No idea, she thought. Bare skies. A thin, wandering life. Nothing to give it any direction, except music. Ten minutes passed, though Celia wasn't capable of counting them.

She became aware, quite suddenly, that somebody was staring at her. The boy. She'd forgotten he was there. He was showing signs of being less complacent; struggling against the seat belt, trying to twist himself out of it.

'What is it?' she said sharply. 'What's wrong?'

'I want to go home! I'd like to go home now.'

Wouldn't we all? Celia thought. She ignored his pleas, put her foot down harder on the accelerator. Began to sing again. A voice like an angel, she thought. That's what they used to say. Heaven. I'll go there. Might fit in better. Lucian was making a noise now – bawling his head off – fists pressed hard against his cheeks, tears streaming. Celia stopped the car. Drew it with a screech of the brakes into the grass verge. They were in a country lane, pitch black. 'Stop that,' she said. 'Stop crying.' She had never cried since – not since Edward – but she couldn't finish the thought.

Lucian stopped crying. He said, 'I'm going to be sick.'

'Don't be silly. My father used to say it was all in the mind. If you think hard, you won't be.'

'Where are we going?' Lucian asked suddenly. 'I want to go home.'

'No, you don't.' We're both freaks, she thought. She had this pain in her head. Was having difficulty concentrating, remembering, making decisions.

'Where are we going?'

'I'm taking you—' A smile crossed Celia's face. Or was it a grimace? 'I'm taking you to see your brother.' The idea had only just occurred to her.

'I haven't got a brother.'

He was being tiresome. Celia told him to go to sleep and drove on through the night.

Chapter Forty-Four

At eight thirty the following morning, Elizabeth rang Jan Finney. 'I heard the News. Have they found him yet? Lucian?'

'No. They haven't.' Jan sounded frantic.

'I'm so sorry. And I was sorry to hear about your husband.' Trite, empty words, but you had to say something.

'Marcus? I don't give a damn about that. It's not important. But Lucian – he's my life. I'm his life.' She was crying now.

'I'm sure he'll be OK. Is there anything I can do?'

'Nothing. The police are searching. If anything has happened to him—'

'Try not to fret. I'm sure Celia—'

'Celia Hannaford is a lunatic. She doesn't know what she's doing. Her own sister said so. They could be anywhere. She could have done anything.'

'I don't think she'll harm him.'

'And what do you base that on? Lucian . . . he's not like other ten-year-olds. He needs special care. He'll be terrified by now. What can I do?'

She could do nothing.

They could do nothing.

It was in the lap of the gods.

*   *   *

Next, Elizabeth phoned Max. and told him what Rose Mulligan had said. 'So that's that,' she said.

'You think?'

'Well, she's not going to pay any more bills. So I guess it is.'

'Oh, come on!' Max sounded irritated. 'After all the work we've done on the case? We can't pull out now.'

'I don't want to.' She had to admit that.

'It's just getting interesting.'

'I know.'

'So what say we keep going another day or two anyway?'

She knew what he meant. Once you'd got the bit between your teeth . . .

'There's only one thing . . .'

'What's that?'

'I should warn you, there might be fireworks at the office this morning. I'm still at home, by the way.'

'Any particular reason?'

He told her about Ginger's car.

'You mean to say you might have caught up with her last night? Celia?'

'Sorry.'

Elizabeth used some strong language. She didn't do it often, but for once she had reason.

Max decided it might make the morning easier if he rang Ginger with yet another heartfelt apology. He dialled the office number.

'Shepard Agency.' She sounded snappy. In fact, he almost put the phone down again.

'Er . . . Ginger. This is Max.'

A silence you could have cut with a knife.

'Look – I'm really sorry about last night. Your car.'

The silence went on.

'I rang the garage. They'll have it ready by lunchtime. And I'll foot the bill.'

'Too bloody right, you will!'

'So there's not too much harm done . . .'

'Only my whole evening ruined, but I suppose we don't count that?'

'We weren't that late back.'

'Oh, no?'

'It's not my fault they didn't have anyone to give us a lift.' Nothing.

'Or that the cab didn't turn up.'

'If you hadn't borrowed my car, none of it would have happened.'

'I said I'm sorry.'

'Sorry's easy to say.'

'I mean it. I really mean it. Look—' He had this brilliant idea. It was now or never. 'As recompense, what would you say if I cooked you supper tomorrow night? My place. Eight o'clock.'

She said he had to be kidding. She turned him down flat. Max got quite aggressive himself at this point. In fact, they had a shouting match.

Nine thirty a.m. Elizabeth, still at the cottage, was on the phone. She was on it for quite some time . . . for an hour and ten minutes, in fact, with her feet propped up on the coffee table and the *Yellow Pages* open in front of her.

At the end of the session, she looked mighty pleased with herself.

D.I. Andy Cooper wasn't too pleased with his lot. He was interviewing Ashley Lewis, who had, two hours ago, been pulled in for questioning. They'd gone through all the formalities, the preliminary questions; but they weren't getting anywhere. Tough nut, Lewis. Pale blue eyes, the kind you couldn't see into. Jeans, blue t-shirt, stubble. And an annoyingly frank and alert expression. Deliberately jokey. Andy was getting irritated, which, of course, was just what Lewis had intended.

There was one thing in Andy's favour. The more he got annoyed, the better he worked.

'Not married yourself, sir?' he asked next.

'God forbid! No . . . I'm enjoying an extended adolescence. Highly recommended, Constable.'

'Detective Inspector, actually.'

'Blimey! I am impressed.' Lewis found a charming grin, but Andy sensed a terrific control under the cocky manner.

Let's hope he isn't half so clever as he thinks he is. 'And you weren't in town at seven forty-five p.m. on the night Miss Gregg was murdered?'

''Fraid not.'

'I should tell you that we have a witness who says you were. Who saw you driving your car into Alfred Buildings . . .'

Lewis shot a look at Andy. 'You're joking, of course?'

''Fraid not, sir.'

'Then your witness is lying.' Lewis's eyes were now possessed by – something. A coldness.

'You think so?'

'I know so. I was at home with my parents all that evening. They've already confirmed it.'

'I'm sure they have.'

'Do you know who my father is?'

'I expect you're about to tell me?'

'He's a solicitor. Very well respected. He's not in the habit of lying to the police.'

Which is more than one can say for his son, Andy thought. I don't like you, sunshine. I'm going to put you away if I possibly can. 'So how does he feel about having a son who was convicted of breaking and entering?'

'I thought that might come up.' Lewis's voice became perceptibly more vicious. 'Well, it's irrelevant . . . my so-called record. It was a long time ago and you'll have a job pinning anything else on me. Ever.'

'Is that so?'

'Yes, it is. I wasn't in town that night. Who told you I was?'

Andy paused. Then said, 'Someone who should know your face when she sees it.'

'She?'

'A Miss Fraser. Glory Fraser.'

Hard to describe the expression that now crossed Lewis's face. Discomposure, followed swiftly by speculation, aggression and finally insolence. 'Glory Fraser? That tart? You're not taking anything she says seriously?'

'I was actually. Yes.'

'OK.' Lewis was gathering his thoughts. 'You want more proof that I was at my parents' house at seven forty-five that evening? Ask our local bobby.'

'You have local bobbies up there?' That was a turn-up for the book.

'Actually, he happens to be a Chief Superintendent and a great friend of my father. Chief Superintendent Francis Powell. He lives just across the road from my parents and he called in for a chinwag that night at around seven thirty. Stayed for about half an hour. As a matter of fact, we all had a jar together. Satisfied?'

Alice Hannaford was washing the kitchen floor when the door-bell rang. Not that it was dirty. (Nothing in Alice's kitchen was ever dirty.) But if she didn't keep active, she'd go insane.

The waiting was unbearable.

But it was almost at an end.

She ran down the stairs wiping her hands on her apron. 'Celia?' she said, flinging open the door.

It wasn't Celia. It was a young policewoman come to tell her they had found her sister's car. It had hit a telegraph pole in a farm lane in the wilds of Gloucestershire. Yes, they were very much afraid that Celia was dead.

The boy? Lucian? No sign of him as yet.

Chapter Forty-Five

Ashley Lewis walked at considerable speed out of the police station. He looked neither right nor left until he reached the corner of Richmond Parade. There, he allowed himself to stop for a moment and draw breath . . . to get himself back together. It was a long time since he'd been so angry. Shaking with anger. And all because of Glory bloody Fraser. She was not the kind of girl Ashley liked to be bested by. Bloody half-caste. Black whore.

Ashley's politics were about as right as you can get.

Well, he'd show her how to play tricks on him. She'd wish she was dead by the time he'd finished with her.

Elizabeth was making another mysterious phone call, this time to a number she had written down in her notebook.

'Miss Shand? This is Elizabeth Blair. I wonder if we could meet? Well, anywhere you like really. Suggest somewhere. What's it about? I'd rather not discuss that on the phone, if you don't mind. Five o'clock at Cheyneys? Yes, that'll do splendidly. I'll see you later, then. Thanks for being so cooperative.'

Could the girl do anything else, under the circumstances? You have to go with the tide in her situation. Protect yourself (and others) as best as you can. And if the tide turns against you, why, to be frank, there's nothing much you can do except paddle like hell. And pray.

The paddling was probably more use.

And more interesting to watch, as an impartial observer.

Love is not a sensible emotion, Elizabeth reflected. It gets you into deep waters. Little Immy knew that now, but would she learn from it? Very few of us do, more's the pity.

By lunchtime that day, Max had had enough. He was thinking of getting right out of it; there was only so much a man could take. He still felt bad about Ginger's car. He'd apologised on the hour, every hour, practically, but she still wouldn't speak to him. Which was a relief, actually, after the initial onslaught. Boy, could she take a man apart! It's all true, he thought. That stuff about redheads and temper.

Elizabeth had given him a pasting, too, which was hardly fair, because he hadn't put the sodding diesel in on purpose. Everybody made mistakes, didn't they?

At least Andy was relatively normal. He'd called at noon to say they'd had to let Lewis go. 'He's got another watertight alibi for the night of Finney's murder. He was seeing some interior design chap about getting the bar done out.'

'His name wasn't Rupert, by any chance?'

'Sorry?'

'Nothing. Stupid joke.' Ginger wasn't laughing. She would never laugh again, by the look of her. Her mouth was set tight as she hammered away at the keyboard. 'Any news of the kid? Lucian?'

'Nothing.'

That was the worst thing of all. Not the car. Not the dirty looks he was getting from the office staff. (And he vindictively included Elizabeth in that category.) It was the guilt about Lucian. I could have got to him. Should have got to him. Would have done if Ginger hadn't yelled at me. So it's as much her fault as mine if anything's happened to him.

Which it probably had, or else they'd have found him by now. He tapped his pencil on the desk and said, fairly abruptly, 'The Mold report. Why hasn't it been sent off?'

Ginger dragged back her hair from her face, looked at him as if he was something the cat had brought in and answered in that light, crisp voice of hers, 'Because you didn't complete it. That's why.'

She always had the last word, no matter what.

The work on the B 426 was supposed to have been finished at the end of September. But as is often the case, it had dragged on. Not enough money; insufficient labour; the wrong kind of weather; arguments between the gas board and the water company about who was to get in there first. Be that as it may, the workmen's hut was still there at the side of the road in the middle of October.

It seemed to be a fixture.

'Bloody eyesore!' remarked Farmer Weedon, standing in the middle of the road and fixing it with his gloomy gaze. He stood there with both hands clasped on his walking stick. 'I've a good mind to ring up about it. Or else shift it with the tractor.'

It was as well that he avoided the latter action, for at that moment, there came a movement from inside the red-and-white plastic flap.

'What the devil——?' Jacob Weedon exclaimed. Someone was coming out of the thing. A boy with scruffy hair and a dazed look.

'My name's Lucian,' the boy said. 'I think I've been asleep.'

Chapter Forty-Six

Almost a week after Lucian was found, Elizabeth said to Richard Timms, 'He says Celia stopped at a crossroads. Told him to get out of the car.'

'Thank God.' The Reverend Timms stood by the church door in a characteristic pose. Head slightly bent, hands clasped around the prayer books, like a figure out of some Victorian woodcut. Two p.m. The spire of St Bartholomew's against a windy blue sky. The bell tolling. The church already full for Miss Hannaford's funeral. 'She was very well known,' Richard Timms said. 'Very well liked. She wasn't always ill, you know. Not so very ill.'

'There's something I have to say.' Elizabeth's heart moved uncomfortably. She stood holding on to the nosegay she had brought from her garden. 'If we . . . If I hassled her . . . made life more difficult for her, then I'm sorry. I'd hate to have that on my conscience. But I honestly don't think—'

'Neither do I. When I rang you the other day . . . Well, it was precipitate. You've always been the soul of tact.'

She'd been called some things.

'My turn to apologise.' He touched her arm in a gesture of understanding. If she'd had any sins, they were absolved.

Nice man. Man of God.

After that, she went through the funeral with less of a sense of strain. Which was more than could be said for poor Alice Hannaford, who sat, grief flooding out of her, in the front pew next to the coffin.

Somebody else played the organ, but without Celia's touch. Johann Sebastian Bach. The salve of music, Elizabeth thought. Music in your heart and your brain and your stomach. Pushing the triggers that can reduce the most hardened to tears.

Poor Celia. Elizabeth's mind went back to the Linley lecture. Unfolding tragedies there too. Thomas junior's death had merely been the first act in that family's distressing decline. Young Samuel, the talented oboist, caught a fever and died on board ship, while Maria and Mary succumbed to consumption not many years after. And Elizabeth, the dazzling Elizabeth, was to fare no better. Her passionate marriage to Sheridan the playwright fell apart in mutual infidelities and she died shortly after giving birth to a daughter by Lord Edward Fitzgerald, the future 1798 Rebellion leader. Causing Sheridan enormous guilt and grief.

A cold wind found its way into the nave as the coffin was carried out.

The wind bloweth where it listeth. Elizabeth sat in contemplation. Celia had gone. God rest her soul.

Jan Finney said, 'He's OK. He's fine.' She looked a different woman. Her face half-euphoric, half-relieved.

'Thank goodness.' Elizabeth said, 'Mrs Finney . . . I'm sorry to bother you again, but do you mind if I ask you something? To your knowledge, did your husband have any appointments on the night he died?'

'What?'

'Did he have any appointments? Only I was thinking about the person who arranged to meet him at the shop the night Kat was murdered—'

'I'm sorry.' Jan picked up Lucian's sweater, shook it out and folded it into a neat square bundle. 'I can't be bothered with that now. It's over. I'm starting a new life. We're starting a new life . . . my son and I.'

Was it all over? Elizabeth wondered.

She knew evasion when it came sniffing round her heels. There was something Mrs Finney was hiding, even now.

I'd give anything to know what it is.

The old dear sat on the edge of her bumpy bed, looking through the window at the street below and wondered why Max kept going on about an accident that had happened twelve years ago. How on earth did he think she could remember that far back? Things just melted away these days. Going, going, gone . . .

Blanche Muir (for that was her name) brought her gaze back from the window and looked Max straight in the eye. 'I didn't see anything. I told them that at the time. All I heard was the bang. I was doing my tapestry and I cursed, because I knew I'd have to go and look and that would throw me all out.'

'So you were wearing your reading glasses?'

'For the tapestry. Yes.' She explained it as to a simpleton. 'They magnify. You know. Make things a lot bigger. I couldn't see clearly out of the window with them, but there wasn't much to see anyway. Who sent you on this lark, anyway? You're not the police?'

'No. I'm a private detective.'

'I'll tell you something. It was a very big relief when the police came that night. Then I could forget all about it. Somebody else would see to it. I didn't have to bother.'

'How long before they came?' Max asked. 'After the accident, I mean?'

'Oh, ages, dear. I had time to go and fill my hot-water bottle and turn the bed down. Of course, I was less crippled then. But even so, it must have been . . . well fifteen minutes.'

'That long?'

'Easily.'

'Was there any activity out there between the time you heard the bang and the police arriving?'

'Not much. There wasn't anybody around really. This is a very quiet area. Not like some.'

'So who called the police?'

'I don't know, dear. Not me. I didn't have the phone back then. I just thought . . . well, someone else must have done it.'

'Like who?'

'Like one of the neighbours, I suppose. Or the young man himself.'

'Doubt if he could move. He had a broken leg.'

'Maybe he had one of these mobile things.'

Maybe he did, Max thought. Must check who made the call to the police.

'Can I get you a cup of tea?'

'No, ta.' Max saw the walking frame and the pot of cold tea and cold toast crusts on the tray beside the bed. Been there since breakfast, by the look of it. 'Let me get you one,' he said.

'What's the time?'

Max looked at his watch. 'Four thirty.'

'A little bit early, but I'll take you up on your kind offer. Not supposed to let strange men wander round, but you look harmless. Milk and lots of sugar. Watch yourself with the kettle. The handle's loose.'

An hour later, Elizabeth and Max were facing Glory Fraser in the front room of the house in Highland Road. Naomi Tilbert had gone off to visit a sick neighbour. Her grand-daughter had seen to that. Elizabeth placed the tips of her fingers together and gazed silently at Glory. A girl with gifts in plenty; a girl who deliberately put out a false image of herself as dipsy extrovert; but who was very determined, very focused deep inside.

As bright as Glory.

Yes, Glory had a first-class brain, was sharper than them all. Efficient. Always was. Had to be. What was more important, she was a hugely strong character. Her stare said, come and have a go if you think you're hard enough. And as Naomi Tilbert had said, Glory paid everybody back sooner or later.

Elizabeth finally broke her silence. 'I expect you're wondering why we're here.'

'I was actually.'

Liar. Elizabeth said, 'It's very simple. I want to know why you invented this story about Ashley Lewis. You did invent it, didn't you? You wanted the police to arrest him.'

Chapter Forty-Seven

Glory seemed to shiver. Her eyes were fixed on her long, slim ankles. 'I never wanted anything more in my whole life,' she said at last.

'You had a score to settle?'

Silence.

'I have to warn you. I'll stay here until I get the full story. Your grandmother—'

'Leave my grandmother out of this!' But Glory knew when she was defeated. 'If I tell the truth, will you leave us alone? Will you promise it won't get back to Gran?'

Elizabeth thought she could do that.

'OK. So I did want Ashley Lewis to suffer.'

'Why is that?'

Slowly her golden, almond-shaped eyes came up to meet Elizabeth's. A dark pool of a look. Dark depths. 'Because he raped me. That's why.'

Elizabeth looked startled. What have we dived into here? Some things you expect and others you don't. But she was too old a hand to show any great reaction. 'When was this?'

'On my twentieth birthday. After we'd been clubbing.'

'You went clubbing with him?'

'No. We were in a group. He offered me a lift home. I didn't like him much, but I saw no reason to be afraid of him. Not then.' A shaky pause. 'He said he was going my way and that he'd drop me off. But instead of driving me home, he drove us out of town on the Frome road. I told him it was the wrong way. I tried to get him to stop . . . grabbed the wheel a couple of times, but he just laughed. I think he'd planned it all along.'

The shiver had moved up to her fingers. It was all over her now. Elizabeth said, 'Take it slowly. There's plenty of time. Try not to upset yourself.'

Glory hadn't heard.

'The world went cloudy grey that day. It's been like that ever since. He made me feel different inside. He's dirty,' she whispered. 'He stopped the car in a country lane and he dragged me out and into the back seat and then he raped me. Plenty of juice, that's what I remember him saying . . . Johnny Mulligan's precious friend. Over and over . . . Black girls got plenty of juice. They're a right pair. Johnny was just stupid and weak, but him — Ashley Lewis — he's vicious. He's the worst kind. Afterwards, you know he acted like it never happened. I was hysterical . . . crying my eyes out, but he didn't give a shit. Get your clothes on, he said. I'll take you home. You'd better not tell anybody. I'll just say you started it. You asked for it. You're a dirty black whore.'

Elizabeth reached for the girl's hand. It was as cold as ice. 'You didn't report the offence?'

'What do you think? He's a solicitor's son. They'd have made out I was lying. He told me he'd lie about it if I said anything.' The shivering was now turning itself into retching sobs. 'I hate him. I hate him . . . I can't tell you how much.'

'So you set him up.'

After a few minutes, the weeping came to an end. A shivering sigh. 'Why not? It was my revenge. It made me feel good. It came to me in a blinding flash when he . . .' she waved a hand in Max's direction, '. . . was questioning me. Even if that bastard denied it, I knew the police would take him in for questioning. That was some kind of revenge. When they came to check my story, I told them he'd once attacked Kat. I pretended she'd told me about it.

I invented all the detail and she wasn't around to deny it. Believe you me, I landed him in a lot of trouble. Let him have a taste of fear and shame, I thought.'

'You aren't afraid he'll . . .'

'Attack me again? He wouldn't dare. The police are watching him. And his name is plastered all over the papers. That won't please his mummy and daddy.' Glory is no longer smart and sassy. She sits there like a nervy teenager. She nips at the side of one small, white nail with her teeth. 'Since the rape, I feel so alone inside. You know? Like there's this great hollow. Like I'm an outsider and nobody can do a damned thing about it. It's a prison . . . racism. I can't wait to step outside. When I'm a doctor . . . it'll be different then. They'll have to respect you. Dr Fraser.'

She had set the sign up in front of her. It was there to keep her going.

'But there are good people,' Max said. 'More of them than the others.'

'I know that. With my head. The Makepeaces. Anna paid for my abortion.'

'Abortion?'

'Oh, yes. He got me pregnant, that bastard. I couldn't tell Gran. How could I? She was so proud of me. I wasn't going to let anybody or anything spoil it for her. She's had a hard life. Harder than you'll ever know.' Glory examined the chewed nail. 'I didn't know what to do. I was worried sick. So worried that I broke down at work one day and Anna looked after me. She's great. He doesn't really deserve her.'

'Aidan?'

'I can't tell you any more. I just can't.'

'You don't need to. I know he had an affair with Kat . . .'

Silence.

'Among others . . . I can guess that much.'

Glory's face was pale and stony now.

'OK. I don't expect you to spill the beans on him. Tell me something. Is he paying your university fees?'

A pleading silence this time.

So he was. In return for what?

'OK. Just tell me one more thing and then we'll leave you alone. Marcus Finney . . . Did he know you'd had an abortion?'

Her face gave her away.

'So how did he find out?'

'I don't know. He just came up to me one day in the health centre and started dropping hints.'

'And the hints turned into threats?'

'Yes. He threatened to tell my Gran. He knew my whole life history. God knows how.'

'He was blackmailing you?'

'Not money. I didn't have any.' Shame and disgust written all over her face. There was worse to come. A hot flush was spreading over her.

'He wanted sex?'

'He was disgusting. A dirty old man. But I had no choice.'

On demand. Elizabeth thought, God, what squalor there is when you look under the stones. 'OK. It'll go no further. He's dead and gone now.'

'I didn't kill him.'

No, I don't think you did.

'But I'm glad he's dead. I hope he rots in hell.'

Secrets tumbling out of cupboards all over the shop. Many small lies to make a truth, Elizabeth thought. Track down the lies, and why they're told, and eventually you'll get to the centre of things.

Max looked shell-shocked as they walked back to the car. 'Sicko!' he said.

'Lewis or Finney?'

'Both.'

She had to agree with him. She unlocked the Citroën and got in. They sat there in silence for a moment or two, looking south over the river, still harnessed to what they had heard in Naomi

Tilbert's front room. Elizabeth couldn't bring herself to switch on the engine. Then, no good brooding, she thought. That way lies depression. 'Tell you what,' she said. 'Why don't you throw that little supper party tonight. The world needs lightening. I'll bring a couple of bottles of wine. Ginger can bring some dips. We'll have a laugh or two.'

'Don't feel like laughing.' The boy was surprisingly tender at heart, though like most men, he'd die rather than admit the fact. 'Anyway, Ginger's not speaking to me.'

'I'll fix Ginger. It's only a car.'

'It is, isn't it.' Max looked brighter. 'She won't come, though.'

She will, Elizabeth thought, if I have anything to do with it. Can't stand an atmosphere. Never could.

She turned the key in the ignition.

Chapter Forty-Eight

———⋙◦◆◦⋘———

Eight thirty p.m. Elizabeth stood on the steps of Aidan Makepeace's seriously sumptuous four-storey town house in St James's Place. A Palladian gem, with central Corinthian pillars, surmounted by a plain pediment. Shining wet city streets set it off to perfection.

She stood for some moments perfectly still, arms folded, looking up at the graceful, mannerly skylight. At the handsome doorway and the iron railings that hedged it round on either side. There were lighted windows on the first floor, but the curtains were three-quarters drawn. Elizabeth could just glimpse a glass case filled with china (and a bust on top). An unnaturally bright chandelier throwing out sparkles, but there was no visible sign of any occupants.

At last, she rang the bell.

The evening was decidedly cool and rain was falling again. Its pitter patter on the steps, the damp wind, the dank air gave a distinctly melancholy feel to the evening. Money aside, what had they got, the Makepeaces? Compared, say, to your average, ordinary couple? Consider now. A big, empty house. A marriage which must have come close, more than once, to falling off the edge. Successful careers, both of them. Now you can't deny that. Yes, but at what a cost. And to what end?

Careers quite often fill a gap . . .

In this case, I imagine, a damned great chasm.

The door opened. Anna Makepeace stood there. She pushed her hands into the pockets of her woollen jacket. Unsmiling, the grey eyes steady, enquiring.

Elizabeth said, 'I asked at the hotel. They said you'd gone home.'

'Is it urgent?' Mrs Makepeace said, eyebrows raised. Expert at repelling invasions.

'Rose Mulligan might think so.'

'Rose?'

'Her son's on a murder charge, remember?'

'I'm not likely to forget. I put up his bail . . . if you remember.'

Touché. 'You must have read my thoughts. I was wondering on my way over here if you would do it again, knowing what you know now?'

'I'm sorry. I've done my best to help Rose, but beyond that, her family problems have nothing to do with me.'

'No?'

'No. Now if you'll excuse me . . .' She was about to shut the door when Elizabeth drew something out of her bag. A green folder.

'You're a busy lady. Now that's a great pity. You see, I thought you might be interested in taking a look at this.'

Anna Makepeace paused. 'What is it?'

'It's a report that was given to me by Ed Harper of Harper's Bizarre . . . brilliant name, don't you think? In case you've forgotten, he's a private detective you've been employing for the last five years.'

That got through her armour. She looked at Elizabeth quickly, looked away. 'You'd better come in.'

The hall was dimly lit; a warm glow under the imposing staircase came from a blue porcelain lamp. A brisk walk down to the second door on the right led them into what seemed to be a breakfast room hung with eighteenth-century coloured prints of racehorses. On the table by the window, an exquisite arrangement of dahlias and chrysanthemums. Yellow wallpaper and two large Regency bookcases.

'You'd better sit down.'

Elizabeth said she would prefer to stand.

'As you wish.' Anna took a chair herself, the one over by the fireplace, and sat with her hands lightly clasped around her knee. 'So . . . how did you find out about Ed Harper?'

'I'll tell you something. In this game, you spend your whole life asking questions. Those photographs I showed you . . . The ones of your husband and Kat Gregg. I was thinking about them one night and I suddenly asked myself who took them. I also asked myself what I would do if I found myself in your position. If I suspected my husband was having an affair. And the answer came to me. I'd want proof. I'd use a private detective. So, I made a list of all the detective agencies in Bath – our own excluded, of course – and I rang each of them in turn.'

'I congratulate you. You're a clever woman.'

'You're pretty clever yourself, Mrs Makepeace. You didn't panic when you found out that your husband was a serial adulterer. He is, isn't he?' She dropped the file on the table. 'Quite a list Ed got to compile in five years. You have my commiserations.'

She smiled a little sadly. 'Oh, I'm used to it by now. It doesn't upset me any more. Well, not so much.'

'You just decided that you'd like to be one step ahead of him?'

'I need to know what's going on.' A long sigh. 'It's like looking after a new-born babe. He doesn't realise what trouble these women could lead him into.'

'You're still in love with him, I presume?'

'I'm not in love with him. That went out of the window years ago. But I love him.' Defiance in Anna's voice now. 'We've been together a long time and there's a loyalty. Yes, I wanted to protect him.'

Ain't love heavy? Heavy as lead sometimes.

Elizabeth put her head a little on one side and said, 'So let's move on. You employed Ed Harper. I guess what I'd like to know next is why, on the Monday morning after Kat Gregg was killed, you suddenly told him you would no longer require his services?'

The answer came in a flash. 'That's obvious. Kat would no longer be a problem to my husband.'

Elizabeth made her next statement very carefully. 'But your husband's little fling with Miss Gregg finished eighteen months ago. It's in the file.'

Across town, Ginger was standing in Max's chaotic (very chaotic) kitchen, saying, 'What's it meant to be?'

'Buttered Kedgeree.'

'Chargrilled?'

'No.'

'I can't see any fish.'

'It's mixed in. Have a taste.'

Ginger dipped a spoon into the blackened mess (no other words for it) and tasted. Then rushed to the sink.

'What's wrong?'

'Hot!' She seemed to be choking.

'That'll be the curry powder.' Max said happily, 'I got the hottest there was and doubled it up to make quite sure.'

'Quite sure you killed somebody?' Ginger by this time had downed two glasses of water.

'Perhaps I left it on the heat a bit too long. It said fifty minutes covered with a folded tea towel.'

She gave him a look. 'Where's the recipe?'

He gave her the soggy-looking cookery book he'd borrowed from the girl in the flat above.

'*Five* minutes . . . you idiot.'

'I'm sure it said fifty. Hang on a minute—' He took the book from her and scraped something from the relevant page. 'You're right. It wasn't a zero. It was a blob of . . .' He wasn't sure what.

'Open the second bottle of wine,' Ginger said. 'Quick. I need a drink.'

'You sure?'

'I'm sure.' Her throat was burning like mad.

'Only we'd better leave some for Betsey. She said she'd be here by eight thirty.'

'It's ten to nine. She won't mind. We can always go out to the off-licence. She gave me a right rollicking, you know, at tea-time.' A resigned look. 'Of course, you're her blue-eyed boy.'

Max went to get the corkscrew. Good old Betsey, he thought. Helps pay the bills, causes trouble in all the right places, has her blinding moments. I'll drink a toast to her any day.

A flush of anger now on Anna's fine-featured face. 'Harper had no right to give you that. It's my property.'

'Really?'

'Give it to me.'

'I don't think so.'

'Let me . . . have it.' Anna moved suddenly, snatched up the file from the coffee table. Opened it, was dumbfounded to find that it contained only empty sheets of paper.

'I must apologise for that little deception. You don't think I'd risk losing vital evidence? The real notes are in a safe in my office. Now, might I suggest you find a truthful answer to my question. Why did you suddenly give poor Ed the push? I'd guess it was because you didn't want him sniffing into your husband's business any more. Because you were scared of what he'd unearth. Scared he'd find out that your husband had committed a murder . . .'

'No!'

'Perhaps it was for the same reason that you had Rose call us off the case last week. You thought we were getting too close to the truth for comfort. By the way, I called in on Rose on my way here this evening. It wasn't too difficult to get her to talk. She was very drunk. And she happens to love her son dearly. As you love yours.'

Anna began to twist the rings on her fingers.

'Rose is a very nice woman, but an alcoholic. Unpredictable. She's been loyal to you up till now, but if she had to choose between you and Johnny . . . well, I have to say there's really no contest.'

'Rose has worked for me for twenty-five years. She'd never—'

'Never tell on you? I wouldn't bet on it. As a matter of fact, she blurted out some very interesting things while I was there today. I gather you supplied her with a case of good whisky and told her the Shepard Agency was pretty useless. You'd find her someone better to investigate her case. I think I rather object to that.' Elizabeth went on, 'And I have to say, the whisky may not have been such a brilliant idea. Alcoholics tend to rabbit on, you know. Rose also came out with a very interesting story about finding a note in this house when she was cleaning. A note Finney sent your husband . . .'

'A note? Saying what?' Anna appeared to be very cool.

'I think you know, Mrs Makepeace. A note asking for money or else Finney would tell the police your husband lied to them about the car accident your son, Oliver, was involved in three years ago. Lied to protect his only surviving son's career in the Met . . .'

Anna did not answer, but she shot Elizabeth a look of pure fear.

'I could go to the police right now. I have enough evidence. It would make a compelling story.'

'All right.' The other woman looked back at her with a mixture of pain and defiance. 'Finney was blackmailing my husband. It's true. And it was all my fault.'

'Your fault?'

'Yes.' She spoke the word with a kind of despair. 'I provided that bastard with the information. Unwittingly, you understand. I'd have cut my tongue out rather than tell him. But he overheard me talking to his wife. Jan and I . . . well, we were friends from years back and we were both carrying heavy loads. In my case, it was Aidan and his women. They've always been around. Always will be. He gets a kick out of winning court cases and an even bigger kick out of the women who line up to fall into bed with him. For years I suffered in silence. I'd find out about some affair or other, he'd swear it would never happen again. But it always did. The only difference was that I got older and they got younger. And then Jan came back here to live. We'd always confided in each other at school and when we found each other again . . . I can't tell you what it was like to have a friend to talk to.'

Elizabeth was beginning to see the light.

'I don't make friends easily, Mrs Blair. Not real friends. It gets harder as you get older. And work takes up so much of my time. But when Jan came back to Bath, well, we sort of fell on each other. We started to meet regularly . . .'

'To unload?'

'It was such a relief. She would talk about Lucian. How much she loves him . . . how much Marcus hated him. She told me about the physical abuse. Well, I'd guessed anyway. There was this look in her eyes when he was around. Like a dog that's afraid of its master . . .'

Elizabeth knew now what was coming, but she did not attempt to comment. She merely waited.

'And I told her about the hell of losing Rory . . .' She paused for a moment, shook her head and then went on, 'And about Oliver's accident. I wish to God I hadn't. It must have been one night last January or February. Jan said come to supper. Marcus was away on a buying trip or else she would never have dared invite me. Anyway, to cut a long story short, the sale he was going to was cancelled. He came back early. The taxi dropped him off at the end of the road and he came in by the back way. We didn't hear him. We were having a right old heart to heart. Pouring it all out. God knows how long he was out there in the hall, listening . . .'

'That's how he found out your husband lied to the police?'

'Yes.'

Elizabeth leant forward in her chair to ask another question. 'Glory Fraser. She had an abortion . . .'

'Yes.'

'Which you paid for?'

'Yes.' Puzzlement.

'Could Finney have learned about it from eavesdropping on your conversation that night?'

She stared hard at Elizabeth from across the room.

'Did you mention it to Jan that night?'

'I . . . may have done.' Mrs Makepeace searched her memory. 'Yes, I think I did, as a matter of fact. I was telling Jan about Aidan's affairs. How difficult it was . . . how jealous you become. How you suspect any female he even looks at. Yes, I remember telling her how I'd found Glory sobbing her heart out in the hotel office. She was pregnant. And I asked her — this is awful — I actually asked her if Aidan was the father. I knew by her face that I'd made the most terrible gaffe. No, of course not, she said. It turned out that she'd been raped.' A look of horror now crossed Anna's face. 'He didn't . . . He wasn't . . .'

'Blackmailing Glory, too. I'm afraid so.'

'But — she's got no money . . .'

'There are other methods of payment.'

'You don't mean—?'

'I'm afraid so. She didn't want her grandmother to know about the rape and the abortion.'

Anna was very pale. 'Then he deserved to die.'

'Maybe so.'

'But my husband didn't kill him.'

'Naturally you would say so.'

The silence of the room was broken by a movement behind them. Aidan Makepeace stood in the doorway. 'All right, darling. I'll take over now . . .'

Chapter Forty-Nine

Makepeace had been doing some eavesdropping of his own. He looked weary and strained. The lines on his face seemed to have deepened. He's as nervous as hell, Elizabeth thought, underneath that oh-so-mellifluous voice.

He said, 'I knew when I first saw you that you were going to be a nuisance.'

'I'll take that as a compliment, shall I?'

'If you like.' He moved further into the room. 'Is the heating on?' he asked his wife.

'Yes.'

'Must be me then. The house feels cold.' He turned the full force of his gaze on Elizabeth. 'So . . . you know all about us? Or at least, you think you do.'

'I know a great deal. Yes.'

'I wonder . . .' He said suddenly, 'It's never as cut and dried as all that. Family life . . .'

'I'm aware of that. I've got a family of my own.'

'You have?' He seemed to be speculating, one hand on his chin. Making it up as he went along? 'Well, then . . .' He seemed to have made up his mind about something. 'Come with me,' he said suddenly. 'Upstairs.'

He must have noticed her expression. He said almost mockingly, 'It's all right. Your virtue's quite safe.'

'It is?' She actually felt a moment of disappointment.

'I want to show you something.'

'Aidan—'

'It's all right, Anna. You can trust me. On this, at least.'

Aidan Makepeace led Elizabeth up the silent staircase and up yet another flight. 'This floor belonged to the boys,' he told her. It still did, by the look of things. The rooms were more homespun, shabbier than the three storeys underneath. The childhood years had stayed. They lurked in the creaky varnished floorboards, the bookshelves still packed tight with *Blue Peter* and *Beano* annuals, the cricket bats propped against low, cushioned windowsills. In Action Men and jigsaw puzzles and board games still lying in piles on the chest of drawers in the long, atticky room which he now led her into.

He patted the chest with a loving hand. 'This once graced my own nursery bedroom. Long ago. Too long.'

Next they moved on to a long, polished table. 'We used to sit round this playing Monopoly together. The four of us. Rory always finished up getting mad because he was losing and Oliver invariably pointed out that it was only a game and it didn't really matter. Character is born, not made. That's what my father used to say. And he's right. How else can you explain the enormous differences between our two boys? They were brought up in exactly the same fashion. Rory was by far the brightest academically. Too bright, perhaps, for his own good. Flamboyant, restlessly inventive, the more difficult of the two. Yet less capable of coping with the practicalities of everyday life.

'The thing he had hated most was being bored. And so many things seemed to bore him. You talked about asking yourself questions. Yes, I was listening in the hall. Well, I've asked myself question after question about why Rory should have sought escape in drugs. Developed a heroin addiction . . .' Aidan walked over to the window and stared out at the cars parked three storeys below. 'It was a waste of a young and gifted life.'

Elizabeth for once said nothing. She felt rather helpless, to tell the truth.

'Every time I come up here now, I see Rory's face. I had to identify him at the morgue, you know. It was the worst night of my entire life. The worst year.' He turned now to face her. 'And I ask myself another question. How would we have got through that dreadful time without Oliver? The solid, ever-hopeful, always helpful Oliver . . . There was one winter afternoon after Rory's death, when the nightmare seemed to blow itself into enormous dimensions inside my head. We were in this room. I'll never forget it. And Oliver, in his own fashion, brought it all simply and stolidly back down to earth. He was standing just about where you are. I'd broken down and he came and put his arms around me, but he refused to cry any more with me. "Enough, Dad," he said. "No more giving in to it. Because if you do . . . well, that's like saying Rory never lived. What you've got to do – what we've all got to do – is just keep on batting." ' Aidan's bright blue eyes were filled with tears. 'Keep on batting. Such tender, serious advice. God, I love that kid. He saved my life.'

'So you decided to save his?' Elizabeth moved towards him. There wasn't a sound of any kind in the house. You were curiously cut off from the world outside. Impossible to tell you were in the centre of the city. She kept her gaze on Aidan. What was it they said of him? He has this wonderful facility to talk to the jury as if he's one of them. No one ever forgets him. They were right. She never would.

'Yes. Now I'm going to save his. Because Oliver's career is his life, which is why I made that stupidly impulsive decision three years ago on a wet night in December.'

'You perverted the course of justice in order to protect your son from a drink-driving charge that would most certainly have resulted in him losing his job?'

'I knew it was stupid almost as soon as I'd made it. It was a moment of madness.'

'You claimed that you were behind the wheel of your son's car when he was returning from a friend's Christmas party. A practising barrister, you practised deception against the public justice. Your son was three times over the drink-drive limit—'

'It was the anniversary of his brother's death. You do know that? Rory had been found dead a year earlier to the day. That was why Oliver was so drunk.'

'Nevertheless, the boy wasn't fit to be behind the wheel.'

'He was just two streets away from home – from this house – when he hit a parked car. When he got out and was walking around the damaged vehicle to assess the damage, he was spotted by a constable in a passing police car, breathalysed and arrested.'

'But after an emotional phone call from the station, you spoke to the officer in charge and told him that you'd actually been driving the car.' Elizabeth had done her homework. 'That you'd left Oliver there in the road with the car while you went home to telephone the police. Only they got there first. It was a beautifully improvised lie, which you got away with at the time.'

Makepeace said, 'It was a foul night and there were no witnesses, either outside the house where the party had been held, or at the scene of the accident. Don't look at me like that. I've regretted it hundreds of times since, not least in these last interminable weeks. But it's done and can't be undone. I love my son desperately and he's a damned good police officer and nobody – certainly not you, Mrs Blair – is going to bring Oliver's life (or mine for that matter) crashing to the ground. Finney didn't manage that and neither will you.'

'No?' Elizabeth could charm, too, when she chose. Could sound sunny, cheery while opening coffins. Or cupboards with skeletons in them. 'So how would it be if I held the floor for a few moments? You've had your turn. Now it's mine. I'd like to talk about the murder of your friend, Kat Gregg.'

She moved away from the table and as she did so, saw the

force of emotion that hit him right between the eyes; the pain simmering just under the surface of that handsome face. There was a heavy silence, until he forced his beautifully controlled expression back.

'A mistake, of course. You were aiming at Marcus Finney.'

'Prove it. You don't have any evidence, I imagine?'

'I can put a case, though. You couldn't take any more of Finney's threats. Not to mention the fact that he was bleeding you dry financially. And so you planned to kill him, or have him killed. Unfortunately, your friend, Kat, got in the way of the bullets.'

Silence again. He didn't like the question, she could see that in his face. Not too many people turned the tables on Aidan Makepeace. It seemed to surprise him. He looked at her with quick calculation and walked over to the window. Parted the curtains and stood looking out for a second or two.

Elizabeth continued with her story. 'Kat Gregg is dead. The mistake has been made and can't be unmade. Once the first panic is over, you realise that the luck is still on your side. The police pick up Johnny Mulligan. He has a motive. Boy, does he have a motive! They even found his watch lying by the body. I mean, what more could you want?'

Elizabeth turned to face him head on. 'So let's consider the second murder. You get it right this time. Somehow you arrange to meet Finney down by the canal. Did you tell him you wanted a pow-wow? That he was demanding too much from you? That you could no longer afford to finance his very plush little antiques shop? Whatever. The plan works this time. He finishes up at the bottom of the Kennet and Avon. And you're safe at last.'

His calm in the face of her exposition was quite impressive.

'You're remarkably silent for a man of your profession.'

'Sometimes pays, I find. Don't admit anything unless you have to. So how are you going to prove all this . . . rubbish? I have a whole cast of witnesses who will swear I was at the hotel the night Kat died. All night. With my wife. And in London when Finney was shot.'

'You could have used a contract killer. I imagine you come across the odd dodgy character in your line of business.'

'I didn't use a contract killer. I had nothing to do with those murders.'

Elizabeth now played her trump card. 'Actually, I believe you. But your mistress, now. The woman you've been carrying on with for the last twelve months. That's quite another matter.'

'My mistress?'

'Louise Shand. It's all in the file downstairs . . .'

'Chuck it out,' Ginger said.

'My culin . . . culinerary experiment?'

'Your yuck.' She didn't mince her words, even when they were slurred. 'We'll phone for a takeaway. When Elizabeth gets here.'

'Where the hell is she?' Max reached rather wildly for the bottle and almost fell off the stool. 'More wine?' he said.

'Yes, please,' said Ginger. Wonderful idea . . .

After that, they stopped talking. Not quite so capable of it as an hour before. Sat there just drinking really. And thinking. Like her, Max told himself. Why? Various things. Hardly any make-up. Not obvious, like Jess was. A certain unconvention-ality. Good job I don't have to say that. Green shirt thing. White skin, blobbed with freckles. Sleepy-looking. Wouldn't mind kissing her on the nose. Careful. Don't go milking the golden egg . . .

Something wrong with that, but he was too pissed to work out what.

He bought the old dear a new kettle, Ginger mused. Like that. Like kind men. A lot of awful blokes in the world . . . like my ex. Dying for a pee. Can't get off this stool. He's taller than Glyn. More fun. More sparks. Dazzling blue eyes. That kedgeree thing! He's little-boy appealing, Bloody hell, that's pathetic.

It's the booze. Back to normal tomorrow . . .

Elizabeth looked at Aidan Makepeace and he looked right back. She thought: that wiped the arrogance off your face. So.

A long pause. Then, 'Who told you about Louise?' He answered his own question. 'Silly me. My wife has been employing a private detective.'

'And, of course, Glory knew, though she kept your secret quite admirably. Glory's a smart girl. How did she find out? Did she spot the pair of you?'

'I sent Louise some roses. The stupid flower shop got in a muddle and sent the account to the hotel instead of my office. Glory was a good girl. Very discreet. She slipped it to me before my wife saw it.'

'And you rewarded her discretion?'

'I help her with her tuition fees. Anything wrong with that?'

'Nothing at all.'

'The relationship is entirely platonic.'

'Makes a change.'

'You think you're very clever, I suppose?'

'I pride myself on doing a good job. Yes.'

He was silent, considering. 'So how much do you want?'

'Want?'

'To keep quiet about all this.'

'I don't want anything.'

'Oh, come on! Everyone has a price.'

'Not me, I'm afraid.'

'No?'

'No.'

'You think I'm going to let you walk out of here and ruin my son's life?'

So what was he going to do about it? Elizabeth walked

steadily across to the window, seeing the fine rain drifting down over the rooftops, the scattered drops on the panes. It was a mournful night. Perfectly dismal.

'I'm sorry for your boy, but I don't think you've got any choice about letting me walk out of here.'

'And why's that?'

'Because a police car has just parked outside. Dead on time. I rang them earlier . . .'

Chapter Fifty

Louise Shand sat facing Andy and Elizabeth in her sitting room in Pulteney Place. She said, 'Where is he?'

'Aidan Makepeace? He's down at Manvers Street.'

'You've arrested him?'

'He's helping us with our enquiries. As is Mrs Makepeace.'

Louise said, 'Dear God!'

'You were having an affair with him? Aidan Makepeace?'

She reached for a cigarette. 'A relationship. I hate the word "affair". It sounds cheap. Temporary. I loved him and he loved me. Loves.' She corrected the tense. Her voice was defiant. 'We met when Immy took me up to Cheyneys for a surprise birthday lunch. What you have to understand is that I don't love easily. Men, I mean. Used to, but my late husband knocked that out of me.'

'Knocked? You mean . . .?'

'He was physically abusive. I got regular beatings. Just like Jan Finney. That's one reason why I was so against Immy marrying Mulligan. It wasn't just snobbishness as everyone thought. That he was dragging her down in the world when she could have married anybody. Anybody. You've seen her, Mrs Blair. She's such a beauty. If he'd been a decent young man . . . Well, things might have been different. But when Immy started seeing him, I made it my business to find out about him. I heard about the drinking and the womanising and I feared it would lead to the other thing as well. Better no man than that, I told her.' She was tight-faced no longer as world-weariness washed suddenly over her features. 'Immy knew what her father used to do to me. Even though she was a small child at the time and I tried to hide it from her, she became aware of what was going on.'

Elizabeth thought. So our naive little girl turns out to have been personally acquainted with the wicked ways of the world. More than she ever let on.

'But I was wrong about Mulligan on that score, as it happens. She told me last night that the reason she stayed with Johnny even after she found out about his affairs . . . the reason she went on with the marriage plans regardless – well, apart from still being in love with him – was that he was always so gentle with her. She said he would never do to her what her father did to me. She trusted him implicitly on that score. I suppose I have to give him that.'

But reluctantly.

Louise Shand went on, 'You see, I do know how powerful a draw gentleness can be. It's the reason I eventually gave in to Aidan and became his mistress. He's soft-centred.' She must have seen Elizabeth's expression. 'You're a cynic. But you've read how he takes on all sorts of waifs and strays, hopeless cases that he really shouldn't touch with a bargepole. His heart leads his head, even though he's such a successful barrister. Perhaps that's why he's so successful. He really believes in people . . . And he's so incredibly generous.' Her face had, for the first time, become lively. A confusion of faith and love. 'He'd buy things on impulse, you know, and have them sent over here. Flowers, chocolates, clothes. I made him stop it, because I was afraid people would notice and talk. Immy in particular. I hadn't told her about Aidan and me. I didn't want her to know. Better to hold it all inside for a while, I thought. Until I'm sure of him. After what I went through in my marriage . . . well, it's hard to trust any man one hundred per cent. And there was his wife to consider. Yes, I did think of her. Still do – though you might not believe me.'

There was a silence. Elizabeth almost admired the other woman's steely resolve. Sometimes concealment is the most powerful thing. All that baring of the soul gets you nowhere.

Andy said, 'And Miss Gregg? Did she think of Mrs Makepeace when she was having a fling with Aidan?'

A look of pure venom. 'I know about that. He told me. But it was ages ago. Just a fling.'

'So how many of these flings do you think he's had during his thirty-year marriage?'

'I don't know and I don't care. Our relationship is different. I knew in my own mind that it was permanent.' A look came across her face like a child who's pushed out alone into the dark night. 'It won't be now, that's for sure. It's all over for us both. I was trying to help – I'd have done anything for him – but I messed it up.' She began to weep, tears streaming down her face. 'I've ruined him.'

Justice, Elizabeth thought. It's like a line of dominoes. Push one little one and they all come tumbling down.

Louise tried to recover her composure. Andy said, 'So would you tell me exactly what happened on that Saturday night? The night that your daughter should have been away on her honeymoon.'

'Oh, God. There were so many conflicting emotions. And in the end, something snapped, you know? I'd hated the idea of her marrying Mulligan, but when she came home absolutely distraught – you should have seen her lying on the bed crying her heart out. Such hard, painful sobs. I couldn't help her. All I could do was sit there and hold her and smooth her hair and tell her that she'd forget in time. Which isn't true, is it? The pain doesn't go away. We bury it, but every now and then it bobs back up to the surface.' She looked at Elizabeth with tear-filled eyes. 'I felt for her. I really did. Such a public humiliation. The press wouldn't leave us alone. They were out there under her window like vultures. And then in the afternoon, Aidan came round. He had a perfectly legitimate reason. Immy worked for him and he wanted to know how she was. Anyway, it never rains but it pours. That morning, Aidan had received another demand from Finney for an exorbitant sum. Aidan was worried sick . . . almost in tears. If he couldn't find it, that bastard would ruin Oliver's career. He didn't care about his own. That was immaterial. He'd had a jolly good run. But the boy . . . Aidan dotes on him. Finney knew that, too, of course; but he didn't give a damn.'

'So you made up your mind to kill him?'

Louise's mood changed suddenly. There was anger instead of grief. 'I'd been clearing out my father's house. He died last year. And I'd found the gun, with some ammunition, in a trunk in the attic. He'd farmed in Kenya for a number of years and had always kept the gun for his own protection. It got a bit dodgy over there at one time and he insisted that we all knew how to use a firearm – even if we were only over there for a few weeks' holiday. Anyway, I'd been intending to hand the gun in, as you're supposed to do, but I hadn't got around to it. And after Aidan had gone home that afternoon, the thought just popped into my head. Bastards like Finney are no good on this earth. Wife-beater, blackmailer, sponger. Somebody should finish him off. And suddenly I remembered the gun. I must have been out of my mind. The only excuse I can offer is that it had been such an extraordinary day. And Aidan had also been telling me how worried Anna was about Jan Finney and the boy. Lucian. He was terrified of his father, you know. And suddenly . . . well, this plan popped into my head. It was just like that. Like a dream or something. Instantaneous.'

'You rang Finney, pretending to be a customer, and made an appointment to meet him at his shop?'

'Yes. I didn't actually intend to go to the shop. Too confined, I thought. Too risky. But I knew about the garage in Alfred Buildings. Aidan was told to meet him there one night to hand over some cash.'

'Imogen didn't know what you planned to do?'

'Good God, no. I made sure she was asleep before I went out. I slipped one of my sleeping pills into her coffee.'

'And Makepeace? Did you tell him?'

'No. I decided against it. The less he knew the better. I didn't want to compromise him. And I thought . . . well, the wedding fiasco was good cover. If it affected me afterwards – killing Finney – if I looked shaky, if I was smoking or drinking too much, well, they'd assume I was upset about Immy.'

'So you parked your car in Alfred Buildings and waited.'

'Yes. I was scared he'd park somewhere else for once, but along he came, right on time at ten minutes to seven and drove the car into the garage. I almost had a go there and then, but there were one or two people passing. Not many, but the weather was getting worse, so I reckoned later would be better.'

Unluckily for Kat Gregg.

'I waited until he'd walked down Bartlett Street to the shop and then I got out of the car and hung around in a doorway just up the alley. There's an empty department store. Used to be an antiques centre. Anyway, I could see him in the shop. I enjoyed watching him wait for a customer who wasn't going to arrive. I felt this enormous sense of power. I'm in charge, you pig, I thought. You won't hurt anyone else or knock around any more women. I've got your future in my hands. I saw him come out of the shop at ten minutes to eight. I saw him put up his umbrella – it was tipping down and getting dark fast. And I shot ahead of him, got back in my car and got the gun out. I saw him turn the corner into Alfred Buildings and open the garage door.'

'At which stage, he must have had his back to you?'

'Yes.'

'So why didn't you do it then?'

'I'll never know. Except that I think I wanted to see his face as he went down. I thought, I'll wait until he's driven the car out and I'll get him as soon as he gets out to shut the garage door.'

'But it all went wrong?'

'Horribly wrong.' Hers hands were shaking and she clasped them tight in an effort at self-control.

'You thought you saw him come out again under the umbrella?'

'I didn't know it was her. I didn't know she was in there. How could I? And how could I know he was going to lend her the umbrella? And she was tall and wearing a dark raincoat just like Finney's. I panicked. I thought that he was going to leave the car in the garage for some reason and walk away from me. It was only when I fired and she went down and the umbrella went down with her that I saw her blonde hair—'

Now the tremors had moved down to her legs. She was shaking all over. Only the eyes were burningly steady. 'I couldn't believe it. I really couldn't. It was like your worst nightmare. I dropped the gun on the passenger seat . . . somehow got the engine going and I shot away down the road.'

There was a long silence. Louise's eyes were closed and she had gone very white. 'It was as well that Immy slept for most of the evening. I was hysterical when I got home.' She fumbled for a cigarette. 'But not half as bad as Aidan. He came down next day in a hell of a state. I had to tell him to pull himself together. To go straight home and not to come back until I told him to. Immy was a bit suspicious that day. I could feel it.'

'Did you tell him what you'd done?'

'Not that day. How could I? He was so upset. I felt dreadful.'

Doggedly, Andy said, 'And the second murder?'

'The second murder . . .' Weariness now in Louise Shand's voice. 'That was easier in a way.'

'May as well be hung for a sheep as a lamb?'

'Exactly. And I hated Finney even more by now for wasting that poor girl's life . . . for turning me into her murderer. I couldn't stop dreaming about her and . . . and the child she was carrying. It got worse and worse. Actually, it was some sort of relief when I did kill him.'

'Tell me how.'

'It wasn't difficult. This time it went like clockwork. I knew it had to. For Aidan's sake . . . and Kat's.'

'You arranged to meet Finney down by the canal?'

'At seven thirty. There's this quiet little spot. Aidan and I used to meet down there and walk and talk. I knew there would be nobody around.' A slightly bitter laugh and a glance in Elizabeth's direction. 'And she gave me the perfect hook.'

'I did?'

'You told me that some woman had been writing to him about her child. I knew how he hated Lucian, poor little chap. How bitter he felt that his only child was handicapped. So I guessed he'd jump at the chance to get in touch with a normal child that he'd fathered. I typed a note. If you want to get in touch with your other son, meet me tonight down by the canal. It worked like a charm. He turned up on the dot. And this time I was more in charge of myself. It was quite amusing really, stringing the bastard along. He didn't know me, of course. I pretended to know him. Don't you remember me, I asked? I gave him a false name and pretended we'd known each other years ago. Remember that night we got drunk, I said? No? God, you were out of it that night. And still he stood there with this stupid look on his face. I'd have felt sorry for him, if I didn't hate him so much. He was quite surprised, I think, when he saw the gun. Someone had caught him napping for once. It gave me great satisfaction. Anyway, I lifted the gun and I pointed it at him. He still didn't move. He seemed rooted to the spot, And I said, this is for Aidan and for your wife, you shit. And I shot him—'

For a minute, there was silence.

'He went backwards into the canal. And as he hit the water, I fired a second shot, just to make quite sure. He didn't stand a chance. He went under and didn't come up again. It was easy. Really so easy.'

No qualms, Elizabeth thought. But then she lived with physical abuse for years. She's cold at the core. Never loses her head. Not any more.

Louise Shand said, 'I stood there for ages staring at the water. It was very quiet. Nobody heard and nobody came. Then I turned around and walked away. Back to my car, which was parked a quarter of a mile away. And I drove home. Imogen wasn't there. She'd gone off to Paris with Tim. So I went upstairs and I put the gun into a polythene bag and placed it back in the trunk. I took a shower, and I rang Aidan.'

'You told him what you'd done?'

'I had to. I couldn't keep a thing like that to myself for ever.'

'And his reaction?'

'Absolute shock at first. But the relief that it was over. He was tremendously worried about it, of course, but there was nothing he could do. I hadn't involved him. And I can live with it, I told him. I've lived with a lot worse.'

You couldn't really approve, but you had to admire her courage.

'Aidan . . . he's the most moral man I know.'

Moral? Well, it's subjective, I suppose.

'That's why I hated Finney so much for doing this to him. He's such a good man. So bloody honourable. All he did was try and protect his son.'

Unadvisedly, Elizabeth thought. But we all do things on impulse. And who's to say what I'd have done in the same circumstances?

Andy said, 'I shall have to caution you. You know that?'

'Yes,' she said wearily. 'But let me call Immy first. She's out with Tim.'

Andy was leading her out to the waiting car when the message came through to him. Elizabeth knew from his face that it wasn't good.

'What is it?'

'Glory Fraser. She's in hospital.'

'What's wrong with her?'

'Ashley Lewis was waiting for her outside the Student's Union bar last night. He beat her up. She's a bit of a mess, I'm afraid.'

Chapter Fifty-One

A day of cold sunshine . . . great calmness and peace. Except in the office, where all hell was breaking loose. 'Where's my pager?' Elizabeth was asking.

'In the kitchen window.'

'What's it doing there?'

'God knows,' Max said. He waited for her to find it and chuck it in her bag. 'So tell me something,' he said. 'What put you on the track of Louise Shand?'

'She was on Ed Harper's list. That's how I found out about her relationship with Aidan Makepeace. So I decided to find out more. I had a little chat with Imogen. Not so as to alarm her, you understand. There were just one or two casual questions I wanted to ask.'

Questions . . . questions.

'Such as?'

'Such as whose idea it was for Immy to take that sleeping pill on the Saturday night when her world fell apart. Hers or her mother's. And I found out – surreptitiously – that Louise, after talking Immy into taking the pill, had sent Tim Kidston back to his mother's house where his French girlfriend was waiting for him. Now I wonder why? I asked myself. And the answer came back that perhaps Louise didn't want anyone to know she was leaving the house that night.'

Elizabeth said, 'Always some woman protecting some guy or other. Have you noticed?'

'Always the woman that suffers,' Ginger said.

'Mostly women with bad judgement,' added Max darkly.

'What strikes me,' said Elizabeth, 'is how chancy life – or death – is. It's so heartbreakingly banale. Kat – and her unborn child – died because she decided to have a bit of a clear-out. And because there was a downpour of rain . . .'

Max said, 'So did you ring the hospital? How's Glory?'

'She'll survive.'

She's young.

Like Kate. Must ring her. Must have another chat with Saul. Quite liked him . . . I think.

Ginger said, 'That poor old lady. Glory's grandmother.'

'She'll survive, too. Has done until now.'

Max suddenly remembered something. 'Caroline gave me a message for you. Rupert thinks the quilt's very . . . spirited . . . yes, that's the word. But if you don't mind, they'll be sending out a wedding list from Debenham's.'

'I hate wedding lists.' Elizabeth set down her bag on the desk. 'They'll get a quilt and like it.'

'So . . .' Max said. 'Time to close the books on our crime of passion.'

'Just make sure our bill goes out and get paid,' Elizabeth told him. 'Passion? All fine and dandy when you're twenty years old. Lovers dallying. Getting themselves all steamed up, getting un- balanced. At my age, I like to know where my feet are going to land.'

'Poor old crock. You'll be in a Bath chair next. We'll have to wheel you out to the next case.'

He was probably right. 'So what happened to my supper the other night?'

'You didn't miss much,' Ginger said.

'Except a hangover.' Max threw a smile in Ginger's direction. A smile that hinted at . . . something. Something he wasn't quite sure about.

Something that might just possibly be explored in the future.

LIZBIE BROWN

BROKEN STAR

Elizabeth Blair, newly widowed, is looking for a tranquil English existence when she leaves Virginia to run a quilt shop in Bath. However, she quickly discovers that there's a lot of secret sin lurking behind the façade of genteel English country life.

Allegations of embezzling the funds for the church roof are already causing tensions to run high in the parish of St Swithin's, near the estate of the unpopular local TV celebrity Larry Aitken. Then the local doctor drops dead in the middle of a parish meeting. A few days later a family friend is viciously stabbed outside the Aitkens' house. Are the deaths linked to the missing parish money?

Broken Star: to Elizabeth it's a quilt pattern, but to the handsome private eye whose office is upstairs, it's Larry Aitken, who desperately needs the young man to clear him of murder charges. Elizabeth soon finds herself becoming Girl Friday to the affable Max Shepard, creating a witty and charming new duo of amateur sleuths …

HODDER AND STOUGHTON PAPERBACKS

LIZBIE BROWN

SHOO-FLY

Elizabeth Blair, a feisty American widow who runs a patchwork quilt shop, and Max Shepard, a struggling young private eye with an office upstairs, are an unlikely pair of sleuths. But they make a great team – at least most of the time. They plunge headlong into another case when they are asked to investigate the murder of spoiled rich kid, Julian Neville, who created havoc when he took a temporary job in the staid MOD establishment at Draycott, on the outskirts of Bath. His battered body was discovered on Beechen Cliff, soon after.

Was Julian murdered by one of the colleagues he enjoyed baiting at Draycott? By one of the women he was said to be having affairs with? By a jealous husband? Why does Elizabeth have the feeling that his mother is covering up secrets? And why, for that matter, does the trail keep taking them into decidedly seedy haunts?

HODDER AND STOUGHTON PAPERBACKS